"If you agree to go home, I will speak to Knut and urge him not to go after Edmund. He'll listen to me," Thorkell said.

"And if I don't?" Branwen asked softly.

"If you won't go, I will lead a troop and personally see to it that Edmund is found and destroyed. Then you will have no reason to wander the roads any longer!"

She knew she should be angry with him for trying to bargain with her but she was not. She would be glad to get home. Edmund would gain nothing by her refusal.

"He will be humiliated," she said.

"It's better than being dead," he said, adding, "but I think he'll just laugh. He's always played lightly for very high stakes."

Looking up at Thorkell's stern face, waiting for her answer, she offered him a plump, juicy blackberry. "You are irresistible, my love." She smiled, popping the berry between his parted lips. He pushed her back into the pillows and kissed her roughly so that the taste of the blackberries was in her mouth as well.

AN UNKINDNESS OF RAVENS

DEE MORRISON MEANEY

ACE FANTASY BOOKS
NEW YORK

To Roberta Delaney,
who never let me use the
children as an excuse

AN UNKINDNESS OF RAVENS

An Ace Fantasy Book/published by arrangement with
the author and her agent, Valerie Smith

PRINTING HISTORY
Ace Original/July 1983

ISBN: 0-441-85450-8

Ace Fantasy Books are published by Charter Communications, Inc.
200 Madison Avenue, New York, New York 10016.
PRINTED IN THE UNITED STATES OF AMERICA

PART I

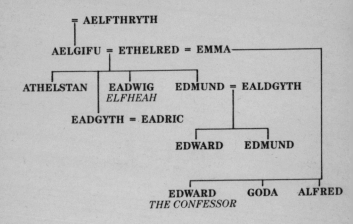

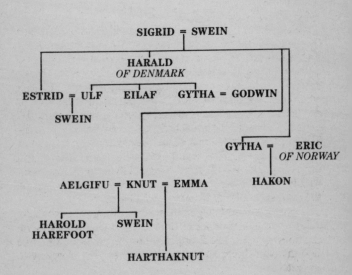

Chapter One

Sherborne, Wessex, 1011 AD

The chill damp of the mid-winter rains had settled into the corners of the room. Heavy woolen curtains were drawn across the shuttered windows and it was dark. Only the fire burning low in the firepit and a single yellow taper guttering in a pool of smoking tallow lit the small room where her mother lay so still. Branwen stood at the foot of the bed, her small hands clenched, nails pressing into her palms. She wanted to reach down, to shake her mother. She wanted to shout, to scream, Get up, get up. You can't die. You can't. You can't. But she stood silent and unmoving, afraid of Wulfnoth, afraid of her father who sat, with his face set like stone, on a low wooden stool alongside the bed, still holding his wife's cold hand.

Branwen's mouth began to tremble. She gave a small cry and turned, running out of the room, leaving her cloak on the floor where it had dropped unnoticed an hour ago. She fled through the great hall and out across the alleyway to the kitchen.

Aelle looked up as the door opened. Her eyes were red-rimmed with crying. She dropped the spoon into the pot of chickens she had been stirring and held out her arms to the girl. Branwen ran to her, burying her face in the soft warmth of the old cook's ample breasts. "There, there, child," Aelle crooned, rocking her gently back and forth.

Elin watched, the half-peeled apple in her hands forgotten for a moment. Snel kept turning the joint spitted over the fire, humming to himself.

But Branwen didn't cry. Though Aelle smelled reassuringly of the garlic which had always hung in a small bag between her breasts, today, for the first time, there was no comfort in her embrace. Branwen pulled away from the old cook and ran back outside.

The mud of the courtyard was ice-rimmed, cracking under her feet as she ran across to the stable. The thick smell of horses reached out to her from the shadows within as she opened the stable door. Her brother had just ridden in. Seeing the wild look of misery on her face, he put down the feed bucket he had been filling and caught her up into his strong arms, wrapping his fur cloak around her.

She was suddenly very tired and let him hold her. He ran his hand over the top of her head, smoothing her dark hair gently. After a moment Godwin spoke to the old man who was wiping down his foam-flecked stallion. "Tom," he said, "get her cloak."

"Poor Branwen," Godwin said gravely, tilting her chin up so that he could look at her, "You're mistress of Thornbury now, you know. You can't go running about like a child anymore."

"No," she cried. "I can't. I won't."

"You must, Branwen," he said. His voice was gentle. "Father needs you now. Someone will have to see to the feast. Someone will have to see that it is done the way she would have wanted it, the way she did for Wulfcen, and for the others."

"Oh, Godwin," she cried. He held her close and she wept. But it was not the same. The comfort had gone from her brother's arms as well. Even wrapped against him, buried in the warmth of his soft fur-lined cloak, she felt alone, separate.

"It will not always hurt so, Bran," she heard her brother say.

She did not believe him. It would not go away, this emptiness. She knew it would not. Hopelessness washed over her, deadening the pain. She stopped crying. When Tom came back with her own blue wool cloak, lined with sheepskin, she looked up at her brother and said quietly, "I'll be all right now, Godwin."

Tears ran down his own face as he watched her walk away, for her feet no longer seemed to dance over the frozen ground and he knew that more than his mother had died that day.

Branwen went back into the drafty kitchen and spoke to Aelle. They sat down together at the thick wooden kitchen table, worn and bleached from years of service, like Aelle herself. As they talked of the preparations which must be made for the burial feast, Branwen's eyes moved restlessly, taking stock of the kitchen as if she were seeing it for the first time. There was the large vat for storing the fish they netted in the Coombe. Long handled utensils—meat hooks, spoons, ladles, skimmers—all hung on the walls, their handles blackened from reaching over the fire. A heavy, locked cabinet stood in one corner holding their spices. I must get the keys, Branwen thought. She felt her lip start to tremble and she frowned hard, pulling it firm.

If the old cook was surprised at the change in the girl, she did not show it. Aelle had seen her grow up, had seen her uncanny strength of will; but then, it was there for anyone to see, there in the girl's eyes. Big and black, like her grandmother's, they had always commanded a respect beyond her years.

The tapestries were hung. The tables were set. The sun was high. The hall was full of the smells of bread and meat and apples. Branwen wore the deep red jumper which she and her mother had stitched and embroidered with fine woolen thread last summer. Everything was ready. Soon Wulfnoth and Godwin would return with the others and the funeral feast would begin.

Suddenly there was a startled shout from the courtyard. Tom rushed in, his face ashen. "Vikings!" he cried. "Vikings! Riding up to the gate!"

Vikings. Visions of bloody bodies—old Aelle, Elin— jarred her. Branwen's heart began to pound.

"They'll kill us all," the old man moaned.

Terror rose up like a wave of nausea. She gripped the windowsill hard, forcing herself to think, forcing a clear deliberateness to calm the panic which threatened to engulf her. Her father had left her in charge; she had to do something. There was no one else, no garrison to defend the manor. There had never been any need this far from the coast, this far into the winter. She must try to keep them safe, Aelle, and Tom, and the others, for a little while, until her father could get back. He would know what to do. If only he would come soon, before it was too late.

Time seemed to slow, taking on another dimension, like cold crystal, as she walked steadily toward the door where the old man stood trembling. Pulling her sheepskin cloak around her shoulders, she went out into the winter sun. The strangers were already reining up in the yard. She stopped just outside the door, surveying the noise and confusion, the dogs barking and dashing in among the horses. She picked out the Viking leader who was preparing to dismount, standing high in his iron stirrups, looking across the filth. He was tall, certainly taller than her father or Godwin, and his hair and beard were brown beneath his helmet. Her eyes caught his and she did not look away.

"Welcome to Thornbury," she said clearly.

A fat man who stood holding the bridle of the leader's horse looked around at her and laughed, "Well now, here's a comely wench, and ripe for a tumble, I'll wager."

She ignored him, watching the tall man dismount. One of his arms was bandaged and he held it close against his chest as he walked toward her.

She forced fear out of her mind, forced a smile of welcome, made her mind fill with thoughts of warmth and welcome. If only she could make them accept her hospitality for just a little while, until her father got back.

"Welcome to Thornbury," Branwen repeated, and there was only the slightest tremble in her voice.

"Where is your father?" he asked.

"My father is not here, my lord," she answered. "But

you have come far and must be cold. Come in and warm
yourselves by the fire."

"A fire would be most welcome."

"How may we call you, my lord?" she asked as he followed her through the door.

"Thorkell," he said.

Her heart turned to lead. Her foot missed a step and she
stumbled, catching herself on a corner of the sideboard to
keep from falling. Thorkell. Thorkell the Tall. It was a
name used to threaten small children when they misbe-
haved. If you're not good, Thorkell the Tall will eat you up.

Elin stood whitefaced behind the table. Seeing how
frightened the woman was, Branwen succeeded finally in
pushing her own fear away. It was up to her. She must buy
time, must keep these people safe. "Serve the wine," she
said quietly. Elin looked around wildly.

"Do it," Branwen said firmly. "Now."

While the frightened serving girl passed among the Vikings, giving each a goblet filled with the warm, spiced
wine which had been prepared for the funeral feast,
Branwen took an ornately worked silver cup to their
leader. When she stood in front of him, offering him the
cup, she raised her dark eyes, meeting his. His hand trembled as he reached out for the cup.

"Your arm troubles you," she said. "Perhaps a clean
bandage would ease the pain."

"Not likely." He laughed shortly.

"Behold the true Viking," a voice behind her said.
Turning, she saw the heavy-set man standing there. "We
shall have to cut that goddamn arm off in another day or
two to save his life, yet still he laughs."

Branwen paled. "It may be I can help you," she said,
looking back at the wounded man.

"You are very young," Thorkell said.

"Not so young," she answered. "And my father says I
have a gift for it."

"What do they call you?"

"I am Branwen, Wulfnoth's daughter."

"Very well, Branwen, Wulfnoth's daughter." He sighed,
sinking down into her father's big chair beside the fire. "As

Olaf has pointed out, it seems I have little choice."

She sent Elin for a kettle of hot water and clean cloths, and began to unwrap the old bandage. A great dog, who had come with them, nosed over to see what was happening. Thorkell rubbed the massive head with his good hand. Branwen was still bent over his arm when her father burst into the hall. She stood quickly and faced him, her voice breaking into the loud silence which had filled the room.

"This is Lord Thorkell," she said. "He and his men rode in while you were still at the graveside. I have invited them to eat with us." She was aware of the Dane's presence behind her and knew that he had risen and was facing her father across the room.

"I had not expected you so soon," her father said stiffly. "If you will excuse me a moment I will dismiss the others." Without waiting for an answer, he turned and was out the door.

What did he mean, she wondered? She had not heard him speak of Danes, or of Thorkell the Tall. Had he been expecting them?

She gently pulled away the last of the bandage, revealing a great long wound, a sword cut probably; an axe would have cut right through the bone as well. It was healing badly, darkly crusted and weeping slowly, but she could smell no trace of disease.

She walked over to an ancient worn cupboard leaning against the wall and pulled out several small drawers. Turning back to the fire where the kettle was steaming, she sprinkled crushed comfrey root, and the agrimony she had picked last spring, into a bowl and poured the boiling water over them. A bitter, dry smell rose as the herbs released their essences. She dipped a clean cloth into the steaming bowl, held up the dripping compress until it was cool enough to wring out, and laid it carefully on the wound. She waited for a moan or a wince, but there was none. Branwen worked quickly and gently while the infusion remained hot. When it had cooled she bound the arm carefully and firmly, bringing the edges of the cut, now soft and clean, together.

After she finished, she went to the cabinet once more,

straining to remember the things her grandmother had taught her so long ago. The cabinet had been her grandmother's then and all the drawers had been filled. Many were empty now and no one, not even the herbalist at the abbey school, knew what was to have been put in them. Branwen knew only the simples of betony and hyssop to ease the pain and speed the healing. She took these out of their small drawers and steeped them in the bottom of the Dane's wine cup. After a few minutes she filled the cup with wine.

"I'm afraid it will have a bitter taste," she said, handing it to him.

When he took the cup from her, his hand was steady.

At that moment, her father returned; Godwin and Leofric, the fosterling, were with him. She stood to one side while the men exchanged greetings. Then her father, seeming to see her for the first time, said gruffly, "See to dinner, Bran. These men are hungry."

Her cheeks were burning as she hurried across to the kitchen. "Aelle," she called, "we are to serve dinner now. Send Tom in with the joints."

The fat, old cook was terrified, unable to work.

"Oh, don't be such a goose," Branwen snapped. "They've only come to speak with my father."

It was late when the meal was over. Wulfnoth had left the hall early, for his burden of grief was fresh. One of the Vikings, older than the others, brought out a small, stringed gittern and began to pick out the haunting chords of a Norse song she did not know. The room had darkened and she motioned to Elin to light more candles. In one corner Leofric sat deep in conversation with Thorkell and Olaf. Godwin, leaning against the wall, was listening. Leofric spoke freely with these men; born in the Danelaw, north of London, along the Wash, the language came more easily to him than to the rest of them—though they all spoke it, this mix of Saxon and Latin with Danish. After a while Thorkell left the group and came over to where Branwen was clearing away the remains of their meal.

"I am sorry about your mother," he said.

"Thank you," she answered stiffly, not looking at him.

His gaze was sharp. "Didn't you know we were coming?"

"My father had not told me."

"But you weren't afraid?"

She was quiet for a long minute and then she said, her voice low, "Yes, my lord, I was afraid. Thorkell the Tall is not a name unknown to us."

"And now?" he said. "Are you still afraid?"

She looked up at him, and their eyes met. "Aelle will be waiting for these things," she said finally, blushing deeply.

In the dark of night, when the work in the kitchen was done, she went silently back into the big hall. The tables were folded back against the walls and the men slept noisily on the benches set against them. One man sat like a shadow on the edge of one bench. He looked up as she entered and suddenly she sensed the throbbing pain in his arm, feeling it as if it were her own pain . . . She stopped, rubbing her arm, and wondered why.

After a moment, she went over to him and said, "I have brought something to help you sleep." When he did not answer, she went on, "My brother told me a wound like yours aches worse at night. Shall I change the dressing for you?"

"Why do you do this for me? You should be sleeping. You must be very tired."

"I would do the same for any man, my lord, who was a guest in my father's house."

Thorkell frowned and took the cup from her. She built up the fire, moving the copper kettle nearer the flames. He drank from the cup she had handed him and watched her work, unwrapping the bandages, applying the hot compresses soaked in fragrant herbs. His eyes grew heavy. The light from the fire made the shadows leap up in the corners of the room.

"What enchantment do you weave, little Branwen?" he asked, his voice thick with the drug.

"None, my lord," she replied, seeing him struggle against sleep.

"Still," he said, "there is a magic about you."

"No, the magic is gone out of the land now. All that is left is in the stories old women tell." Her mother had said that to her not long ago. Memory flooded over her and she grieved silently while she rebound the Dane's arm, but he had fallen asleep and did not notice. When she had done she lowered him carefully back among the cushions and covered him with his cloak.

She woke at first light and, dressing quickly against the numbing cold, hurried into the hall on her way to the kitchen. Again she sensed his pain and saw the tall Dane standing at the window, looking out toward the river, his hand resting on the great dog's head. He was dressed still in his baggy woolen riding pants, his close-fitting blue jacket thrown around his shoulders. He must be more used to this cold than I, she thought, hurrying past without speaking to him.

In the kitchen Aelle was already kneading dough for the day's baking. "Good morning," Branwen said, hugging her quickly. "At least it's warmer in here." She moved the big copper kettle out over the fire to bring it more quickly to the boil.

"And how am I to feed so many today, child?" Aelle asked her, her floury hands on her hips.

"Isn't there anything left from yesterday?"

"Well, we do have the pork pasty which is untouched; I might be able to heat it up. And then, there are some rabbits from the traps this morning."

"That will be fine. They can have those for breakfast, if they're hungry. Then, you know Godwin will be off hunting. He seldom has such a good excuse."

As they spoke Branwen unlocked the spice cabinet and Aelle took what she needed for the day. Like a child playing house, Branwen thought, that's all I'm doing. She relocked the cabinet. The kettle had started to boil. She wrapped the handle in a corner of her apron and went out.

Olaf was watching as she removed the bandages that morning. "By Freya's corns," he said, "it's healing. Who would have thought the little piece could have done that? We shall have to take you with us, girl. There's more than enough work among our kind to keep you busy."

Branwen looked quickly at Thorkell and he laughed at the dismay he saw in her dark eyes. "Would you be so loath to come away with me?"

She was relieved when Wulfnoth came in, rubbing sleep from his grizzled beard. He kissed her absently on the top of her head and said to the Viking chief, "How's your arm today, Thorkell?"

"It seems the cut is healing. Your daughter has magic in her hands."

He had spoken jokingly but Wulfnoth looked at his daughter and said gravely, "Aye, so it seems. Born out of time, I'm afraid."

Branwen picked up the soiled linen strips and left the hall, without further word to Thorkell or her father. She met Snel on her way across the yard. He had just drawn two buckets of water from the well and was carrying them into the laundry for Elin. She was suddenly grateful to him, poor lost half-wit; he never mocked her, nor she him. She smiled and said, "The water must be cold this morning, Snel."

His blank eyes lit for a moment and his mouth gaped into a wide grin, but he could not speak. She held the door open for him and they went into the wash house. Elin was pushing the linen around in a large three-legged iron cauldron which stood in the fire.

"The sun is out, Elin," she said. "We should be able to dry things at last."

She and Elin had grown close since the girl had come to live at Thornbury as Elfric's bride. The only son of Tom and Aelle, Elfric was dead now, killed last summer in a skirmish with Viking raiders near the coast at Wareham, but Elin had stayed on.

"Will they be leaving this morning?" the girl asked.

"No," Branwen said apologetically, "not for several days, I think. Do you want to go away for a while, back to the village, until they are gone?"

Elin dumped a bucket of water into the cauldron and stirred strongly with the long wooden paddle. After a while she said, "Aelle will need help. I'll stay."

"Good. Shall I put these in there?" Branwen asked, holding out the bandages. Elin nodded.

They worked together for an hour. By the time they had hung out all the wet linen, Branwen's hands were red with cold, for the sun gave little warmth. She buried them in the deep fleece which lined her cloak and went out to the courtyard where she could hear the men and the jangle of horses' harnesses. She shaded her eyes with her hand watching Godwin and the others mount up.

Leofric stood in the stirrups and waved to her as he rode out. "Pity the poor stag," he called. "How can we miss with such an army?"

She smiled and waved back at the fosterling. After they had gone she stood for a while looking at the empty courtyard. The long house with its great hall stood along the south side, overlooking the river. The kitchen, wash house, and the cottage where Elin lived with Tom and Aelle were to the east. Looming dark against the northern sky, the barn sheltered the yard from the winter wind, while the stables crowded into the forge and storage sheds flanking the great gate on the west. All the buildings were thickly thatched. The wattle and daub plaster gleamed brightly between the dark timbers. Protecting the whole complex was a stockade of heavy tree trunks sunk deeply into a wide, high berm, leaving a ditch on the far side.

Absently she stroked the little sparrow which had fluttered down to sit on the shoulder of her cloak. She thought of her mother; how different it would be if she were here. Everything had been so easy for her. She always knew what to say, what to do. People found it easy to talk to her; they enjoyed being with her, sitting at her table. "Gilaina bin nybeth," she said to the little sparrow, *not like me*. She spoke in the ancient language of the animals, long forgotten in the memory of men, and the sparrow chirped back to her.

Suddenly she realized she was not alone. Leaning against the sunny wall, Thorkell was watching her. "I was right, after all, wasn't I?" he said gravely. "There is a magic in you."

"My grandmother taught me to call the birds," she said.

"And how did your grandmother know?" he asked, blocking her escape with his tall frame. There was no trace of mockery in his manner.

She looked up at him. Her arm throbbed again in sympathy with his. "She learned in faery long ago, before my grandfather found her."

"And it was she who taught you the herb lore?"

"Yes," she said slowly, "I learned from her and at the abbey school, too. I was six when my grandmother died."

"And the magic of faery has come down to you?"

"Perhaps, my lord. My mother said it was not so. She would never let me speak to the wild things in her hearing. She was very angry with my grandmother for teaching me the words."

"How old are you?"

"Fifteen last harvest time. And you?" she asked.

"Twenty-four. How is it you are still unwed? Are you promised to your father's fosterling?"

"Oh no," she laughed. "Leofric is betrothed to one who will bring more lands to his father, the ealdorman of Coventry."

"But surely there are others?"

"The women in my family have always been free to wed whom they please."

"And?" he persisted.

"I have not met such a one as pleases me."

"Have you not?" he laughed.

The sound was warm and she lingered to talk with him for she found it easier than she had thought. She had never met anyone who listened to her and laughed with her the way this tall Viking did.

When the hunters had returned and a stag hung from the butcher's rack behind the cookhouse, Branwen reached up to take her cloak from the peg beside the door. "Godwin has set out the target, Elin. Come and watch with me."

"For God's sake, Branwen, how can you be so nice to them?"

"Oh Elin, I'm sorry." After a moment she added lamely, "It wasn't these men, you know."

"What difference does that make? They're all the same—vicious, brutal murderers." The serving girl turned away angrily, banging the silver goblets as she put them back in the cupboard. Branwen winced, hoping she would not dent them. Then she wrapped her cloak tightly about her and went out.

There were only two men still shooting. As she watched, Olaf shot well, his arrow embedded deeply near the center of the target. Godwin bent his bow and notched an arrow. He looked over at her and winked, for it was one of the arrows she had fletched for him with feathers from the kestrel he kept. She watched proudly as the arrow flew truer than the Dane's. She wondered idly how her brother came to shoot so well; even in the field, he preferred a spear to bow and arrow.

"Break out the metheglin, Bran," Godwin shouted over to her. "The wind blows cold; we'll need more than a fire to warm us tonight."

That evening, when the men were standing around the fire in the great hall, their cups filled with the rich fermented honey, Branwen sat on a tall stool in the shadows spinning yarn from the basket of wool at her side. It was too dark for needlework, even with the candles lit; but she needed no eyes to guide the steadily spinning whorl as it twisted the soft, carded rolag into fine yarn. Thorkell sat near her, lost in the shadows. She had drugged his drink to ease his arm and was not surprised that he took no part in the conversation.

"So, there's to be no raiding come spring," her brother was saying. "That's too much to hope for."

"By Loki's balls, you may not think so," Olaf answered. "Swein has set the Danegeld at 350,000 pieces of silver. He is taking hostages against the payment."

Godwin whistled. "Will Ethelred pay it?" he asked.

"Aye, he'll pay, the whore's son," his father growled. "What choice has he got?"

"What's he like, Swein Forkbeard, your king?" Branwen asked Thorkell. "Surely he can't be the monster that men say he is."

"Perhaps not," the tall Dane said. "Still, he is a bitter

man, and hard. Merciless."

"How can you serve him?"

"How can your father serve the Unraed?"

"He does not." Branwen laughed. "Except when it pleases him to."

"Even so," Thorkell said wearily.

"Forty shiploads of Vikings are loyal to the great Thorkell the Tall and serve Swein when it pleases them," Olaf said mockingly.

"Would you have it different, Olaf Haraldsson?" Leofric asked.

"If I were king I'd bring the chieftains to their knees."

"It can't be done," Wulfnoth said. "Even Alfred had to be content with less."

Branwen spun in silence while the men went on talking, their voices droning on, going over the old arguments she had heard before. Her mind wandered as the spindle whirled. She thought back over the events of the past years, events she was too young to remember clearly in which her father had played his part.

Central to all of them was the dim figure of the old king—Ethelred—who had come to the throne stained with his brother's blood. He had been twelve in 978, too young, some said, to be blamed for Edward's murder. Still, she thought, it had been done for his sake. And why had the murderers never been found?

King Edward had come to visit Ethelred and Aelfthryth, his mother, at Corfe on that hot summer day long ago— that hot summer day when Ethelred's retainers had gone out to meet the young king, stabbed him, and pulled him from his horse to let him lie in the courtyard. Branwen frowned. Corfe was not far from Thornbury. Father had talked to men who were there that day, who had seen Edward lying there, before they carried his body to Wareham for a hurried burial, one without ceremony or honor. It was a horrible crime and even if Ethelred had been a child, he could not escape its consequences. And twelve was not so young.

People still remember Edward, she thought, Saint Edward now. Father says he was no saint when he was alive. It was just three years ago last March that poor old Ethelred had to sanction the celebration of his feast day. That must have been a hard thing to do. What a miserable life he must live, she thought. Even the queen despises him, they say. She looked guiltily at her father. He had little sympathy for the king.

But he had forgotten her. Leaning together over their goblets around the fire, the men were talking about the coming spring, the coming raids, raids which seemed to have been going on forever. It had become worse in the last ten years, since Ethelred had ordered the Danes killed, all the Danes living on the island. Not all, she thought, there had been too many; but thousands, even the children, killed. She shuddered. The St. Brice's Day massacre, they called it now. What had made him give such an order? No one knew. All they knew was that it had unleashed the full fury of the Danes.

The king of Denmark, Swein Forkbeard, had a sister who, with her husband and children, was among those killed. Raging, Swein had allied himself with the Vikings at Jomsborg, making their chief's younger brother, Thorkell the Tall, one of his commanders. Angry men flocked to his standard from all over the North to avenge the massacre. No place was safe. Exeter was betrayed to them; they harried Wessex and East Anglia, sacked Norwich, occupied Sandwich, the Isle of Wight, raided Hampshire and Berkshire to Reading and across the Chilterns to Wallingford. Only when a tribute of 36,000 pounds was paid did the raiding stop, and then only for a few years.

In that brief respite, the island-born built a fleet of warships to defend their shores from the Vikings. Every three hundred households had been called on to provide a ship of sixty oars; every eight households—an armed man. Wulfnoth saw to the work in South Wessex, and early in 1009 he took twenty ships and their crews east to Sandwich where they were to join the others. There they learned that command of the fleet had been given to Brihtric, a vile, deceitful man, Eadric's brother. They were both greedy, grasping men. No one trusted either of them. Brihtric ordered Wulfnoth and his men to attack the Viking

stronghold on the Isle of Wight. Wulfnoth refused,
unwilling to allow his men to be slaughtered. There
had been a bitter argument. The entire fleet was too inexperienced to attack the Vikings. The numbers were too
evenly matched and the skill was clearly with the Danes.
Finally, Brihtric had called Wulfnoth a traitor. Her father,
child of the South Saxons, thegn among his people as his father had been, and his father's father, for generations into
the dim past—Brihtric had dared to call *him* a traitor.
Wulfnoth had left before dawn and twenty manned ships
left with him. Brihtric followed but a sudden summer storm
blew up, driving eighty ships with their inexperienced sailors onto the shore east of Worthing. Wulfnoth had turned
back and burned the stranded fleet. In the fighting Brihtric
was killed.

Wulfnoth had returned to Wessex a hero. He had defied
the king's man and won. There was no thought that he had
betrayed his country. There was no national feeling. They
were Wessex men, not Englishmen. All their loyalty was to
their thegn, to that part of southern Wessex which was
their home—the hills and rivers, farms and villages they
knew. What did they care for London or Exeter? Those
far-off lands and towns meant little to them. Who was
Brihtric? A fool who deserved death.

Wulfnoth had made his own quiet peace with the Danes.
His was a large holding, stretching from the Crewkerne to
Shaftesbury, from Cerne Abbas to Glastonbury. These
lands paid their share of the Danegeld when asked, and no
more. They sent no men to swell the king's army, sent no
men to court. There were no messages between Wulfnoth
and the king. And Wulfnoth was not the only thegn to oppose Ethelred. There were others. A stronger king would
never have allowed it. But Ethelred had neither the
strength to hold them nor the power to punish them. The
Unraed, they called him, Ethelred of Ill-Counsel.

And now Thorkell the Tall himself had come to
Thornbury to talk to her father. She looked up at Wulfnoth
and saw that the men were listening intently to what he was
saying. She smiled proudly, set down her spindle, and went
over to the fire to refill their cups.

* * *

The next day the Danes made ready to move out. Thorkell's arm would be a long time healing. It would be even longer before he had the strength to wield a sword, she thought as she dressed his arm for the last time. She was pleased that she had been able to help him and did not understand why she was sorry he was leaving.

"What can I give you, Branwen," he asked, "for saving my arm? Tell me, what would you like?"

She thought for a long moment and then she walked to the door and opened it. She looked out into the morning sunlight sparkling on the silver harness pieces of the waiting horses. She called out a word he could not understand and suddenly on her hand was the sparrow. She smiled and turned to Thorkell. "My lord, there is nothing you need give me. You are like the sparrow—just knowing it is my friend is enough."

Suddenly she felt his reluctance to leave wash over her the way his pain had when he first arrived. "There is an old man, Ansgar, with my camp at Weymouth," he said. "For many years he was a wise man, a healer, with my brother at Jomsborg. But now, in his old age, his mind wanders and he has become a figure of fun in the camp. I will have him brought here to you. Be kind to him. If he is cared for again perhaps he can still teach you his wisdom. I have seen him call the birds out of the sky as you do."

"I'll be glad for the old man's company." Branwen paused and then added quietly, her eyes on the floor, "Will you come back someday?"

Lifting her chin with his fingertips, Thorkell looked down into her black eyes. "I will be back, Branwen," he said.

Chapter Two

ANSGAR WAS A strange gift to a young girl. White-haired and stooped with age, his black eyes watched her warily as she tried to make him welcome.

"It must have been cold riding up from the coast," Branwen said when he had climbed down from the cart.

The old man said nothing.

"Aye, lady," the Viking escort answered for him.

She looked at the young Dane and smiled. He wasn't much older than she herself and his chain mail shirt was too big for him, hanging over his hands so that she wondered if he could fight in it at all. "Well, you must come in then, and warm yourselves by the fire. Tom will see to the horse."

Inside the great hall Wulfnoth sat slouched in his chair, deep in conversation with his son.

"Ansgar's come, father," Branwen called. "Thorkell sent him as he said he would."

"Well then, Ansgar, is it?" her father said, getting to his feet. "Welcome to Thornbury."

The old man made no answer.

Wulfnoth went on, his eyes narrow, his voice flat, "How is the Dane? His arm continues to heal?"

"Beg pardon, my lord," the escort said. "The old man don't talk much nowadays."

Wulfnoth glared at him.

"Thorkell is well," the young Viking added lamely. "His arm mends rapidly. Already he can heft his axe."

Wulfnoth wasn't listening. Turning to his daughter, he roared, "God's blood, Bran, I think you have healed his arm and addled his brain. What was he thinking of, sending a daft old man here? As if we've not enough of our own to take care of. Take him back, you! What's your name?"

"Pym, sir. Take him back, sir?"

"Oh no, father, you can't do that," Branwen cried, her mind racing. "Thorkell would be furious. You can't insult him over such a small thing. I'll clean out the old storage shed. He can stay there. I'll take his meals to him. He'll be no trouble, father."

Wulfnoth drained his cup. "Very well," he said gruffly, "but I'll have no part of it. See you keep him out of my way, do you hear? Tell Tom to see to the roof on that shed; it needs mending." Stomping off to the door, he added, "And mind you see young, er . . . young. . . ."

"Pym, sir."

"Mind you see young Pym here fed before you go running off."

"Yes, father," Branwen said, grinning.

Not until the next morning when the chores were done did Branwen and Elin take the old man to the empty hut. The fire which Tom had started for them had driven some of the chill from the deserted building.

"By the good St. Bridget, Bran," Elin said, setting down the kettle on the edge of the makeshift fire pit, "it's not much."

"It will be fine," Branwen said.

They set a straight-backed chair near the fire, covering it with a down coverlet and settling the old man in it. Earlier in the morning Branwen had gone up to the storage closets under the eaves in the great hall to get the bright, thick quilt. There, alone in the smoky winter chill, she had felt her mother's disapproval wash over her. Such a quilt was too fine, she would have said, to give to an old man who would probably wet it like a baby. Oh mother, Branwen had thought, leaning her head against the sloping attic roof, I'm afraid I'm not the daughter you wanted. The sadness she had felt then still lingered as she opened the shutters in the little hut. The window faced south over what would be a kitchen garden in the spring. Even on this cold January morning the sun streamed in; but the air was cold and, reluctantly, she closed the shutters again. Elin swept out the rotting straw which lay heaped in one corner and then brushed the cobwebs from the mud plaster walls with feathers tied on a long pole. Branwen took a broken table, up-ended and long forgotten, across to the barn where Tom was bundling thatch to repair the holes in the roof.

"Can you fix this, Tom?" she asked.

"Aye, Branwen, leave it here."

She carried a great armload of hay back to the hut, piling it in a corner for a bed. When she was leaving the barn with her third load, Tom joined her, carrying the table he had fixed. With the floor swept, the hay covered with an old linen sheet, the table oiled and the colorful quilt draped over the chair, the hut looked at least inhabitable. While they stood there admiring their handiwork, Ansgar said, "The roof will leak."

"Well, old man," Tom said, "so you can talk."

"When I've something to say," Ansgar snapped.

"Well, don't worry about the roof. I'll have it patched before dark. Shall I be seeing to it then, Branwen?"

Branwen nodded.

"Hmph, and where's my box?" the old man asked.

"Elin will get it for you," Branwen said.

When Elin and Tom were gone, Branwen waited quietly, watching the old man. He looked around the room. Ten feet by ten feet. A door in the corner of the north wall, leading to the barn. A heap of straw in the opposite corner. A window, shuttered, but undraped and drafty. A chair with a high back but no arms and an old square oak table about twenty inches to a side. The floor was dirt, the walls were mud daub and sadly in need of attention. The smoke from the hastily constructed fire pit in the middle of the room had no trouble finding holes in the roof to go out ~ough.

"'s not the palace of Llyr," the old man said.

"Llyr," Branwen said softly, feeling the word echo within her. "What is Llyr?"

The old man would not answer her.

Slowly they came to know each other, Ansgar and Branwen. And through the late winter the old man grew stronger, learning to trust her, to know there was no mockery here. His silent withdrawal faded with the coming of spring. By the end of March Branwen was spending long hours with him, learning an herb lore which went far beyond anything she had known before.

Even at the abbey school where she had gone to study with Godwin and Leofric, Brother Francis had not known the secrets she learned from Ansgar. She smiled at the memory of that monk who worked so quietly among the rows of plants he loved. How many dreary hours of Latin and rhetoric, science and theology had she endured for the moment each afternoon when she would be released to go to the gentle herbalist? She recalled how proud her mother had been that her daughter could read and write as well as any nobleman's daughter. She was not so pleased with my enthusiasm for Brother Francis, Branwen remembered ruefully. The pain she felt was still sharp as she recalled how coldly her mother had turned away from her one day when she had returned home eager to share the knowledge of a new healall.

Later, her mother had come, kissing her on top of her head. "I allow you your choice, Branwen," she had said. "Don't ask me to do more."

Branwen had often wanted to ask her what the words meant but, though they could talk easily of other things, around this there was a high wall and Branwen never found the gate.

In the soft green spring Ansgar walked beside her in the high meadows and through the fiddleheads in the still, bright woods not yet full leafed. Together, they went down into the village where Branwen had gone with her grandmother when she was still a child. Now it was Ansgar who brought healing herbs to a child with a bad cough, knowing hands to ease the pain of a farmer's strained shoulder. And

Branwen was amazed at the depth of his knowledge in these matters. Learning from him eagerly, she never suspected that he was only uncovering a skill which was part of her heritage, a skill which had been buried too long.

Whenever they were alone, he spoke to the wild things and they came to him, and to her as she stood with him. She learned the secrets which had been hidden from her since the death of her grandmother. She found the shy, silent way of the rabbit and the deer. Laughing, she recognized the bold, brazen disdain of the raven. They spoke to the brown mice of the field; the otter in the stream amused himself at their expense; fox and badger, hawk and sparrow, each in his turn heard his name called and came to meet the girl who belonged to the earth as few of her kind did any longer.

One warm May afternoon Ansgar began a lesson he had not taught before. Quietly, and with close concentration, he began to impose his will on hers—willing her to feel his thirst. Gently, he reached out to touch her mind.

Instantly she turned on him. "Old man, I do not know what you are doing or why, but stop!"

"So," he said and there was a flash of respect in his keen dark eyes, "you felt my touch. Can you do this thing yourself? Can you touch another's mind?"

"I've never tried to 'touch another's mind'!" she replied angrily.

"Perhaps not tried, but still there are minds you have touched, I think."

"It is an evil thing to do," Branwen said, frowning.

"Not evil, child," Ansgar replied. "The power itself is neither good nor evil—no more than any tool is good or evil. Your grandmother called up this power once and overcame three men who had enslaved her."

"Did you know my grandmother?" Branwen asked, her anger forgotten.

"No, child," the old man said gently. "But I knew another who told me of her."

"Will you tell me?"

"Your grandmother was the only one of her kind to find happiness with a man of the new tribes," he said thoughtfully.

"Why?"

"It is not for me to speak of this. Not now, Branwen."

"Why?" she asked angrily.

"You have much to learn first, before you are ready."

"Then teach me," she demanded.

"I can't teach you what you need to know," he said.

"Why not?"

"Yours is a different heritage, Branwen. It is not mine. I do not know what you need to learn."

"Then how am I to find out? Who will teach me?" she cried.

"I do not know," he said.

They walked on in silence for a while, the May sun warm on their shoulders. Then Branwen asked quietly, "What did you mean 'bend another's mind'?"

Ansgar sighed. "Haven't you ever felt something to be so right you couldn't understand why everyone did not feel the same way?"

Branwen nodded slowly, remembering how angry and sad and alone she had felt when she was still little and first heard the frightened voices of the wild birds netted for pies. No one had listened to her small-voiced protest until she finally gave up and hid in the barn, her hands over her ears, weeping. It was as if her language was as strange to them as the wild things she alone could understand.

"Sometimes it's as if people only hear what they want and there is no way to tell them the vision that is in your head—all the little threads woven together which make a thing so important. No one has the patience to hear you through. After a few words their eyes glaze over and you know their thoughts are elsewhere. Isn't that true, Branwen?"

"Sometimes . . . sometimes, it's true," she said.

"You have a gift, child. Language is a tool which came late to the children of woman. In the beginning, like the animals still do, we shared our thoughts one with the other. It was a sharing which grew much more complex than the sharing among the beasts. They sense fear and can direct each other to food or shelter, they can share a kind of love—at least some of them can—but they don't think as we can. In the beginning we shared our thoughts."

"But we don't anymore, at least most people don't," she said thoughtfully, remembering the odd way she had felt the Viking lord's pain.

"No, it is lost to us—that skill—except to you and perhaps a few others. I don't know. . . ."

"Why? How did we come to lose such a precious gift? To know another's thoughts, to be able to understand her feelings . . . it must have been so easy to get along with each other."

"Do you think so, child? And what if you disliked someone, or did something you were ashamed of, or wanted something which belonged to someone else? How would you keep it secret?"

"Are secrets so important?"

"Yes, they are."

"How do you know all these things, Ansgar?"

"When I was a small boy—many years ago—there was a school, hidden in the hills of the west, where all the traditions and teachings of my people were passed on by word of mouth, passed on from the old to the young, generation upon generation, since the shadowy beginning of time. There are things, Branwen, which can only be passed on by word of mouth—things too sacred to be profaned by pen and parchment, for any eyes to see. Even when I was young the school was dying. The old men who had been teachers were dead—all but two when I first came—and the young men who wanted to learn the deeper mysteries all went to study in the Christian monasteries. Few know the old truths now. I never learned all the lore—the last teachers died before I could complete my studies. I was never initiated into the mysteries. I was born too late."

"And so was I," Branwen said with a whisper.

"Aye, child, and so were you, but to a different heritage, a different line."

"Tell me."

"I cannot. Your people worshipped the Great Goddess. Mine did not."

"Who is there to tell me of my heritage," she cried, "if even you cannot?"

"You will know, child. In time, you will know."

And then he began to teach her to bend another person's

will, to touch another's mind. Setting his mind against hers, they struggled silently, striving with each other as the sun went down and the shadows lengthened, gradually spreading out into twilight. In the end Ansgar rose and fetched water from the well for her to drink. Branwen laughed, hugging him.

"Now you can bend men to your will," he said, his voice old and tired. "You have the power to make a man feel fear or trust, love or hate—even pain. Take care how you use it, Branwen. It is a powerful tool."

"Oh Ansgar, why would I ever use such a tool here?" she laughed.

"I cannot say," he snapped, turning to go. "Come along, child, we have a lot of work to do tomorrow."

The next day they worked in the good, brown soil of the kitchen garden planting the seeds which Ansgar had brought with him: lovage, meserean, and milkwort, lily-of-the-valley, eyebright, and pimpernel. These they set in among the perennial household herbs: hyssop and rue, sage, thyme, mint, savory, pellitory, foxglove, pennyroyal, rose.

Later in the afternoon, the fires in the main hall were put out for the summer. Buckets of whitewash were mixed and painted over the walls to cover the accumulated soot and smoke from the past winter. While the others worked in the great hall, Branwen took two buckets and whitewashed the walls in the little hut. When the winter wheat was harvested in June, Branwen saw to it that the first straw went to rethatch Ansgar's hut. When it was done and the roof was snug and the walls were clean and white, they moved her grandmother's worn cupboard into the little house. It almost filled one wall. When the men left after carrying it in, Branwen stayed behind. The sun, bright through the open window, reflected brilliantly off the new whiteness of the walls. The hut smelled of new thatch. She felt suddenly, overwhelmingly sad and alone.

How much longer, she wondered, until father insists I marry and leave Thornbury? Perhaps he has already talked to one of his friends. Will there be guests this summer? Will I have to pick among them? What would it be like to leave Thornbury, to do another's will? Her mother hadn't seemed to mind. Perhaps she was luckier than most, having a man like Wulfnoth for a husband. For her father, who was a great and fierce man, taking what he felt was his even from the king, had loved his wife. Loves her still, she thought, and how old he has gotten since she has gone.

But all around Branwen love died early. Sickness and death, hunger and need, were a drain that left little room for love. The never-ending year-long calendar of chores that had to be done. The awful sameness of the thing. And then the crushing round of pregnancy, birth and death. There must be more to life than that, she thought fiercely. There must be.

It was still and hot the next day. Supper was light and the alewife's brew, drawn up in its heavy, brown jug from deep in the well, was crisp and cold. When they finished eating, Leofric and Godwin began a game of draughts. Branwen sang lightly while she cleared away the table. She had a true voice, and the melody was a familiar one. When she finished, her father rose from his place, disturbing the dogs which slept at his feet.

"You make a very satisfactory daughter, little Bran," he said. "Come, walk with me awhile. It is still light in the fields."

Although the hour was late, the sunlight lingered with the warmth of the day as they walked across the yard. Branwen, unsure of herself, was silent, lost in thought. He loves me; he will understand how I feel. I won't have to bend his will as Ansgar thinks, she tried to reassure herself.

Suddenly she caught a glimpse of an animal just disappearing into the woods across the field. "Did you see it, father?" she called excitedly. "Did you see it? It was a unicorn. There really are unicorns!"

"Unicorns?" He laughed. "Is that what you see?" He laughed again and she felt her face flush. "And I suppose that one day you'll be off for the mountains to hunt dragons. Well, I'll check in the armory and see if we've any magic swords for you to take with you," he said, still chuckling. "What you need, Branwen, is a husband to dream about instead of unicorns!"

Hurt and angry, she looked at him with her great dark

eyes. Then, concentrating, she began to bend his will. She worked quickly and skillfully and he was not aware that she touched his mind.

As her will became his, he gathered her into his arms and said, "You'll never have to marry to please me, Branwen."

She smiled, satisfied.

But then he went on, "There is too much of the old people still left in you. Your mother saw it, too, and it grieved her," he said. "She denied that part of her, your mother did, when she was young and the shadow of what had been denied was always over her."

"What shadow, father? What is it that has come to me through her?"

"You are of the race of faeries, child. The power of the old tribes still flows in your blood. The Picts were a strange people, closer to the earth than the rest of us. They had a magic—I don't know—it was their blood that your mother denied when she promised to marry me and live as a Saxon woman."

"Did my grandmother give up the old power, too?"

"She never married your grandfather. Caedmon did not ask it of her; he was content to live apart from other men. But I was a fool," he said harshly. "I did not know what price the daughters of faery pay to live among men."

"What price?" she asked, her voice a whisper.

"All magic must be denied, or they are feared and hated. Your mother knew the price. Anuvial pleaded with her; but we were young and we loved each other and so she promised to be my wife, as other women are wives to men."

"And she always kept her promise?"

"Always. Your mother honored the bargain made—and not grudgingly, but with such song as was left to her. I was a very lucky man." His voice caught, and it was several minutes before he went on. "Thornbury is to be yours. It was your mother's from her mother, bought when Caedmon died. It was her will that it go to you in turn.

"Branwen, you will not find the road you seek an easy one. But Thornbury will always be sanctuary for you, providing food and shelter as you have need of them."

They walked slowly back up the hill toward the manor.

Just before they went in Wulfnoth said, "I'm sorry I laughed at you earlier, Branwen. Unicorns are out of place in a world of men and war; and often, many important things are forgotten because we are too caught up in the ordinary work of getting through each day. And I had forgotten, for a while."

Branwen fell asleep that night wondering if she had indeed altered her father's will at all.

The next morning, before the household stirred, she sat with Ansgar in the chill light of dawn. The kitchen garden was a tangle of green: the eglantine over the fence was in full bloom, soft pink petals with glowing yellow stamens alive with bumblebees. She told him of her conversation with her father.

"I did not stop to think whether it was right to go into his mind," she said. "It was so important that he see things my way, and not force me to wed before I am ready. Why do I feel this reluctance? Other women wed; my mother did, and she was happy."

"I am not surprised, child," the old man said. "For you are more like your grandmother—there is much magic in you, the like of which I have not seen in many years." He added absently, "I had thought never to see it again. . . ."

"No one believes in unicorns anymore," she added wistfully.

"No," he said, "no one believes in unicorns anymore. Or magic. Or faeries."

"Do *you* believe in unicorns?"

"Once I did." He hesitated before going on. "When I was a young man, many years ago now, there was a girl. . . . She was not much older than you. She believed in unicorns. Her name was Penardim." Memory seemed to rise up about him like a shadow, and for a while they did not speak.

"But, if you want the answers to your questions, you'll find one, child," he said at last.

"Where should I look?"

"I can't help, Branwen." Ansgar smiled. "I am an old man and old men don't ever see unicorns."

Chapter Three

LATE IN THE summer, when the August sun had ripened the corn, Ansgar and Branwen rode out to the hill overlooking the road running east toward Salisbury. They went out early in the morning, collecting the hairy-stemmed betony with its whorls of red purple flowers. She looked up at one point and saw a cloud of dust moving toward the manor along the road. She wondered briefly who their guest would be for dinner that day. By noon, the rider forgotten, she sent Ansgar on ahead with the baskets of flowers while she walked down to the river. The birds circled high overhead and she called out to them, but they were too far away to hear. Beyond the willows, in a sheltered place, she slipped out of her clothes and into the river, feeling its coolness wash away the dust and the heat of the day. The sand felt clean under her feet and she lingered, until hunger began to intrude on her thoughts and she remembered guiltily that dinner would be waiting for her return. She pulled her thin summer gown on over her wet body and smoothed down her hair with her hand before slipping into her coarse blue linen work shift.

"A pretty sight, Branwen. Does your father know you bathe naked as a fish here in the river?" She turned with a start, and saw a man smiling down at her from the high bank.

"And have you not read in your bible, my Lord Thorkell, that it is evil to leer at maidens as they go to bathe?"

He laughed and she laughed with him, unashamed. He reached down to help her up the bank.

"What brings you back to Thornbury, my lord?" she asked, suddenly shy of the tall Viking.

"That's a long story and I'd rather wait until I can tell you and your father together. They told me at the hall that he and Godwin are at the Hundreds today."

"Yes, but in this heat I think they will be back early."

They turned toward the manor and Branwen asked, "Have you seen Ansgar yet?"

"No, not yet. How is the old man?"

"He's wonderful," she said. "He knows everything. I am so glad you sent him here. We fixed up a house for him by the garden, you know; he is happy there and teaches me more and more every day. We've filled so many drawers in my grandmother's old cupboard. I shall always be grateful to you for sending him to me." She was laughing now and dancing to keep up with his long strides; talk of Ansgar made her forget her shyness. "How is your arm?" she asked. "Is it better? Can you use it properly yet?"

He stopped and turned to look at her. He held out his arm and the sleeve fell back revealing the long red scar, but she could see the muscles already beginning to firm up underneath. She put out her finger to trace the angry red line.

"I've missed you, little Branwen," he said suddenly.

She looked up at him and felt strongly his joy mix with hers. Their eyes held and she replied quietly, "And I, my lord."

There were dark shadows around his eyes and new lines around his mouth. He did not look as if he had done much smiling since she had seen him last, eight months ago.

Thorkell looked down at her. "It's the same," he said, "just the way it was the last time."

"Yes," she said hesitantly, not sure of what he meant but somehow wanting everything to be just the same.

"I thought I must have dreamed it." After a minute he asked, "Does it happen often with you . . . like this?"

"No," she said cautiously.

He frowned, puzzled. "It's not like knowing your thoughts."

"Do you feel it too?" she asked startled.

"Didn't you know?"

"No, I thought . . ." She shrugged. "Only when you feel something strongly; then it comes through . . . how glad you are to be here . . . like a sudden burst of light."

"And you," he said, "you are glad as well."

Branwen looked down at the ground where the weeds had grown late-summer coarse, dark green and heavy leaved. She did not know what to say to him. The moment dragged. At last she looked up, "They will be waiting dinner, my lord," she said.

"Yes, we should go up," he answered with a smile.

In the great hall, as she served the meal, watching him, she was more and more struck with the sense of overwhelming care and worry which seemed to weigh on him. What had happened in the east? Certainly the collection of the Danegeld locally, although a nuisance, was no cause for this kind of concern. Where is Wulfnoth, she wondered impatiently? What has happened?

As they were sitting down to eat Ansgar came in. Thorkell rose at once as the old man joined them at table.

"Ho, grandfather, you are looking well! This Dorset air agrees with you, I see."

" 'Tis not the air, dolt, which eases my old age, but this child of faery."

"So, child of faery, is it?"

"Only a fool questions what he knows in his heart. And mark well, my son, the man she chooses will be blessed indeed."

"Ah, grandfather, but she tells me she has found none that pleases her."

"She will do well to wait for the man whose heart speaks to her own."

Thorkell looked at her. "Is that so?"

They ate roast heron which the falcon had brought

down. They were lingering at table, their mugs refilled with ale from the dark jug, when Wulfnoth rode in with Godwin and Leofric. After the initial courtesies were exchanged, the men sat down to a meal of leftovers while Thorkell told them the news from London and Canterbury.

"All the country east of here is in turmoil," he said. "We took hostages last spring, as you know, against the payment of the tax. I was sent to Canterbury to hold the Archbishop until he raised his share. There is a lot of money in and around Canterbury and the sum was a high one, but it wouldn't have mattered if it had been only tuppence. Alphege would not give anything nor would he ask his congregation to meet the assessment."

"Alphege is a holy man, Thorkell; he has a big following. What did you do?"

"For two weeks we held him prisoner at Canterbury and I urged him to at least appear to be raising the money. I warned him that when Swein found out there would be hell to pay. But he was a stubborn old man and he would not comply."

"Was?"

"Swein eventually found out and, when he did, he sent his own men."

"But Alphege was your prisoner."

"Swein doesn't observe the niceties. His crew laughed in my face, took him out and murdered him in the courtyard."

"So," said Wulfnoth, thoughtfully, "where does that leave you? Swein would not leave you commanding a troop. Even he cannot maintain a chain of command with links he breaks apart himself."

"My men were to be reassigned to other commanders. There are forty ships whose crews are loyal to me and will see Swein in hell before they serve him again."

"Of course," the old man said, nodding. "So you withdrew from Canterbury and sailed into London to join Ethelred."

"You would have done the same."

"Perhaps once I would have, but I know what you do not."

"I know now, too. Now that it's too late. As Swein is mad, Ethelred is a fool."

"Well, what are you doing here? Ethelred is in London, or at least he was the last time we had any news of him."

"Ethelred doesn't trust me."

"I can't imagine why."

"Eadric, the one they call the Grasper, advised him that one way to get me out of London was to send me to meet with Edmund."

"Eadric Streona," Wulfnoth said thoughtfully. "What did you think of him?"

Thorkell frowned. "I don't believe everything I've heard about him. He is ambitious, though, that's clear, and the king relies on his guidance. He would be a dangerous enemy, but perhaps," he said slowly, "perhaps more dangerous as a friend."

Wulfnoth nodded thoughtfully. "And so you are on your way to young Edmund. You will find him more to your liking, I think."

"When Edmund rules then we will have a real king on the throne," Godwin burst out, unable to keep silent any longer.

"My son is Edmund's most loyal supporter. He refuses to admit that Edmund is not even next in line for the throne, having an older brother."

"Pah!" Godwin exploded. "What good is Athelstan, too sickly to leave the cloister."

Wulfnoth laughed. "Please excuse his youthful fervor. He would have joined Edmund long ago but I forbade it. Then it would have been a waste but the time is perhaps drawing near. I will send the young men with you to Holcombe tomorrow."

As the abbey carillion rang out for vespers, Leofric went over to the stables to have Tom saddle their horses and bring out the birds. They would ride for a while before the end of the day, perhaps even get to the hilltop above Holcombe.

Branwen never went hawking. Her sensitivity to the voices of the small animals and birds, terrified by the circling predator, made the sport unendurable for her. But this time she resented being left behind.

She walked over to the drying racks to check on the betony they had picked that morning. Ansgar had them stripped and carefully spread out where the sun would not spoil them. She covered them over with the tightly woven cloth they used each night to keep the dampness from settling on the drying plants. She then went by the kitchen to see what Aelle was making for supper. Supper was much lighter than lunch and there was no need for anything elaborate, but with a guest staying it would be pleasant to have a fresh sweet. She was inexplicably annoyed that Aelle had anticipated her and a lovely gingerbread was cooling on the window ledge. There was even some applesauce from the green apples which had already fallen from the trees. In the hall new candles they had made just last week from beeswax stood in their holders. Why did Elin put those out? The tallow would have been fine, Branwen thought. But she didn't change them.

When she heard the men returning, she slipped quietly out into the kitchen where Elin and Aelle were eating their supper. Snel, too, sat in his corner with his trencher and stew.

"Elin, you serve supper tonight," she said. "I will take a plate to Ansgar." She ignored the lifted eyebrow and, picking up a bowl, put in a slice of the good dark bread and piled two scoops of stew on top of it. She took a mug of ale in her other hand and went out the door, taking the path on the outer side of the laundry through the garden to avoid the men in the courtyard.

The old man had fallen asleep in his chair. She woke him gently, urging him to eat a little. She sat with him while he ate. He said nothing. She worked on drawings of the flowers they picked to be stitched into a tapestry next winter. She would hang it on the cold wall next to the bed here when she was finished.

She looked up at Ansgar to ask him for corrections on her sketch of the late mousebane they had collected earlier in the week, but he had dozed off again, and she helped him into bed, covering him lightly with a linen sheet. When she turned back to her drawing she realized that the light was gone and it seemed foolish to light a candle. She went out and shut the door behind her.

She climbed up the fence which ran around the sow wallow. The pen was empty now. The pigs were all out with the swineherd, fattening in the old oak forest near Nettleden. The wind blew from the east carrying the smell of the wallow away from her. It was a sturdy fence, built to hold a heavy sow who resented being penned all winter. Sitting on the thick top rail, Branwen could see over the stockade, eastward across the darkening valley toward Holcombe, toward Salisbury and beyond that Winchester and then London and Canterbury. Dreaming of distant places she had never been, she did not hear the Dane as he came toward her through the shadows.

He stood without speaking. The moon had not yet risen. The crickets were chirping. Branwen was a small shadow against a sky still grey with the last light of evening. Her features were fine and she had the innocent beauty of one who is completely unaware of appearances. Her hair was thick and dark; her skin clear and smooth. So different, he thought, from Viking women with their yellow hair and rosy skin. He wondered if he found her more beautiful than any other woman just because she was different. He shook his head. It couldn't be just that. Her small, slight body was like a boy's. She moved like a boy, too, he thought with a smile. Even in her long skirts she had an easy way. Walking or working she seemed so strong and sure, like a boy. . . . No, not quite like a boy, he grinned.

"We missed you at supper," he said at last.

She looked up, startled by the sound of his voice. "Did you, my lord?" she asked. There was more she might have added but, as he came near, her head was filled with the rush of his emotion, as she had felt his pain some months before. Instinctively, she withdrew into the darker hiding places of her mind, shutting doors as she had learned from Ansgar.

"I will be leaving in the morning," he said, leaning against the rail beside her.

"Will you be back?"

"Not soon."

"Oh."

They said nothing for a while, watching the moon come up across the valley, an enormous yellow orb, not round, distorted as if pulling its weight into the sky were some gargantuan effort.

"Why does it look like that?" she asked.

He didn't answer.

"In an hour it will be cold and silver, smaller. . . ."

"Bran, I want to talk to you," he said. Looking down at her, he put his hands on her shoulders.

She looked at him, trying to understand what was happening to her. His face was in shadow.

"What is it?" she asked.

He pulled her toward him and she yielded softly against his warmth. She could hear his heart beating. He leaned down and his lips brushed the top of her head.

Her eyes were wide and dark in the twilight. He kissed them closed, slowly and very gently. She waited without moving, not even breathing, as if by holding her breath she could stop time and hold the moment frozen forever. His lips were soft on hers and there was a sweetness in her mouth like the smell of raisins, dark and warm. And then he held her very close and she clung to him, her arms around him, holding him.

"Don't go," she said, her eyes shining.

"I've got to," he whispered.

"Take me with you then."

"Not yet, Branwen. I can't now. There's too much . . ."

She fought tears, annoyed with herself.

"If the war goes well," he said, "I can be back in six months. I'll talk to your father then. . . ."

There, close in the hollow of his arms, where it seemed she had always belonged, she felt her heart grow heavy. "No, Thorkell," she whispered, "not that. Please, not that."

He didn't seem to understand at first. "Will he mind, do you suppose?" he went on, still thinking of Wulfnoth.

"Not your wife," she whispered. "Please don't ask me to be your wife."

He stiffened then as he began to understand what she was saying to him. His arms grew cold around her. "What?" he asked hoarsely.

"Don't be angry."

He turned away, his hands clenched at his side. "Why, Bran?" he asked.

Frantically, snatching for a reason for her reluctance, she gave the excuse Ansgar had given her—one which she hardly believed herself. "Oh, Thorkell," she said, "there is a thing I must do first. I've got to find the unicorn. There are . . ."

"By the Midgard Serpent," he hissed, "you are either a fool or take me for one, lady. There are no unicorns in a world where a man must sleep with a knife in his hand."

"Yes, there are, my love," she said softly, reaching out to touch his angry mouth with her fingertips, tears running unheeded down her cheeks.

But he pulled away from her, striding down the hill into the darkness.

She stood there listening to the sounds of his leaving. "Don't go," she whispered. "Oh please, don't go." When she could no longer hear him, she turned and went into the hall.

Her father came in later that night and said, "We missed you, little one. Thorkell went out to find you when supper was over. Did you see him?"

"I saw him, father, for a few minutes."

She knew he wanted to ask what had happened between them and she wanted desperately to tell him, but she was too close to tears and could not speak of it.

In the morning Thorkell was gone.

Godwin and Leofric had accompanied the Dane; three days later Godwin returned alone. He rode in on his great, grey war horse just before noon while Branwen was in the mews feeding his birds. She fed the last of the chicken bits to a little, brown sparrowhawk. She did not talk to these birds, their minds were too full of dreams of killing, but she loved the freedom they felt despite their bonds. Even while they were trussed and hooded she knew in their hearts they were riding high on the thermals which rose over the valley. She turned to meet Godwin who had come in with Wulfnoth, who was as anxious as she was for his news.

"Well, brother, welcome home." She hugged him and

asked, "Where is Leofric and where," she added with studied coolness, "is the Dane?"

He did not answer her, handing her instead a small, unfledged goshawk. "A gift from Edmund. It's half dead."

She held it in her cupped hands and it quieted. "It may live, Godwin."

"It won't eat."

"I'll try."

"Come, come, son, what news?" Wulfnoth asked impatiently.

"Edmund agrees with Thorkell that we will have war. We spent most of our time devising lists of men to be roused and equipment to be laid by during the winter. The Danegeld will satisfy Swein this year but Ethelred must fight in the spring."

They continued to talk as they walked back to the house. Leofric had gone home to mobilize his own lands. He carried a letter from Edmund to his father, Leofwine, ealdorman of Coventry.

"Thorkell has gone back to London with letters from Edmund for the king. How Edmund loathes his father."

All through the meal Wulfnoth and Godwin talked of the preparations for war. Afterwards they stood together in front of the great gate looking across the road toward the river.

"Wulfnoth and I will not be at home as much this winter as perhaps we should be, Branwen. Father will have to meet with the Hundreds here and at the old holdings in Sussex where we will have to raise a troop. Men will have to be armed and ready to move out. Most of the winter must be spent in preparations. This house will serve as headquarters for the area. I have hired two smiths to come from Salisbury to work here, to forge new weapons and armor. You see, we are lost to the world here in a way that Edmund never can be.

"We will need to enlarge the kitchen staff to feed more mouths each day. The household must be able to sleep twenty or thirty each night, so Elin will need help. We've endured this peace too long. It's finally time to fight. We need to be ready. What will you do?"

"Godwin, are you seriously asking me to run a military camp?" She looked from her brother to her father. "With a staff of three?"

Edmund, Godwin told her, had a worthy thegn with him who had lost his small holding in Sussex to the Danes. He was an experienced man of war and would be invaluable to Thornbury. "If you agree, father, we can bring him back with us next week. He can oversee the work."

Wulfnoth nodded.

The sun was low in the sky. The river glowed.

Godwin turned to her and asked, "What happened between you and Thorkell? He was in black despair as we rode out of here."

She looked from Godwin to Wulfnoth and back at her brother, and said softly, "He wanted to marry me."

Wulfnoth snorted. "And you refused him."

"You know how I feel, father. Why couldn't he accept it the way you did?"

"The man loves you. Is that so hard to understand? He's a good man, Bran," he added, shaking his head. "You'll be hard pressed to find another like him." He turned away from her and walked back into the house.

"This is absurd, Bran. What is going on here? Why would Thorkell want to marry you? He's a Dane, not a Saxon."

"What difference does that make? Anyway," she said softly, "I told him I wouldn't."

"For God's sake, why not? He's a powerful man. How could you turn him down? Do you know what it would mean if you married him?"

"I don't want to marry anybody. Not now, not yet."

It was growing dark on the terrace overlooking the river when they finished talking.

"Well, Branwen, that's all well and good," Godwin said as they turned to go back into the hall, "but what are you going to do now? Thorkell won't be the last man to ask for you. Others may not take no for an answer. You are too good a match, and pretty, too," he said, smiling at her. "I don't know, Branwen. You will have to marry sooner or later. If not Thorkell, it will be someone else."

"Wulfnoth promised, Godwin. He said I could always stay here."

"Wulfnoth is an old man. He has forgotten what men will do when they want a woman," Godwin said gruffly.

They went in to supper but their conversation was stilted. After they finished eating Wulfnoth and Godwin walked out to look over the barns, planning for the harvest ahead. Branwen went out to the kitchen garden with Ansgar. They talked of the work to be done the next day, but she kept losing the thread of their conversation.

"It's Thorkell, isn't it, child?" he said suddenly.

"Yes, Ansgar, it's Thorkell," she said, and tears started in her eyes. "What shall I do?"

"Hush, child, give him time. I have known him since he was a boy. He will be back."

"Oh Ansgar, not soon, I know that, not soon." And she turned from him and went into the house.

Chapter Four

Early one morning while Branwen worked in the herb garden between the kitchen and the stockade, Ansgar called her name. She turned but only saw a very old tom cat sitting at the end of the row, staring at her through unblinking dark eyes.

"Ansgar, is that you?"

The image wavered and dissolved and the old man knelt there, laughing at her.

"How did you do that? Can you teach me? Is it hard?"

"It is not hard, child, but like many things, first you must understand what is done."

"What is done?" she asked. "Weren't you a cat just now?"

"Ah, Branwen," he said, smiling, "if I could truly change this old flesh into a new shape, it is not the shape of a cat that I would choose."

Branwen frowned, puzzled. "And you won't tell me?"

"No," he said simply.

It took two days, but then, on their way back from the village, right in the middle of the cartway, she suddenly stopped and said, "I know. I know how it's done. Close your eyes."

He did.

"Now," she said. When he looked she was gone and in her place was a sleek black cat. The illusion shimmered for a moment and then vanished.

"You will need some practice," the old man said, "but you are right. As you can bend another's mind to your will, so you can make others see whatever you wish them to see. It is one and the same."

"Is that all there is to the magic of the shape-changer?" she asked, disappointment in her voice. "I wasn't really a cat at all. I just made you think I was."

"Yes," he said, "most magic is just that—an illusion, a way of making someone see something that isn't there. There is no magic to change what is real," he added, shaking his head.

"Illusion," she echoed sadly. "Not really magic at all."

He was thoughtful for a moment, as if undecided how much to tell her. At last he said, "There are some who know a deeper magic. There are some who can fly."

"Isn't that the same thing?"

"No," he said wistfully, "flying is not the same. It is not illusion—not *just* illusion."

"What is it then?"

"To truly fly, you must learn to free your soul from the too-heavy flesh that houses it. It's a dangerous thing to do, child. Not only must the soul escape but it must find its way back into the flesh again or be condemned to roam this world forever. Without a mortal body, a soul can never find the door which death opens into the peace of the next world."

"Can you do it, Ansgar?" she asked softly.

"No," he said slowly, "although I've tried. But the power is in you, I think, if you can find the way."

The days passed. Branwen delighted in the simple magic of the shape-changer. In the meadow she would suddenly look like a deer; in the little hut, a furry, brown field mouse. But she never tried to hold the illusion for more than a moment or two and she never tried to fly.

Ansgar was annoyed when he saw how she only played with the magic and would not learn the skill. "Branwen, Branwen," he chided, "have you not thought what the shape-changing will do for you? You could be free, free to go anywhere alone, anywhere you please."

"Alone! Oh, Ansgar, you can't mean that. I'd be too afraid to go anywhere by myself even if I were disguised as . . . as. . . ."

"Then I have been wasting my time," the old man said disgustedly, turning away from her.

"Perhaps you have," she threw angrily after him.

It was a clear, cool morning when Wulfnoth and Godwin rode out of Thornbury on their great war horses, dwarfing Branwen on her ancient palfry. The mist lay heavy in the low fields. The sky was cloudless. Dew had settled the dust on the road.

Behind them Tom drove the cart slowly along the sun-baked ruts, jolting, as mercifully as possible, Elin and Aelle who rode with him. Elin had been up late the night before making garlands of wild flowers which hung all around the big-wheeled cart. Ansgar had not come with them.

They were joined along the road by others coming along the road from Nettleden, and up from the cluster of houses along the brook near the abbey. It was the Feast of the Virgin, the start of the harvest season, and they had all been invited to Holcombe for the celebration.

Branwen wore a tunic she had just finished stitching. The fine rose sandal wool had lain, neatly folded, at the bottom of her mother's trunk. What was she saving this for? Branwen had wondered when she found it there. Loneliness had washed over her when she made the first cut. Today its soft rose color was reflected in her cheeks. Even the light tan she had been unable to avoid this summer did not seem coarse and the curls escaping from her lacy cap gave her an air of innocence which delighted her father, riding proudly at her side.

There were pennants flying from the top of the stockade as they rode through the main gate at Holcombe. Tom left the cart outside the gate and came up to take their horses out as well.

The prince stood under a bright blue awning which had

been stretched along the front of the great hall. He was tall, with powerful shoulders like a plowman's. His hair was black and so was his full beard. His face was tanned from a summer in the field; his eyes deep blue, Saxon blue. Like Godwin, Edmund was not yet twenty. Around his forehead he wore a single, narrow, gold band.

"Well, Wulfnoth, welcome to Holcombe. And Godwin, good to see you again. How's the new goshawk doing?"

"Eating me out of house and home, Edmund. I hope she will be worth it when she is full grown."

"She will be, Godwin, but how did you do it? The other nestlings died last week. And who is this?" he asked, turning to Branwen.

"My sister, Branwen," he said.

"Why have you kept her such a secret, my friend?"

Branwen curtseyed, mortified to feel her face flush scarlet.

"Have a care, Edmund, she's only a young thing." The voice belonged to a small, fragile, old woman, richly dressed in dark brocade and creamy lace and seated to one side under the awning. "Don't mind my great boisterous grandson, child, he has barely learned his manners."

"Nonsense, grandmother, it's always been a royal perogative to leer at pretty maids. Wulfnoth, you know," he said, remembering the courtesies.

She nodded, greeting Wulfnoth with a warm smile of recognition.

"But not his son, Godwin," Edmund went on, "and his daughter, Branwen the Fair. My grandmother, Lady Aelfthryth, who, as all the world knows, has raised me since my royal mother died when I was still a babe." He bent to kiss the old woman's cheek and then said, "Now you must excuse us, the archers are waiting. Come along, Godwin, I've heard you are no mean fellow with the bow. Bring your sister."

Branwen looked inquiringly at her father.

"Very well," he said, frowning.

She smiled radiantly at him and, dropping a perfect curtsey to the old lady, said, "Excuse me, if it please your grace."

Aelfthryth nodded. "You may join the young people now, my dear, but you must promise to come back for a long visit soon. I'll be spending the winter here and you shall keep me from being lonely."

"Yes, my lady," she said.

When she turned to follow Edmund and Godwin through the crowd, they had already been swallowed up. The courtyard, which was much larger than the one at Thornbury, was filled with knots of people: families with their small children in tow, groups of young girls dressed in their finest, men gossiping together, trying to predict the harvest, young boys chasing each other, dodging through the crowd, dogs barking at their heels.

Not far away Elin was standing at the edge of a group of villagers watching two acrobats. Branwen walked over as the crowd roared its approval of a trick she missed.

"They're really good, Branwen. Stay and watch," Elin said.

"I was looking for Godwin. Did you see which way he went?"

But Elin was intent on the performers, watching as the little one, dressed in motley, was hurled into the air, spinning over and over, bells jangling, before landing lightly on the burly shoulders of his bigger partner. They had begun to juggle brightly colored balls back and forth between them before Elin answered, "Over by the tree, I think. Wait, I'll come with you."

As they were threading their way through the crowd, Branwen noticed a harper leaning against the stable wall. "Look over there," she said, catching Elin's sleeve.

His features were perfect; his eyes, cool and distant, watched a group of young boys wrestling with each other. His clothes were draped with the unmistakable ease of fine wool.

"He must be very good. Look at his harp," Elin whispered. "It's banded with gold."

"He's Edmund's harper."

"Lucky Edmund," Elin said.

There was a sudden hush from the crowd around the ancient oak. "They've started shooting," Branwen said.

"Hurry up."

As they moved through the crowd they could not help noticing the deference the villagers showed Branwen. There were few among them who failed to return her smile, nodding respectfully, moving aside for her.

"Well, Bran," Elin laughed, "It looks like I'll have to be calling you 'my lady' before long."

Branwen frowned. "Don't be an ass," she said.

Near the oak, one man moved aside, letting them in. As if to confirm what they had both felt, he said, "Lady Branwen, you're just in time."

Lady Branwen? she thought. When we went fishing last summer, you called me Bran. Oh Wade, have you forgotten? And then she realized sadly that it had not been last summer but the one before that, and many things had changed. "Edmund's not shooting?" she asked aloud.

"No," Wade laughed. "He lost on the first round."

"Oh, what a pity. Was he angry?"

"No, not Edmund. He only laughed and said that archery is for cottars and geneats."

"Who is shooting against Godwin? It looks like Brun, but who is the other man? I don't know him, do I?"

"You will, so I've heard. He's to be your new steward."

They watched in silence as Brun shot first. He was a massive silent bear of a man who lived alone at the edge of the forest where he had inherited the right of woodsman. He shot with a strength which drove the arrows deeply into the target.

"It would take stout armor to turn aside an arrow from that bow," Wade said respectfully.

When Godwin stood to shoot he notched his first arrow, aimed casually and let fly. All eyes were on the flight of the arrow except Branwen's, who watched the fierce concentration on her brother's face with sudden awareness. His shot was true and he notched a second arrow. Again he shot without seeming to aim. Branwen watched the flight of the feathered reed and saw it veer toward the center of the target as if blown by a favorable wind. The air was calm.

So, she thought, I am not the only one of Anuvial's

grandchildren to have inherited the faery touch.

She watched Godwin notch his last arrow. Then, as he released the string, she called out his name in her mind without making a sound. He started, forgetting the speeding arrow which flew wide of the mark. Branwen smiled to herself; dark storm clouds crossed her brother's face when he realized he had lost. She knew how much he hated to lose at anything, especially in front of a crowd like this.

"What did I tell you, Godwin?" Edmund said loudly. "The bow is for fyrdsmen." He roared with good natured laughter and threw his arm around Godwin's shoulder. After a moment's hesitation, her brother, too, laughed and called for a towel to wipe the sweat from his hands and face.

Then it was the stranger's turn to shoot. Clearly the sympathy of the crowd was against him and he stood with his mouth set in a firm line. When his three arrows flew truer than Brun's, there was only a low murmur and Branwen was sorry because he had shot well.

"Come on, Elin," Branwen said, walking over to where the men were pulling their arrows out of the target.

"Sorry, brother dear," she said, teasing him gently, knowing from years of practice just how far to push him.

"Are you?" he said, an edge to his voice.

Ignoring the edge, she asked sweetly, "Won't you introduce me to the winner? Wade told me he's to be our new steward."

"Aye, my lady," the man answered for himself, "if you're Branwen, Wulfnoth's daughter, then it will be my pleasure to serve you."

"You speak as well as you shoot. Dyffed, isn't it?" she asked, noting the square, strong face smiling through the thick bush of brown beard. His clothes, although worn, were not of the coarse wool Wade wore and indeed there was an air of command about the man. He would be most welcome at Thornbury.

The crowd had thinned out when the four of them turned back toward the hall.

"Edmund will have Bran and me at the head table,

Elin," Godwin said, walking across the yard. "Will you see that Dyffed is not lost among strangers? There were some who were not too pleased to have their champion bested out there this morning."

"They'll get over it soon enough," Dyffed said. "But I'll be glad for your company, Elin, if you've a mind."

Elin colored slightly and said, "I'd not mind."

And so they went in and found their places in the hall.

"Ah, there you are, my dear. Your father and I were worried that you had gotten lost."

"Oh no, Lady Aelfthryth, my brother was introducing me to the man who is to be our new steward, Dyffed. Do you know him?"

"Dyffed?" she repeated slowly. "Yes, I know him. A pity—he lost everything to those godless Vikings. He was to have made a very good marriage, too, I'm told, but now, of course, that's impossible." She gestured with open hands.

They rose to their feet as Edmund made his way through the crowd to take his place at the center of the head table, which was set up on a platform at one end of the room.

"Well, shall we begin then?" he said as he reached his place. "Father Anselm, the blessing."

Through the drone of the priest's voice, Branwen listened to the clatter of cauldrons and kettles, the restless movements of the villagers waiting for their food, the rumblings of the dogs milling around the room, all finally overwhelmed by a chorus of "Amen" as Father Anselm finished. The mugs were banged on the table and the joints were brought in.

"Who is your handsome harper, there at the end of the table?" Branwen asked Edmund as they attacked the enormous meat pasty in front of them.

"Handsome harper, is it? I shall tell him you asked. That's my brother, Elfheah. He fancies himself a harper. You know," he said, lowering his voice, "he claims to have seen Taliesen himself. I think he is quite mad. Shall I ask him to sing for you?"

"Would he mind?"

"What does it matter if he does?"

"Perhaps later, Edmund."

He laughed, turning his attention to Godwin, who sat on his sister's left. "Now, Godwin, you must tell me what you have done to keep the young goshawk alive." He spoke with his mouth full of savory pie. "The other nestlings have died, you know."

"It's Branwen," her brother said. "She has a way with birds. I've even heard her talk to them."

"And do they talk back?" Edmund laughed.

"Do they, Bran?" Godwin asked, getting even with her for the arrow.

"Sometimes," she answered softly, her eyes lowered, staring at the table.

"You don't say?" the prince asked, pausing to look around at her. "And the little goshawk, what did she say?"

"She was hungry, my lord, and frightened. Once she knew we would not hurt her she was content, and began to eat."

"Well, well," Edmund said thoughtfully. He laid down his knife slowly. After a moment, the mood passed and he roared across the room, "More wine here."

Branwen looked at her brother. "You're an oaf," she said in a low voice.

"Is that so?" he said, holding out his cup to the pourer.

Later, when the servants were bringing in the great bowls of pudding, Edmund leaned forward and shouted to his brother, "Elfheah, a song for the Lady Branwen."

Elfheah looked down the length of the table. His hair, cropped short, curled carelessly around his face. There was a look of casual disdain in his eyes as he met her own. She smiled uncertainly. His gaze slid past her without a flicker of acknowledgment and she found herself grinning foolishly at nothing.

"Your pleasure, Edmund," the harper said, standing up. He put his foot on the bench and rested the harp on his knee. He ran his fingers lightly over the strings and the room was filled with music. He sang a familiar ballad which began,

King Easter wooed her for her lands,
King Wester for her fee,
King O'Luve for her comely face,
And for her fair bodie.

His voice was clear and true and the song well chosen.
There were whistles and foot stampings when he finished,
so he sang again, moving through the hall, between the tables while they ate. When he had returned to his own seat
and put down the harp, Edmund said, "Well done,
Elfheah. Well done."

The villagers shouted, banging on the tables with their
cups.

When the noise subsided, Edmund gave the word for the
dancing to begin. There was an eager rush for the doors as
flutes and recorders began to play in the courtyard.

They danced the great circle dances, holding hands in
lines which wove in and around, turning and twisting, while
the pipers played their high-pitched dance tunes, a drum-
mer tapping out the beat on a pair of small goat-skin
drums. They danced and danced and when they grew tired
or out of breath, they dropped out to stand in groups,
watching those who were left, until the call of the music
drew them back into the circle once more.

It was a warm evening. The stars shone overhead, a light
breeze ruffled the leaves in the great oak. Pale-winged
moths flew around the flickering torches, falling eventually
to the cobbled courtyard with singed wings. Branwen
danced without stopping, trying to banish the silent, empty
ache that made her feel unaccountably alone in the midst of
the happy, laughing crowd.

It was quite dark when finally they took torches for the
trip home.

The next morning at dawn, while the household was still
sleeping, Branwen slipped into the meadow outside the
stockade. There was a strange clarity in the early light,
outlining each leaf on the top of the old oak, glowing coldly
in the low lying mists. She walked through the glow, a being set apart from all others, alone in the silent world.

Then, suddenly, the sky began to fill with the cry of larks waking hungry with the sun. Wheeling, they called to her. She stood quite still, the mist swirling around her feet, her head in the dawning light. She looked up at the sky, yearning to be one of them. She shuddered, a small, almost imperceptible movement, as her soul broke loose. She was free among the larks, high over the walls of Thornbury.

There was a lightness upon her spirit. No weight of loneliness bore her down. No wild yearning, no hunger disturbed the pure, fierce joy of flight. Higher and higher she flew until the meadow was only a small square in a mosaic of fields below her.

Then she saw her brother bending over the shape she had abandoned. He must have followed her out. Ansgar's warning rang in the air: "The spirit must find its way back into the flesh," he had said, "or be condemned to roam this world forever."

Godwin was walking toward the walls of Thornbury carrying her body in his arms. Quickly, she dropped from a great height. She opened her eyes and looked up at him.

His face was grey. "My God, Branwen, are you all right?" he asked. His voice was raw, grating on his fear.

"I think so," she said innocently. "I must have fainted, that's all."

"You lie," he said angrily, putting her down with a jolt. "I've seen you with that old man. He is teaching you more than healing skills."

"There was so much the old ones knew, Godwin. So many things that are lost now."

"It's a good thing they are," he said. "There's too much danger in that old magic. Leave it be."

Her voice was very quiet but there was a hard edge that cut through the morning stillness. "And will you set aside your spear and never hunt boar again? And the shaley corner on Wyllum Hill, you'll never again race around it—because it's too dangerous?"

"That's different, Bran."

"No, it isn't," she said. "I am not a child, Godwin."

He looked at her for a long moment. Her jaw was set; she held his gaze and did not look away. "No, that you are not," he answered grudgingly. "But for God's sake, be careful."

The harvest began in earnest now. The days were long and filled with work for everyone. Each evening Branwen left her chores and took supper to the old man. He, too, was busy, working in the garden behind the kitchen, tying the household herbs in fat bunches to hang from the rafters in the kitchen, digging out the root vegetables to bury in the sandy floor of the root cellar. Two young boys had been hired to help him with the digging, but they laughed at the old man and he was helpless to catch them, so he worked along at his own pace. Only in the evening, when Branwen brought his supper in to him, could he rest.

Although the little hut was snug now and the roof and walls tight, they both knew that the winter would be especially difficult for Ansgar and that they might not share the seasons round again. There was a kind of subtle urgency to her lessons as she worked by candlelight on her drawings and notes. Not flowers now, but the roots which had to be dug each fall in the fields and woods and how to clean and store them; roots like gentian and restharrow, witch grass and shepherds knot.

Dyffed and Godwin went everywhere together. Their backs aching, their hands blistered, they worked with the cottars, harvesting the oat crop with short sickles. Everyone was glad to get that crop in and move on to the wheat fields. The mill turned endlessly, grinding first the wheat and then the rye into coarse, brown flour. The straw was piled high around the barn to shelter it from the north wind.

The two smiths Godwin had hired from Salisbury arrived and set up shop in one corner of the courtyard where the ancient forge was cleared off, the fires lit, the rotting leather of the bellows replaced with newly tanned oxhide. The cooper worked in a shed across the way, near the well, turning out the barrels they would need at hard frost when the herds of swine came in from Cowstead and Nettleden. While the weather held the hogs remained out in the oak forests where they were being fattened on acorns. Soon all that pork would have to be smoked or salted down to keep it through the winter, ready to be sent to Edmund when his army began to assemble in the spring.

Elin's father, Bynni, worked at Thornbury that fall, too. The pig sties and goat barn had to be enlarged to hold more live animals. Several sows would be bred, instead of just one, to keep up the production of piglets. The goats would have to be milked; they could not be allowed to run dry for their milk would be needed for cheeses. The manor seemed to bulge at the edges.

The long hours in the field in September weakened the old man and early in October he collapsed. They carried him into his hut and laid him on the fresh straw. Branwen sat with him, holding his head on her lap all afternoon. In the evening he drank some of the oxtail soup Aelle sent from the kitchen. He seemed to feel better and sat propped up on the pallet talking softly with her. "There is one thing more, child, I would have you know before I leave you," he said. "The birds can bear a message across the land for you."

"I don't understand, Ansgar," she answered softly. "You can't leave me—not yet."

He hardly seemed to hear her. "Mark my words well," he said, "they can fly swiftly carrying your words when you have need of them. There was another Branwen, many years ago, who taught a lark. . . ." His voice trailed off. He dozed.

When he woke he had drifted away from her, back into his youth. He talked of the land he came from. He told her of the fields and marshes of Denmark, of the frozen winters. As the sky grew dark and the fire died down in the hearth, he began to talk to her of the hills he had come from before he was captured and taken to Denmark. He talked of the hills where the old people lived, under the shadow of the dragon caves. He talked again of the girl called Penardim who believed in unicorns.

As the night wore on, he began to fade from her even as she held him. By cock's crow he was dead.

They buried Ansgar that morning at the foot of his garden. Branwen wouldn't let them erect a cross over his grave and hunted instead for a suitable stone along the brook in the valley. After she had seen it carried in and set in its place, she turned, her eyes red with crying, and went into the hall.

She gathered her things together and went back with them to the little hut. She hung her cloak on the door and tossed her quilt on the straw pile. She set her comb and a bit of mirror on the table; the red wool dress which she had worn the day of her mother's funeral hung next to the soft rose one on a peg on the side of her grandmother's chest.

She kindled the fire and sat in the big chair. Let Godwin and Dyffed share the hall with Wulfnoth. Let them talk of war and battles. There was no place for her in their world. They treat me, she thought, as something handy, to be picked up and then put down as suits their need. There has to be more to life than that. There has to be.

That evening, after her father had drunk deeply of the fresh peary and had run through the day's news with Godwin, he turned to Branwen and said, "I'm sorry, little one. The old man will be sore missed by you, I fear."

"Yes, father," she said softly, her eyes brimming with tears. "There was so much to learn from him. Father," she added, "I have moved my belongings into Ansgar's hut. I am going to live there now."

"No, Branwen, it wouldn't be safe. There are all manner of men in and out of the walls these days."

Godwin snorted alongside of them, choking on his laughter. "God's Blood, father, she would be safe in the middle of an army camp. Do you know what she can do?"

Branwen looked at him in alarm. He was drunk and she reacted instinctively, silencing him with her will. Godwin looked at her, startled and suddenly sober, as he tried without success to bring the words out of his mouth. It only took a second or two and Wulfnoth never noticed. He had walked over to where Tom sat finishing his supper wearily. They spoke a few words and Tom nodded, wiping out his bowl with his last crust of trencher.

Then Wulfnoth turned to her and sighed. "All right, child, if you are sure that drafty hut is what you want, you may try it."

"Thank you, father," she said and reached up on her toes to kiss his grizzled beard.

She went over to the livery cupboard. Unlocking the door with a key from the ring she carried on her waist, she removed a long, yellow tallow candle.

"Good night, father," she said as she went out.

Tom followed her into the night. "You'll be sleeping here regular, Branwen?" he asked.

"Yes, Tom."

"Well then, if ye've no objections, I'll be sending Bynni in the morning to put a bolt on the door for you and see to strengthening the shutters."

"Thank you, Tom. Good night now."

She added a few small pieces of wood to the glowing embers but did not light the candle after all. The day had been long after a night with so little sleep. She slipped off her tunic and put on her warm woolen sleeping robe. She lay down under the quilt and was asleep in minutes. She never heard the small sounds that Tom made as he rolled himself up in his blanket to spend the night outside her door.

She woke from habit before sunrise and dressed absently, her mind dulled, unable to face the starting of the new day. She stopped to splash cold well water over her face and hands before going into the kitchen which was already busy. Although the sun was not yet up, fires had been lit in the wall ovens in preparation for the day's baking. She sat at the table watching Aelle move assuredly through the morning routine.

After a while she went across to the stable. She saddled the small palfrey and tied the panniers securely behind the saddle. They were filled with the healalls she had learned to use. Today she rode slowly, unable to shake the leaden mood which had settled over her. It had been almost a week since she had ridden down to the village with Ansgar, that last time, and she knew there were several people who would be looking for them. They had come to welcome Ansgar's visits. Would they welcome her now that she was alone, she wondered?

They did, at least the two she tended that morning did, and the others would as well, although she didn't know it yet. Ansgar had been reassuring with his great store of knowledge, but it was Branwen they had begun to look for; Branwen, who had the hands of a healer.

She had lunch on the open hillside where she could look down at the abbey and the river beyond, at the road that ran east/west. All of it seemed grey and empty. She fed the scraps of her coarse dark bread to the birds. Lost in her loneliness, she did not talk to them. She thought of the old ones and wondered. If she travelled north, into the mountains, could she find them, any of those who still kept the ancient ways, who still knew the runes of wizardry? Were there any left of the people who had raised the great stones to mark the far points of the moon's path? Were there any left in all the world who still knew where the unicorn grazed? Were there any left who had seen a dragon spread its wings over the high crags? She knew in her heart that she would have to find out. She knew that was what Ansgar had meant her to do when he taught her the art of the shape-changer. He had shown her the way, the way she could travel any road, the way she could search for the answers she needed. She knew that this was what her grandmother had intended, so long ago.

What kept her here, she wondered? She thought of all the sensible reasons for not going and then laughed at herself for being afraid. But it wasn't only fear that kept her and she knew it. It was Thorkell. She had to see him again. The one thing which kept her at Thornbury was the knowledge that, sooner or later, he would come back.

Chapter Five

THE SUN HAD set when Branwen rode back through the wide gates and into the courtyard. The new stable boy, Cobbe, took her horse from her and she walked wearily into the hall to say goodnight to her father and brother.

Wulfnoth sat hunched over in his chair near the fire. His head was bowed. She went up to him softly, not wanting to disturb him if he slept. But he was awake and looked up as she came near.

"I didn't hear you come in, Branwen. You've been gone a long time."

"I stopped at Holcombe to see the Lady Aelfthryth, father."

"Well, I'm glad you've come home at last." He smiled gently at her and she could see that he was deeply disturbed.

"What's the matter?" she asked, frightened. "Where's Godwin?"

"He's gone," Wulfnoth said wearily. "A messenger from Eadric Streona arrived this morning, soon after you'd gone, with an invitation to a harvest festival at Cray. Godwin was rude to the man and when I rebuked him, he lost his temper. He's gone. Rode off to join Edmund."

"Oh, father, I'm sorry. But you mustn't blame yourself. Godwin was anxious to be gone. You know that. If it hadn't been today he would have found an excuse sooner or later. You know that he felt he was missing too much staying here."

"Yes, you're right. I was the same when I was his age. But I'm afraid he will stay away too long." Wulfnoth was silent for a long moment and then went on, "First your mother, then Ansgar. The grim reaper is not far off. Oh, Branwen, I feel the coldness of winter in me."

He was so low that Branwen could not bear to leave, but sat there with him in his great hall, a warrior's hall that rang in the stillness with the echoes of men's voices, the tread of booted feet, the clang of weapons set aside for a few hours while fighting men talked of battles. The men of his command were all old now or dead. His glory was faded by the sun of many summers but his hall was large and his son was strong. Hundreds of men would answer the fyrd call in his name; not only from Thornbury but from estates he seldom visited which owed him fealty. Wulfnoth knew this power was passing to Godwin and the embers that glowed where fire had raged flared up against the coming night.

She learned more about the scene between her brother and father early the next morning as she sat in the kitchen talking with Elin across the worn wooden table top.

"Godwin lost his temper," Elin said. "He felt Eadric was mocking Edmund. Your father's been sleeping poorly for several weeks. He was tired and snapped at him, telling him, in front of us all, that he was still lord of Thornbury."

Branwen could well imagine the scene and Godwin's shame which had forced him to save face by leaving rather than backing down. There was no need to go into the details.

"What do you mean, Elin, that my father has had trouble sleeping? Why didn't you tell me before this?"

"Oh, Branwen," Elin answered, looking down at the newly swept floor. "It was only that he told us not to tell you. Aelle and I have brewed him many different tisanes to help him sleep but nothing seems to do much good."

And it was true. Branwen was angry with herself for not noticing it earlier. It was written clearly on her father's face that morning. She would have been able to see it easily if she had ever taken the time to look at him. If he didn't want her to know he was sick, however, she would not speak of it. But she did not ride out that morning. Instead, she sat with him at breakfast, noticing what he ate.

Over his second cup of wine, which seemed to revive him, he turned to Branwen and said, "I am going to send you to Cray for the feast tomorrow. Eadric cannot be snubbed regardless of how Godwin feels. I am too old to stir up trouble with Ethelred over a triviality. You will go and I will send Dyffed with you. I think even your brother would have accepted that compromise if he had not been so hot-headed."

"Yes, father," she said.

She tried, out of loyalty to Godwin and Edmund, not to become excited at the prospect of going to Eadric's, but it was difficult to sympathize with Edmund's hatred for his father's councillor when she understood so little of the cause of the bad blood between them.

Late in the day she built a fire in the laundry room and set the big wash kettle on to heat. The pot was bigger than any they had in the kitchen. It took Snel twelve trips from the well to fill it for her. When they had finished supper she went back to the laundry where the fire had burned low and the water in the cauldron was hot. The small room was warm. When she bathed, the soft mutton fat soap, which she and Elin had made only last week, lathered into great billows of bubbles. Soft and sweet smelling, she sat by the fire combing her hair until it dried. Then she dressed and went back into the hall to tend to her father.

She mixed a sleeping draught of hawthorne and balm, steeping the herbs in hot wine. When it had cooled a little, she added a few drops of attar of damask rose so that the steam rising from the cup would make him drowsy. It was a fine, strong brew. She was confident, watching him grow heavy-eyed as he drank slowly from the cup she handed him.

She helped him to bed and watched as he dozed off. She

wrapped herself in a blanket and sat in the big chair listening to the crackling fire and Dyffed's soft snores across the room.

How much longer before Elin sleeps here with him, she wondered, feeling more alone than ever at the thought of the happiness they had found in each other. Then she laughed, a little ruefully. Isn't that what I want? They can run Thornbury and I'll be free. But free for what? Free for what?

She looked at her father, who slept peacefully. How silly of Elin not to tell me. See how easily he sleeps.

She, too, grew drowsy in the warm, dark room with the flickering firelight. She must have dozed for a little while because her father's soft groans woke her. She rose and went silently over to him. He was still asleep, but his sleep gave him little relief from whatever tormented him. He lay curled on the bed, softly moaning.

It had been a strong decoction she had made for him. He should have slept until cock's crow. She was frightened; only severe pain would cut through his sleep like this. She began to examine him gently, not wanting to wake him. She was afraid if he woke he would send her away. She was afraid, too, of what she would find. And it was there, as she had feared: a large hard lump rising out of the still firm flesh of his abdomen. Gently she covered him and quietly left the room.

Wax dripped on her hand from the tallow she held to light her way to the small hut in the corner of her father's rich holding, but Branwen felt nothing. She set the candle down in the holder on the table in the center of her room, went over to her grandmother's cabinet and opened the left door. Pausing to think for a moment, she opened the second drawer from the top. She pulled it all the way out because it was high, over her head, and she needed to see what was in it. She set it down on the little table. It was not quite half full. How long would it last her father? A month? She wondered how long the lump had been growing there.

"Dyffed will have to get more from Salisbury," she said aloud in the chill dark of her room. She would leave instructions with Elin in the morning to prepare some of the narcotic so that it would be ready to measure out when she returned from Cray.

Branwen lay down on her bed in the corner, but sleep eluded her. *What will I do when the poppy is gone? The pain will grow worse. What if there is no more in Salisbury?*

There was no answer but the one she could not face.

As they rode through the crisp, glittering morning on the frozen cartway to Cray, Branwen explained to Dyffed what she needed and why.

"I'm sorry to hear this, Lady Branwen. Your father is a fine man. I will ask about the opiate you need, but . . ." He gestured with open hands.

"You must send someone to Salisbury. The apothecary there will have some. You must do it tomorrow." Her voice was firm.

"Yes, my lady," was the only response Dyffed could make.

Talking of the miserable business at hand, Branwen forgot the nervousness and excitement she had felt yesterday. It no longer mattered what she would say to the great lord from the king's court. Her mind was full of her father. She had no care for Eadric or his dinner. Her eyes were particularly dark and haunted. The cold ride brought a glow to her cheeks, contrasting with the winter whiteness of her skin. Her hair, soft and dark, framed her face under the hood of her cloak.

A groom took their horses from them as they rode into the courtyard at Cray, and they were shown into the hall. Branwen held back a little as they made their way through the crowd, her eyes scanning the room, surprised at a lavishness she had never encountered before. There were small groups of beautifully dressed men and women glowing among the darker villagers. Great long beeswax tapers were set out on the arches waiting for the early darkness. The walls were completely covered with colorful tapestries and even underfoot woolen weavings had replaced the rushes she was used to.

She realized that she had been separated from the page who had been leading her. He and Dyffed had disappeared. Branwen stepped back into the shelter of a thick carved oak column, watching the crowd as if from a great distance. She stood quietly, unthinking and uncaring. She didn't notice Eadric until he was right in front of her.

"Well . . . so you are Wulfnoth's daughter," he said. His eyes were icy green. His hair was brown, cut short, curling softly over his ears and framing his face. He was slightly built, taller than Branwen so that she looked up at him but only because she herself was so small. He had an aura of easy elegance, of power, as he stood in front of her, the power of one who was used to having his own way.

"My lord, I am Branwen, Wulfnoth's daughter," she said, her voice calm, almost cold. She noted the arrogance in his manner but it was nothing to her. Her cloak was open and the Celtic jewels which had been her inheritance from her mother and grandmother flashed around her throat and waist. "My father is not well and could not come himself. He hopes you will hold him excused. I am sent in his place."

"But, of course," Eadric said slowly. "We are delighted that Wulfnoth would send you to grace our feast. You must give him our regards when you return home. I hope he will recover soon."

"Thank you, my lord."

He stood in silence for a moment, looking at her as one might appraise a fine silver goblet which could be worth acquiring. He mistook her distraction for disdain and it intrigued him. Suddenly he turned away from her and she was left alone.

Soon Dyffed returned and said, "This way, Lady Branwen." His eyes were bright. He seemed pleased with himself.

They made their way between the tables until they reached one which stood first along the wall leading from the head table on its dais. There Branwen recognized the men of the fyrd of Thornbury. There, standing at the table, were fourteen men who served her family when called. Brun and Wade were there. Old Manni, who had lost an eye fighting the Danes, was there, and Bynni, too, Elin's father. She greeted them all solemnly.

"Why aren't your wives here with you today?" she asked.

"Yer brother isn't the only man loyal to the prince, lady," Manni said. The others nodded in agreement. "This Eadric's a bastard. We all know it. Yer father's taken much from him and his brothers in the past, but not today."

"What do you mean?" she asked, horrified. "You're not going to make trouble?"

"Nae, nae, dinna fret so, lady. It's only that he thought to slight yer father by seating you among the villagers this afternoon. The head table is filled with his rabble from court. Well, there'll be none of that. Ye sit here with us and we'll see to it ye are treated as yer father's child should be."

"Oh," she said relieved. "That's very good of you, I'm sure. My father will be pleased that you cared." But, she thought, can it really matter? Look how pleased they all are with themselves.

The meal progressed from pumpkin in ginger broth, spicy and hot, through a sweet fruit and salmon pie, to skewered larks with venison in a dark, rich, savory sauce, each course washed down with goblets of good wine imported from Normandy. As they ate, Branwen found that Eadric was watching her. Each time she lifted her eyes to the head table he would be looking at her. She began to feel uneasy. I will not look up there again, she told herself, but the more she tried not to, the more she did. The wine, too, began to have an effect and she realized to her dismay that it had been served almost full strength. This was not the usual spiced and watered wine she served so often at home. This was a fine Norman wine that needed no help to make it drinkable. Her worry over her father faded into a haze at the back of her head. The merrymaking around her grew brighter. Her laughter became gayer, no longer forced, but no one noticed. The whole affair was gradually becoming quite drunken.

As the last of the sweets were cleared away, the musicians began to play. There was a general scraping of benches as the tables were folded back to clear a space for dancing. In the uproar, she was never quite sure how it happened that Eadric stood beside her pouring more wine into her goblet. She only knew that he was very attractive. His face was like a lonely child's, wary of hurt, hungry for love. His eyes watched her, lambent, and she could not still the pounding in her breast.

"No more wine, Lord Eadric," she said. "I'm afraid I've had too much already."

"Come and dance, then. It will clear your head."

"Oh yes, I'd like that," she said, too eagerly.

But when she stood up, Eadric did not move back as she had expected him to. He remained close to her so that she was caught off balance. His arm went around her waist to keep her from falling but he did not step away. She felt her body come alive as her own desire rose up, catching her by surprise. His body felt warm, close and hard. There was a scent, too, rich and undefinable, like that of some dark root whose use no one had ever explained to her. She never noticed the look of easy victory curling up the corners of his mouth.

They danced together then, and when the music paused Dyffed was there and they danced to the wild quick tempo of the country dances she had always know. And there were others when Dyffed tired and she danced, laughing, her father forgotten for a small hour that afternoon. Eventually her youth outstripped the wine, her head cleared, and the wild desires of an hour earlier began to subside.

"Dyffed," she said, when the music stopped for a moment, "we should go home."

"Aye, lady, whenever you're ready."

Her face was flushed from dancing and from the heat of hundreds of candles burning on the archways. Her eyes still flashed with excitement, although her head was calm and thick-walled against the sudden shame and sorrow she felt welling up in her.

Seeing her pick up her cloak, Eadric moved away from the group of courtly women he had been standing with. He stood alone near the door as she made her way through the crowd toward him.

"You had a good time this afternoon, Lady Branwen?"

"Yes, my lord, it seems everyone did. Edmund will be hard pressed to keep the affections of the villagers when you offer such rich diversion."

"And you," he asked with polished slickness, "where do your affections lie?"

"My heart is yet my own," she said quietly.

"Well, perhaps I shall ride over to Thornbury before I leave, to pay my respects to your father."

"If it please you, my lord. I am sure my father would be honored."

"Eadric, Eadric, come see what Willibrord can do," called a doll-like creature with a whiny voice.

Eadric grimaced. "Good-by for now then, lady."

"Good-by, my lord."

Wulfnoth slept peacefully that night, drugged with the opiate Elin had prepared earlier in the day.

Branwen wondered at his stoicism as they sat together over bread and wine the following morning. He admitted not to even the smallest sign of the pain she knew he must feel. She offered him his jeweled goblet which contained more of the drug.

"Here, father, drink this. It will ease the pain for you."

She held her breath, waiting for the storm to break. His eyes swept her face, reading her dismay and misery.

"So," he said, "it's true. I'm dying." He stood up and walked over to the window. "It comes at last to us all," he added, turning back to look at her.

Her eyes filled with tears and she could not answer him.

"Come, come, Branwen. I expect better from you. You've tended more than your share as they died around here. Tell me what you can. How long?" He held the goblet in his hand without drinking from it.

"I don't know," she admitted. "But the medicine Elin prepared yesterday seems to ease you. Come, drink it, please."

"And sleep the morning through only to be drugged again and sleep once more? Would you have me die before I die?" He put the cup down on the table. "It is not so bad, child," he said, running his hand over her head, smoothing the curls. "It is enough to know that the cup is there. Don't fret. If only Godwin were here." He turned and went out of the hall to begin his morning rounds of the manor buildings.

Branwen went into the kitchen. Elin, working over the last of the jelly, looked up when she came in. "Dyffed sent Wade to Salisbury this morning to try to find some poppy."

Branwen was not encouraged by her tone. Trade was very slight with the East these days. Their surpluses had been drained away by the Dane's tax. There was little left to trade with foreign ships and they came only infrequently to port.

Out in the courtyard, she found Dyffed going over a supply of new spear points with Wigbeorht, one of the new smithies. "They're not sharp, not one. Look at this," he said, flinging it on the coals. "When we go to battle I hope you march with one of these. Then you'll know quick enough what a difference it makes to a man's life." He looked over and saw her standing against the wall waiting for him to finish. "See to it they're sharp," he snarled. "Bastard," he grumbled, walking toward her, "he should be standing in a bloody field trying to shove a dull point through boiled leather while the other man is trying to shove one into him." He spit for emphasis.

"Dyffed, I need some help," she said, thoughtfully.

"I sent Wade to Salisbury this morning."

"We've got to get Godwin home."

"Oh, that'll take a while, lady," he said, shaking his head slowly. "Even if I leave now, it's bound to be a week's riding to get to Coventry and then it's hard to say where they'll be."

"No, Dyffed," she said. "We need you here. And I'd not ask any man to ride that road alone this time of the year."

"I'd be safe enough."

"That may be true but I can't risk it, and it would take too long."

"What then?"

They had been walking in the direction of the side gate which led through the stockade near the little hut into the field beyond. They stepped through it into the meadow, pale green with the new growth of winter wheat.

"Dyffed," she said gravely, turning toward him, "will you help me?"

He looked at her steadily. "Aye, Branwen," he said

carefully. "What do you want me to do?"

She stretched her arms up and out at the skies, calling a loud, wild cry that hung in the grey sky, echoing off the far hills. The sky was still as the echo faded but then a black speck appeared, rising out of the trees, and then another, and two more.

"They're coming," she cried exultantly. "It worked. Are you frightened, Dyffed?"

"Not yet. Should I be?" he asked warily, watching the sky. "What have you called?"

She laughed. "The ravens. I've called an unkindness of ravens."

"An 'unkindness,' " he asked archly, "not just a flock, uh?"

"When one deals with ravens, Dyffed, one must observe all the proprieties. No raven would admit to being part of a 'flock.' Oh no," she laughed, "ravens assemble as an 'unkindness' or they won't assemble at all."

"Oh, I see," he said smiling. "Now tell me why you've called them."

"We'll ask them to get Godwin. That's where I need your help. You'll have to tell them where he is, how to find him."

"But Branwen," he said practically, "I don't know how to talk to birds."

Branwen watched the sky without answering him. There were ravens all around them, settling on the field, their great wings folding, their hooked beaks pulling idly at the young wheat. The wind died down and everything was still. They waited.

"Now what?" Dyffed asked.

"Watch."

The bird was enormous, with a wingspan wider than any raven's she had ever seen. Like a black eagle, it circled lazily around to land on the bare branch of an oak in the middle of the field thirty yards away.

"Come on," she said, leading the way across the field.

She stopped well back from the tree and called to the bird in strange, unrecognizable sounds, neither the tongue of the rook nor the tongue of man. And the great raven answered her. Back and forth it went until, at last, she said, "He's agreed. Watch."

The king of the ravens spread his wings and, gliding low over the birds waiting in the field, spoke hoarsely to them. Then, as he turned toward the hills, his wings beat powerfully and he rose into the low-lying clouds. The rooks in the field rose to follow him. The air was filled for a moment with the sight and sound of their black wings.

When the sky and field were empty, they saw that one bird remained, having settled unnoticed in the upper branches of the oak, where he perched, pecking disinterestedly at the feathers of his left shoulder. He's still young, Branwen thought, somewhat disappointed. His ruff is not full-feathered.

"Greetings, Blaec," she said aloud in the ancient language, using the name told to her by the king.

The bird uttered a deep, guttural croak.

"I need a message taken to my brother who is many leagues distant. The old one says you are strong and clever. He says you will take it quickly."

The bird was silent, eyeing her, his head sideways, his eye red and glittering.

"Was the old one wrong then, that you sit silent? Are you afraid to leave the nest, fledgling?"

The bird, having only birdly wisdom, rose up then on the branch. Spreading his wings, he arched his neck, glaring out over his strong, curved tearing beak. Suddenly she knew why the old king had chosen this one to carry her message. This was the new king-to-be. The old one must be hoping he never gets back, she thought. Already the young bird's wingspan was wider than her outstretched arms and his shaggy throat feathers, still growing, would be a noble ruff under that powerful, threatening beak.

I will take your message where you will, flightless one. Your brother is not unknown to me, he-who-has-another-hunt-for-him.

She turned to Dyffed and said, "He was well chosen. There's not much danger to a bird like that between here and the eastern sea. Now we have to tell him how to find Godwin. Tell me where he should look, the rivers, the towns, the mountains and hills and I'll tell him what you say."

Then Dyffed, well trained in language in this age when storytelling was still an honored art, described in great detail the border lands of Mercia and the Danelaw. And Branwen told the bird what the soldier told her.

At last the raven, beating his wings, rose into the sky and flew off to the northeast. It was past dinner time. When they returned to the hall, Elin, seeing them both come in together, turned abruptly and left the room.

" 'Sblood," Dyffed swore. He put down the trencher he had just picked up and followed her out.

Wade had been gone for four days and it had rained every day since he left. Branwen spent an hour or so each morning in the little house spanning the loom. It was tedious work, stretching the linen thread evenly, back and forth, between the frame pieces, and it helped pass the time while she waited for him. She had worked all summer with Ansgar on her sketches for this tapestry. She had planned to spend the winter here with him, learning from him, escaping from her father and brother whenever possible.

Today, when she heard the abbey bells ring sext, she looked up and was surprised to see the sun breaking through the clouds. She had just put the thread down when Elin came in.

"It's Eadric, Branwen," she said breathlessly. "Lord Eadric, he's ridden in just now. All alone, he is. Dyffed has shown him in to the hall but your father is sleeping and . . ."

"Eadric?" she said. "He said he might come, but I thought. . . . Tell Aelle we'll have dinner as usual. Oh, and put on a clean apron."

When Elin had gone, Branwen removed her own soiled linen apron, hanging it over the back of her chair. She removed her woven belt and slipped the household keys off it. Reaching into her chest she took out the heavy silver belt which had been her grandmother's. The plates, joined together with flattened links, were heavily engraved with birds and large-eyed gripping beasts. Slipping the keys over one end, she buckled it to hang loosely over her warm blue winter tunic. She ran her new boar bristle brush quickly over her hair and hurried through the yard into the main hall.

Just outside the door Dyffed caught her by the arm. "Keep him in the hall. Your brother and Edmund won't want word of what is going on here to get back to Ethelred."

"I'll try," she said.

Eadric was standing at the window looking out over the river. He was dressed in trousers and a tunic of rich dark red wool, simply cut, unadorned with the furs and jewels he had worn at Cray earlier in the week. His sword and the jeweled belt it hung from were his only ornaments and they hung low over his narrow hips. A falcon sat quietly on his wrist.

He turned from the window and stood there, the light behind him, staring at her across the flames which burned between them in the long, low central hearth. The detail of her belt was not lost on him. She was glad she had not put on an apron.

"How thoughtful of you to come, my lord," she said. "I am sorry my father is too ill to receive you."

"Good day, Lady Branwen," he said, bowing slightly. "What a pity he is not better."

"May I get you some wine?" she asked, walking over to the livery cupboard.

"Thank you," he said.

She poured out a goblet of wine which she had mixed with balm and honey several days ago. It was not the fine Norman wine he had served at Cray but it was a good drink and one which they served often at Thornbury.

"Now, if you will excuse me, I'll go and see how father is. I'll only be a moment."

The opiate she had fixed for Wulfnoth that morning was gone. He lay unconscious across the bed, his boots still on. She tugged at them until they came off. Covering him as he lay, she struggled to keep back her tears. She felt lost and inadequate and very alone.

The hall had filled during those few minutes she was gone. The three village women who were weaving in the women's room under the eaves had come down for their dinner. The smithies had come in, Wigbeorht and Swetmann; the stable hands and Tom were there; and even Brun, who had brought in a cartload of wood today, had stayed to eat.

Branwen sat next to Eadric, hardly tasting the spicy pork and raisin tart or the venison stew with pepper sauce. The flush of excitement she had felt at his arrival had died out, leaving only an ache of worry for her father. She knew she was poor company but she did not care.

Eadric, too, was quiet as he sat beside her at the center of the long trestle table. "You set a good table, Lady Branwen," he said, finally. "Your father must be proud of you."

"Thank you, my lord," she answered absently, picking at the broken trencher bits in front of her.

"Is he dying then?" he asked her.

She turned quickly to him, angry that he would be so unfeeling, but her anger died when she saw the honest concern written on his face. He covered her hand, lying on the table, with his own.

"Yes," she said, struggling to control her feelings.

"Where is Godwin? Why isn't he here?"

"My brother left before we knew"—she hesitated—"before we knew that father was sick. We've sent word to him but whether he'll get it in time, I don't know."

They sat in silence until Eadric said, "Will you hunt with me this afternoon? Surely the air and the exercise will be welcome after all the rain."

She knew without looking up that Dyffed was watching her. She would have to go, to keep Eadric away from the yard.

"If you'd like, my lord, although I'm afraid your tiercel will find little prey here this time of the year," she said, knowing that wherever she rode the small game would not flush, lying hidden as she commanded.

She was right. No bird, no rabbit, nothing moved except his hawk circling around in the sky screaming its disappointment. They rode for an hour, until the sun began to drop in the western sky. They saw no game.

"I've never seen the fields so cleared," Eadric said.

"My brother says the hunting is much better in the spring," she lied, as they turned back to Thornbury.

"In the spring you must come to London. You would be a welcome breath of freshness at court," he said. "Would you come?"

"The spring is a long way off," she said. "But I think not, my lord. This is my home. I'd be lost in London."

"I'd be there. You would not be lost." His smile was warm and open. There was nothing sinister or threatening, and Branwen wondered why she had felt so challenged by him earlier. Gone was the arrogant courtier and in his place was a friend. This afternoon she felt desperately in need of a friend.

"Tell me about the court, my lord," she said.

"That would take a while, I'm afraid." He laughed. Reining in his horse, he dismounted and led the animal to where Branwen had halted several yards ahead. He helped her dismount and they began to walk slowly back to the manor whose stockade they could see rising above them on the hill across the valley.

As they walked he told her about Ethelred—what a difficult person he was to serve, lacking the strength of mind necessary to run the government. How often he changed his mind; how impossible it was to depend on anything he said; how his mood changes were swift and deadly; how the spectre of his brother's murder haunted him waking and sleeping. The slightest mention of the dead king was enough to drive him into deep depression.

"And the queen is no help," he said. "Emma can't stand the sight of him. At first we thought it would be better, that she would lend him backbone and courage. When they were first married, ten years ago, our hopes were high. But she is too much of a woman for him; he can't control her at all and she despises him for it. I think she can't even stand the sight of her own children because they are his. God knows she hurried them off to the priests at Oxford when they were hardly weaned from their wet nurse."

This last held the trace of the sneer Eadric had shown when they first met. It was an echo that tripped her up as she tried to understand the man who walked with her toward Thornbury.

"And what of your wife, the Lady Eadgyth? I've heard that she is very beautiful."

"The Lady Eadgyth is my wife for political reasons only," he said coldly. "We see each other as little as possible; she has her estates, and I have mine. Were it not that there was no way to refuse the king when he offered his daughter in marriage we would not have indulged in this farce."

"Poor Eadgyth, she must be very lonely."

"You jest," he said angrily.

Branwen blushed as she realized that her simplicity had led her roughshod over what was apparently very tender ground.

"Oh, I am sorry, Eadric." She reached out and touched his arm. "Please excuse me, I meant no offense."

He walked on in silence for a way before saying quietly, half to himself, "I think you must be the only one on this island who does not laugh at me. Streona, 'the Grasper,' they call me. 'He overstepped himself that time and look what it got him.' " His laugh held no mirth at all.

As they entered the courtyard, Dyffed was waiting.

"What is it?" she asked. "Wade is back?"

"Aye, my lady, he rode in a few minutes ago. There was nothing," he said gently. "The apothecary laughed at him. There has been no opiate in the market for months and none is expected."

She sagged visibly under the news so that Eadric reached out to support her. She leaned against him heavily, her face pale. "Thank you, Dyffed. Tell Wade I'll speak with him shortly." She turned to walk back to the gate with Eadric.

"What does this news mean to you?" he asked. "The opiate, was it for your father?"

"Yes. I have only a little left here. I had hoped to get enough to ease his dying—but now I don't know what I'll do. It is hard to watch him suffer. He knows I can end it for him—but how can I?"

"My dear," he said gently, taking her by the shoulders and then lifting her chin so that their eyes met in the gathering twilight, "surely there are limits to what is asked. My own physician who travels with me is at Cray even now. He will send you the opiate you need in the morning."

"Would you do this?" she asked. "How can I repay you?" She hugged him then, laughing and crying together.

"Lady Branwen"—he laughed—"your man, what will he think? There will be plenty of time for repayment. For now it is enough for you to keep your own counsel when you hear the things people say of me. There is little love lost between your family and mine. Your brother is Edmund's man and that makes him harsh in his judgment of me. Don't let them sway you to their side completely, my lady." He took her hand to his lips and, holding her eyes with his, kissed her palm. "Go in now and tend to your father. I will see to it that the drugs you need are sent in the morning. And you must promise to send word to Cray if you need me; otherwise, I shall spare you needless gossip. I will be back in the spring. Come to London with me then."

He covered her mouth with his finger so that she could not answer him and then he turned and rode out the gate.

Chapter Six

IT WAS COLD and the rain came down steadily as they stood under the bare branches of the rowans in the churchyard. A solitary raven perched overhead, watching.

"It seems longer than a twelvemonth since we buried father here," Godwin said.

"God, what a bloody awful year!" Edmund swore bitterly.

"I'm glad he didn't live to see it," she said softly, remembering their humiliation as Swein had swept unopposed across the length and breadth of the land.

The first of the Viking army had landed at Sandwich early in July while Swein and the fleet had gone around East Anglia into the mouth of the Humber. At Gainsborough all Northumbria had submitted to him without a fight. In a matter of days the people of Lindsay and the Danelaw had knelt to him as well. Uhtred, Sigefirth, Monkere—all the great nobles surrendered and gave him hostages. Swein had then moved south unopposed, taking what horses and supplies he needed as he moved through Leicestershire and across Watling Street. Oxford and Winchester surrendered to the approaching army and gave hostages. Nowhere had there been any resistance.

Edmund had tried to gather an army to oppose the Dane

but pitifully few answered his call. Ethelred had remained unseen behind the walls of London, making no attempt to defend the land, not even acknowledging Edmund's right to carry the royal banner into the field. Edmund found himself scorned—the younger son of a king now married to a second wife with sons of her own. His claim on the common man's loyalty was too tenuous to raise an army, especially in the face of such overwhelming numbers.

By September Swein had crossed the Thames and was camped outside the walls of London, demanding its surrender. But Thorkell and his men held the city for Ethelred and would not yield it. Poor Thorkell, how he must be chafing inside those walls, she thought. Swein abandoned his siege of the city almost before it had begun and went off in search of easier sport. If Thorkell and Ethelred wanted London so badly, they could have it. He would settle for the rest of the island.

Just before the winter rains closed in, Swein swept across Wessex, north to Bath where he was acknowledged king by the conquered nobility. In triumph, he returned to the Humber where his young son, Knut, waited with the fleet and seven hundred hostages. They were still there, celebrating.

There was no news from London. All roads were in the hands of the Danes and travel in and out of the city was impossible. Only Thorkell's fleet kept the city open to supply through the river gates.

"I pray the new year will be better, Edmund," she said.

"Amen to that," he answered bitterly.

They stood in silence a while longer, looking at the dripping grave stones until the cold seeped through the shoulders of their thick, woolen cloaks and they turned toward the horses and home.

When they rode into the stable at Thornbury, Leofric, coming from the mews where he and Elfheah had been feeding the falcons, asked, "And how was the good father this morning?"

"It wouldn't have hurt you to have come yourself," Branwen answered, "or Elfheah either."

Leofric laughed. Elfheah, leaning carelessly against the

wall watching Cobbe take the stallion from Branwen, said nothing.

The hall was filled with the aroma of roast venison and stuffed goose. The walls were hung with the tapestries taken from their storage chests for the feast. A great fire burned in the fire pit and candles burned extravagantly throughout the room. Under the table, the dogs lay gnawing on yesterday's bones. The raven Blaec flew in through an opening at the roof peak and perched, dripping, on the back of a carved oak chair.

"Well, what next, Edmund?" Leofric asked, filling a mug.

"Hell, I don't know. Swein won't be able to consolidate his victories until spring. Until then we are safe enough. If my father will stay in London through the winter. . . ."

"He'll stay, Edmund," Branwen said. "He won't just abandon us. He can't. Then, in the spring, perhaps the ealdormen will unite against the Danes," she finished lamely.

"Not likely," growled Godwin. "They were all too ready to deal with Swein last year. Nothing will change them, short of a miracle."

"There won't be any miracles while Ethelred sits on a throne stained with his brother's blood," Leofric said.

"We don't need a bloody miracle," Edmund snapped. "We could have stopped Swein and held at least Wessex if our royal father had taken the field. But he just sat there all year, behind those thick London walls, and the rest of the country be damned. No wonder the ealdormen wouldn't rally behind their king," he ended bitterly.

"No man is king," said Elfheah coldly.

"He held London, at least," said Branwen quietly, trying to dispel the gloom.

"He didn't hold London, God damn him. Thorkell held London, as he bloody well might. Swein will have that Dane's still-beating heart if he gets a chance."

Branwen shuddered. She got up from her seat and walked over to the window, looking out through the glass toward the river beyond. How wonderful that glass was. She remembered when her father had found these prized pieces; how pleased he had been to be able to build this window for her mother. Looking out now into the cold, wet January noon, she thought of Thorkell, wondering what he looked like, what his voice sounded like. It had been almost two years and she had quite forgotten. He would be twenty-six now, she thought wistfully. Perhaps he had married.

She turned from the window as Dyffed came in. He looked tired but pleased and she guessed that the brindle milk cow had finally calved. She caught his eye; he grinned and held up two fingers. And then Elin came in carrying the pork pasty, covered with a cloth against the rain. She was big with child and struggled awkwardly with the door and the pie. She and Dyffed had married last spring only days before he had ridden out with the fourteen armed men of the fyrd from Thornbury. A pathetic handful riding to join Edmund's campaign against Swein—the campaign that never was.

Elfheah began the long Song of Beowulf as they were finishing dinner. It was a good choice for a cold, rainy afternoon. The whole company sighed as one and leaned back against the walls, stretching out their legs, settling in.

Beowulf slew Grendal, tearing off his beastly arm. Just as he descended into the murky waters of the swamp in search of the vengeful mother, Branwen heard hoofbeats in the courtyard.

Dyffed had dozed off, snoring quietly in the shadows. Young Cobbe sat wide-eyed on the floor listening to the singer. Rather than disturb them, Branwen rose quietly and slipped out into the yard.

A rider had come in. The stable door was still open. She wondered who it could be, out on a day like this when everyone should be home with friend and family. She pulled her cloak around her and ran across the yard. It took a few moments for her eyes to adjust to the gloom of the stable and she stood inside the doorway, silhouetted against the lighter grey outside. Suddenly she knew who it was. She walked silently past the stalls to where he was rubbing down his horse.

"My lord," she said quietly, "welcome back."

He turned and she held out her hands to him. She had

forgotten how tall he was. He took her hands in his and stood there for a moment before saying, "Happy new year, Lady Branwen."

She felt suddenly shy under his gaze; her heart began to pound. Thorkell looked haggard, mud-spattered, and bone weary. To hide her confusion, she turned to his great war horse, already unharnessed. She filled the feed bucket with grain from the sack in the corner. When she had finished, she said, "Now it's your turn, my lord. Let me get you warm food and water to bathe. Edmund is in the hall with my brother but surely they can wait."

"What news I have Edmund is not anxious to hear."

She led him around the puddles and through the yard to the little hut that had been Ansgar's and now was hers. She built up the fire from the few glowing embers deep in the ashes until it was crackling and snapping, licking at the dry wood, sending flickering light into the corners of her room and over the ceiling hung with bunches of dried herbs whose redolent odors mingled with the smell of wood smoke. As she tended the fire Thorkell stood, leaning against the closed door, watching her.

When the fire was going well, Branwen stood up and turned to him, chiding him in the way young girls learn from their mothers for not taking off his wet things. And still he stood and watched her until she removed his cloak herself and spread it over the back of the chair to dry. She unfastened the heavily embossed gold buckles that held his stiff boiled-leather armor at the shoulders and along the sides and stood it carefully on top of Ansgar's old chest to dry slowly away from the fire.

He laughed, a hollow, unpracticed laugh, and drew her to him. "Branwen, Branwen, you've not changed. I was afraid to hope."

"Haven't I?" she asked, looking up at him.

"Have you married?" His voice was forced.

The question hung in the air and she was silent for a moment, leaning against him, feeling his strength and the warmth of his body. "No," she said finally, "I've not married. There is only one man whose heart speaks to mine and he has been gone for too long."

"He was a fool." He bent down and kissed her. Lifting

her up into his arms, he held her close. Suddenly she felt a wild despair wash over her, a hopelessness which poured out of him, rising around her. She didn't pull away the way she had two years before. She had changed, she knew her strength now and was no longer easily frightened. Listening with her heart, she reached out to him, touching his abandon, recognizing then the wild freedom which comes to a man who has nothing left to lose.

"Oh Thorkell," she cried, her face against him. "What's happened to you?"

"The fleet," he said, his voice carefully controlled, "it's gone. Gone to Normandy with Ethelred. Olaf commands them now."

"Your fleet?" she asked, her voice hushed by the enormity of his loss.

"The flagship holds at Wight," he said. "Only the Raven's Wing refused to go."

"Why?"

"There was no other way, Branwen. Swein would have hunted us down. I couldn't let my men die for nothing."

"Why didn't you go to Normandy with them?"

"I've had my belly full of Ethelred," he said bitterly. "Better to stay here and die. Besides," he said, shaking the black mood from his soul, "*you* were here. I had to see you again."

There were tears in her eyes. "I was afraid you'd never come back."

His mouth found hers and she was swept up once more into the wildness which raged deep within him. Now his despair was suddenly ecstasy—an unbounded, unreasonable happiness. But she knew that both his despair and happiness were the same—burning too brightly, like a fever, in his soul.

After a while she said in a small voice, not really knowing what to do for him, "When did you last eat?"

"Yesterday morning," he said.

"Yesterday morning?" she asked, surprised.

"Aye. I've ridden straight through from the coast."

"Stay here and warm yourself by the fire. I'll get you something."

"You are food and drink enough, Branwen," he said, pulling her toward him.

She laughed and slipped out of his grasp. "I'll only be a minute," she said.

But when she returned carrying a covered iron kettle with leftover goose, several slabs of bread and a jug of new wine, he was asleep across her bed. She set the pot to one side of the fire to stay warm. She took a goblet from the cabinet on the wall and set it next to the wine and bread on the small table. She fussed with the fire a minute, adding another log. Finally, she set her copper water kettle on to heat so that he could wash. Then she stood quietly just watching the man as he slept. He lay defenseless, vulnerable, and she knew he must feel it, too, even waking. He had been a great leader with forty ships and their crews at his command. They were gone now, taking his power and rank with them, leaving only part of a man behind. Could he heal himself? How could she hope to help him? After a moment she went over to him and brushed a strand of hair off his forehead. She went out again into the late afternoon. The rain had stopped. She walked back to the hall where Elfheah was beginning the final battle between Beowulf and the dragon.

> His name was Wiglaf, he was Wexstan's son
> And a good soldier. Watching Beowulf, he
>   could see
> How his king was suffering, burning. Re-
>   membering
> Everything his lord and cousin had given him,
> Armor and gold and the great estates
> Wexstan's family enjoyed, Wiglaf's
> Mind was made up; he raised his yellow
> Shield and drew his sword
> Then he ran to his king, crying encouragement.
> As he dove through the dragon's deadly fumes:
> "Beloved Beowulf, remember how you
>   boasted,
> Once, that nothing in the world would ever
> Destroy your fame; fight to keep it,

Now, be strong and brave, my noble
King, protecting life and fame
Together. My sword will fight at your side!"

They were her favorite lines. Across the room she noticed tears glistening in Edmund's eyes. Poor Edmund, she
thought, even Wiglaf couldn't help you slay your dragon
now.

When Beowulf's ashes had at last been sealed in the
great tower at the side of the sea, Branwen said, "The
rain's stopped. I'll race you all to the big oak at Nettleden.
Loser gets to rub down the horses."

It was a good idea; they were ready for a fast ride after
being inside all afternoon. They pulled on boots and cloaks
and went out to saddle the horses.

"What's this, Branwen?" Godwin asked, nodding at the
new horse standing quietly at the end of the row of stalls.

"A surprise for the evening, brother."

He went up to the horse and took hold of the harness. "It
can't be good news that brings Thorkell here," he said absently. "Did he tell you? The king has fled?"

"Now Godwin, let's ride first. The news will wait and
he's sleeping after having ridden all night." She was de-
flated that Godwin had recognized the harness so easily, although it was distinctively worked in silver set with amber.

She saddled a young stallion, smiling to herself as she remembered the fuss Dyffed had made the first time she had
ridden out on him. "Ladies do not ride stallions," he had
said. But she had established a rapport with this animal she
had chosen from the eight the men had broken last fall.
When they rode, it was as one. He knew what she wanted
from him at the smallest signal and responded eagerly. She
called him Beornwig, Little Warrior, because he was too
small to be a war horse. He was beautiful and as fast as any.

Today he sensed her excitement and was anxious to be
off. Twelve furlongs to the oak and twelve back over frozen
and rutted road. She and Beornwig led all the way, although she could hear the great horses of the others thundering close behind. By the time they made the turn at the
tree, she was frozen to the bone. When they reined up in

the courtyard her face was reddened with the cold and she was laughing with delight.

"God's teeth, Branwen, you ride like a man," Edmund said, slapping her on the back. "I haven't been beaten in a horse race since I was old enough to grow a beard."

"Listen to him, will you," roared Godwin. "What about . . ."

And then Thorkell stepped out of the shadows and all the laughter of their youth and freedom vanished.

"So," Edmund said softly, "it's over already. He couldn't hold on even . . ." His voice broke and his eyes glittered. In the sudden silence he reached up with a hand to either side of his head and lifted the thin gold band, holding it poised for a few seconds as if reliving a day long ago when, as a raven-haired toddler, he had first received a golden circlet from a father he had not yet learned to despise.

"You take it," he said, tossing it to Branwen. "A prize for a horse race."

Remounting, he rode slowly out of the yard.

Later that evening Godwin and Leofric returned. Edmund remained with his brother at Holcombe, their fate seemingly sealed, condemned to banishment or death.

When at last the household was asleep, Branwen and Thorkell stood alone looking into the darkness outside the hall. She could feel a restlessness in him, like the sea washing up onto the shore and then running out, never still.

"A long time ago you asked me to help you find your unicorn, and I refused. I'll take you now," he said.

"The unicorn," she whispered. "I'd almost forgotten." She was silent for a few moments and then she said, "There were always so many reasons not to go, so many things that needed to be done, little drips that fill a barrel until it is too heavy to move." Staring out into the darkness beyond the window, she went on, "You see, I *have* changed, Thorkell. I've stopped believing that anything is possible, the way children do. I've found that the best we can hope for is the satisfaction of doing a job well each day." She paused and then went on. "Hunting for a unicorn means giving up even that small satisfaction. I am needed here. If I leave, what would my life mean?"

"Am I too late?" he asked.

"I don't understand, Thorkell. Too late for what?"

"I'll take you there," he said, putting his hands on her shoulders. There was a wild, haunted look in his eyes that frightened her. "I'll find a unicorn for you. I know where to look, don't you understand? Everything will be all right."

His hands hurt her shoulders but she hardly noticed. Her eyes filled with tears, not with pain, but with the knowledge that he was a man who had been pushed to his limit, a man whose defenses were cracking. She clung to him. Finally, afraid to argue, no longer caring, knowing that he needed her and that it was enough, she said softly, "I'll come. In a day or two," she added, "when you're rested. . . ."

"No. We must leave at first light. Every minute my men lay over at Wight they are in danger. Swein will be looking for us."

"I'll be ready," she said. There was no other answer. He had nothing left now but her—and this wild quest. Perhaps he just needed something to believe in.

The room was still. The burning logs settled on the coals with a soft sound. After a while, Thorkell kissed her dark hair and, laughing quietly, he said, "It's too bad you weren't looking for a great, green, scaly dragon sitting on a mountain crag with a horde of gold and jewels."

"Why?" she asked. "Do you know where there is one?"

"No," he smiled, "but dragons don't hold out for virgins the way unicorns do."

"Oh," she said with a little laugh that broke the tension and pushed back her fear, making her glad once more that he was there. "I hope we find one quickly," she said, reaching up for his kiss.

It didn't take long for Branwen to gather her things together that night. She stopped at the stable where Beornwig greeted her, surprised at the extra measure of corn she doled out to him. She took the saddlebags her father had always used. They were soft and dark with the oil of many years.

In the little hut she quickly packed one of the bags with the herbs she found most useful. In the other she put a change of clothes. There was still room so she added the old red wool jumper which she had worn when Thorkell first rode into Thornbury. Wrapped inside, she carefully packed her grandmother's silver belt. The narrow gold crown Edmund had given her that afternoon she placed in the bottom of Ansgar's small chest.

She lay finally on the straw of her bed and waited for sleep to come. The raven perched unmoving atop the tall cabinet against the wall.

"Well, Blaec, will you come with us in the morning?" she whispered. The bird didn't stir. She smiled, knowing he would follow her anywhere; it would be impossible not to take him with her. "I've always thought your flight to Coventry last year turned your head, you know. When you got back you were too sophisticated for the local girls." But Branwen knew it was her fault as well. What ordinary raven could compete with her when she soared through the skies, her feathers iridescent in the sunlight? If Blaec were confused by her shape-changing, he didn't let it bother him. In whatever form she chose, his devotion to her was unswerving. To Branwen he was not a pet but a good friend. She spoke with him often, learning from him, for the rook was a very smart bird and would undoubtedly be king but that he aspired to greater glory.

They rode hard the next day, pushing the horses through the cold, raw winter fog. The cold bit through the layers of wool and only Branwen's pride kept her from crying out to Thorkell to stop. She wondered if he meant to ride through the night. That thought only made her more miserable. Beornwig snuffled softly, sensitive to her mood, questioning the relentless pace. Long after dark Thorkell turned off the road into a grove of trees. They rode a short way along an overgrown trail until they came upon an abandoned building. Four walls still stood, more or less, and in one corner part of a roof still spanned the distance.

They brought the horses out of the wind into the shelter of the walls. They fed and watered them, rubbing down their heavy coats. Then, kindling a small fire, they huddled together under the roof making a meager meal of the bread and cheese they had brought with them. They sat there, hugging their knees to their chests, each wrapped in a thick wool blanket. Gradually warmth came back into Branwen's body, and the misery of the unending ride that day gave way to such an excitement and sense of adventure that she could hardly sit still.

Sensing her emotions, Thorkell laughed gently. "Do you affect everyone like this?" he asked.

"No," she said, looking at the fire.

They sat in silence for a while and then she added softly, "Don't you see? The threads of our destiny are interwoven too tightly. That's why we can't hide our feelings from each other; why you are the only one I have ever met who. . . ." She tried to find the words but she was very tired and could not.

He leaned toward her and kissed her. "You're right, little one," he said gently. "But we have a long, cold way to go. It won't be easy. Sleep now, while you can."

Wayworn, Branwen slept easily on the frozen ground between their small fire and the crumbling walls of the decaying hut. The sound of the horses, snuffling and moving around as Thorkell tended to them, woke her some hours later. The fire had burned out and their shelter was dark in the early dawn shadows. It was bitter cold. She lay there, wrapped in her blanket, feeling for the first time the hardness of the ground and the ache in her shoulder which came from sleeping on it.

There was a sudden rush of wings as Blaec, who refused to fly after sundown, caught up with them. Settling on the crumbling wall, he preened himself, pointedly ignoring them.

Thorkell looked up curiously. "Friend of yours?" he asked, nodding at the raven.

"His name is Blaec," she said, and then added, "I think he's in love with me."

"Oh ho!" he said, grinning. "First, the horse, and now a raven. Tell me, are there others?"

They pushed the horses hard as the sun rose that morning. When they reined up at last on the top of the dunes overlooking the south coast, a church bell in the distance

began to ring, calling the monks for morning devotion.
They gathered driftwood and seaweed and lit a smoky signal fire. The Isle of Wight lay on the eastern horizon lightly
veiled in fog.

Seeing a Viking longboat making for the cove at their
feet, Branwen felt an uncontrollable flash of terror.

"Now, Bran," Thorkell began, laughing at her fears.

But the laughter was instantly frozen and his voice became harsh. She felt a violence rise in him beyond any she
had ever sensed before. "Fenrir take your manhood,
Swein," he growled between clenched teeth. "Wait here,"
he commanded. "If I live I will come back for you."

"I don't understand, Thorkell, what is it?" she cried,
even as she saw, sailing out of the mist in the southeast, the
striped sails of two Viking ships.

"They can't see them. They're still coming in. May the
raven fly with us this day."

Making up her mind instantly, she spoke a word to
Beornwig, confident that he would find his way safely back
to Thornbury.

Thorkell turned on her angrily when he realized that she
had no intention of waiting for him on the dunes. "You
can't come with me, lady."

"Don't tell me what I can or can not do," she snapped,
having been pushed too far already. "This whole thing was
your idea and you're not leaving me here. I won't lose you
so easily, not any more." She picked up her saddlebags and
started off, running lightly down the path to the beach. She
heard his heavy footfall behind her.

The Viking longboat had a shallow draft but there was
no way to avoid wading out to it through the January surf.
Oh God, I hate being cold, was all she thought as the water
rose around her legs. She tossed her bags into waiting arms
and was pulled unceremoniously aboard.

The ships Swein had sent were closing rapidly, cutting
them off from the open sea. Thorkell strode to the bow,
taking command, leaving her without a thought.

Branwen stood on the tossing deck, holding tight to a
cross brace supporting the helmsman's deck high in the
stern. The waves were crashing onto the shore behind them

as they pulled out of the shallows. The brilliant blue mid-morning sky was charged with the same wild note she had sensed in the Dane before: Thorkell's joyous abandon.

His voice was low but it throbbed through the ship like a heartbeat. His swift chant, like an invocation, marked the beat for the oarsmen. She watched their faces as the men of Thorkell's flagship prepared their hearts for bloody battle and violent death. She felt her own soul, too, being drawn in, caught into his will. And as she watched, she saw the fear of death leave the ship. Like a grey cloud, it left, and behind was a glory of brightness, a living light. Drops of water on the rigging shot fire like precious stones in a diadem. The sky and sea became a burning intensity of blue. Her gaze swept down the two banks of rowers and saw the grinning wild faces of men now gone berserk. And still the chieftain's chant throbbed through the ship. Her eyes caught his and she surrendered herself to his joy. Her soul, freed, soared into the sky, a raven iridescent in the sun, screaming from the masthead where the raven banner flew. Then a second great raven answered her call, flying out from the shore. She rose into the sky to meet him. They flew up into the sky, circling higher and higher.

A mighty shout went up from the men of the Raven's Wing. Heartened by the omen, they felt for a moment as if they might clear the point and gain the open sea. Then, inexorably, the gap between the ships narrowed. The closing ships were newer; the men bent over those oars were younger. Thorkell's men were seasoned veterans who would outlast any crew over a distance but in this sprint the advantage was clearly with the younger men.

Now they could see the grinning faces, hear the chants of Swein's captains. Thorkell's hand tightened on his axe, the roar of battle already in his ears, the blade already thick with blood.

Suddenly the pursuing ships broke cadence, their oars clattering against each other.

"Pull, men, pull. The ravens of Odin fight for us this day."

Even as he spoke, the men could see the two great birds darting among Swein's seamen. Wild oars toppled men from their benches, cracking ribs and heads. One rook rose and flew at a helmsman. Clutching his face, he let go of the long sweep.

Thorkell's ship rounded the point and without a pause, headed southwest into the open sea which lay between them and Land's End at the westernmost tip of Cornwall. No crew in the world could catch them now.

Then Thorkell raised his gleaming battleaxe above his head, saluting the ancient god of war, one-eyed Odin, guarded by wolves, counseled by two ravens. The tall chieftain laughed. "By Odin's ravens, we'll see Swein in Hell."

But his laughter rang hollow through the still sea air. His men, plunged suddenly back into the chill of mere mortality, watched him, pulling steadily now, the distance increasing rapidly between the boats.

In vain he tried to break the mood as he strode the length of the deck greeting each of them. On the last bench, Ragnar leaned into his stroke. "Odin didn't send them ravens, Thorkell," he said.

"It's her doing," said another, nodding to the space under the steerage. "They do her bidding. We seen 'em."

"Well then," said Thorkell, standing firm on the rolling deck, his legs apart, "we're lucky to have her with us." His eyes were steel, daring them to disagree.

Even as he bent over the small figure tucked among the bales under the deck, he knew something was wrong. She was too still. An awful, sinking dread rose in him until he could taste its bitterness in his mouth. Branwen lay unmoving, the salt water freezing on her boots and skirt. Her eyes were open but unseeing. Only the soft sound of her easy breathing reassured him that she was not already dead. He pulled her out onto the deck and began to strip off her frozen clothes—whistling a sharp call as he did so. There was an unmistakable groan from the other side of the coiled rope. A great dog labored to his feet and walked stiffly over to Thorkell.

Obediently, the dog lay beside the small, inert body, letting the heat from his great bulk warm her. When Thorkell returned with dry clothes from her saddlebags, the blueness was less pronounced. Clumsily, the Viking chieftain pulled on the dry tunic, woolen stockings and boots, dressing her as if she were some strange doll. His face was set; not a flicker betrayed his feelings. The men watched uneasily. When he finished, the dog still curled around the motionless form. Thorkell covered them both with a rug of wolf pelts and walked away.

A following wind came up toward evening and they raised the sail, shipping the oars. Thorkell stood in the bow, watching the shore for the narrow break in the dunes that opened to a salt marsh where they could lay over, hidden from sight. As the sun went down, the temperature dropped steadily and the salt spray began to freeze on the lines and over the plunging bowsprit.

Safe at last in the marsh, they built their fires on the shore in the shelter of the dunes. There they ate and drank from the ship's stores, but they were cold and tired and there was little on the frozen beach to shelter them from the wind.

Pym sat next to Thorkell, hunched inside his furs, watching the flames. They had been together a long time. After a while he asked, "What's wrong with her?"

"I don't know," Thorkell groaned. Rising to his feet, he tried to peer into the darkness back the way they had come. "I think that damned bird won't let her go." And he walked away, leaving Pym more puzzled than before.

Thorkell crossed the gangplank. A blue cover had been spread to make a roof over the galley. He wrapped himself in his blanket and sat watching the still figure of the girl. He dozed off almost immediately. The last hard days finally demanded their toll. He was never able in the days and weeks which followed to sort out his waking and sleeping that night.

He had a dream that a great raven landed on the high stern of the ship. Even in his sleep he had felt an overwhelming sense of relief. Branwen's back, he thought and struggled to wake. Then the image of the great rook faded and the girl stirred. She sat up slowly. He tried to call out to her but he couldn't make a sound. She turned and looked at him. Her smile was radiant. She rose and came silently toward him. Gently she touched his forehead and kissed him. The dream gave way to the darkness of sleep.

In the morning, when he woke, she was there, sitting on the coil of rope, eating a ship's biscuit, stroking the dog.

"Good morning," she said.

"So, he let you go after all."

"Blaec is a very intelligent bird, but it never occurred to him that any raven, however unnatural, would fly at night."

"What will he do now?"

"Go back to Thornbury, I think. He is king of the ravens there, you know."

They were both very aware of twenty Norsemen watching them, some boldly, others over-busy with their gear.

"I'm glad you're here," he said quietly.

"Me, too," she whispered with a smile.

A stiff breeze blew from the northeast and they sailed a long reach across the water toward Land's End. Seated high in the prow or standing at the tiller, Thorkell watched Branwen move among the men that day. She sang songs so bawdy, even these hardened sailors laughed; she took thread and needle from Pym and neatly finished his mending for him; she helped the men rubbing rust from their swords with wood ash. The wind blew steadily throughout the day and by late afternoon they rounded the tip of Cornwall and turned north along the Atlantic coast.

Lowering the sail, they rowed into the bitter wind, harboring at sunset in a cove which sheltered them from the long Atlantic swells. There was skim ice on the rocks at the bottom of the low sea cliff.

They lowered the gangplank over the side and ate a meager meal of ship biscuit and dried fish around several driftwood campfires on the beach. It was a very dark night, the moon was hidden by a thick blanket of cloud and it was bitterly cold. The little warmth from the fires was blown away by the winter wind and the mist which had begun to fall with the dark was gradually turning to rain. Branwen wondered if the stories of Jomsborg were true. Did the rigorous training produce men who were unaware of this bitter, knifing cold?

As she watched Thorkell move among his men, talking

to them, laughing with them, she felt tired and very alone. All day she had struggled to bend the minds and hearts of the men around her for his sake. That same aura of peace she had radiated unknowingly when she first met these Vikings on the day of her mother's funeral, she used again. It was a skill she had learned well. By landfall not even Ragnar remembered his fear of her magic.

When Thorkell finally left his crew and walked over to her, she was too tired and cold to care. Seeing how unhappy she was, he smiled and picked her up into his arms, carrying her toward the ship. "Come on, little one," he said. "Let's find a warm place for you to sleep. Only one more night like this," he added as if to comfort her. "We'll be in the Severn in two days and then there will be shelter for us all."

The cold was all around, coming through the sides of the ship from the sea and blowing over the top, still from the northeast. The rain froze on the rigging; the deck was slippery with ice. The cold could only be endured. Wind blew the rain under the deck cover. They all slept together in the center of the ship, burrowing under the furs, sleeping poorly, disturbing one another all through the night. The men were eager to row at first light. They rowed all that day, under the dripping blue canvas, grateful for the warmth their work brought them. Branwen sat in the lee of the ship's stores, the dog at her side, singing their rowing songs with them. It rained unceasingly.

They reached the wide mouth of the Severn early on the second day as Thorkell had said, and rowed steadily up river until late in the afternoon. Rounding a bend, they came within sight of a large timbered hall surrounded by a sprawling village of thatched huts. The men on board the Raven's Wing gave a loud cheer. Thorkell leaned strongly on the tiller and the longboat grounded sharply on the broad gravel beach.

Chapter Seven

BRANWEN STUMBLED AS they led her across the frozen ground up to the big house. Her feet were beyond feeling. When she walked through the doorway the warmth struck her suddenly, like a blow. She staggered and would have fallen but for a small arm which reached out to steady her.

"Welcome to Tottenness," the woman said. "I'm glad you're safe. Word came that Swein had sent ships after you. We were afraid he would trap you at Wight."

"He damn near did, Winfrith," Thorkell said ruefully.

"Well, apparently he didn't succeed," she said. "After you are warmed, you must tell me all about it."

She was a gentle woman with dark hair braided around her head like a coronet. Her clothes were rich and her hands soft. She led them toward a small room off the main hall where a fire was crackling merrily.

"This is Branwen, Wulfnoth's daughter," Thorkell said as they stood around the fire.

"Thank you for your hospitality, my lady," Branwen said, sinking down on a little stool by the fire.

"Why she looks positively frozen, Thorkell! What were you thinking of, bringing her around by sea in this weather?" She clapped her hands and called to the servant who answered, "A large kettle of hot water and be quick about it."

"It was the only way," Thorkell answered. "We couldn't wait until spring. We were almost too late as it was. But we'll stay here a while," he added, "until she's ready to go on. A week or two won't matter now. When she's ready . . ."

Just then the serving girl returned with a large copper kettle of water which she set to one side of the fire.

"Leave us now, Thorkell. Botta and I can do what needs to be done and there's food and drink in the hall. You're just in the way here," Winfrith said.

"Aye," he said slowly, not anxious to be gone. "I'll send in her things." He turned at the doorway and added, "I'll be back after supper."

As he returned later that evening he heard sounds of laughter coming from the small room. He pulled aside the curtain and Branwen rose from her seat by the fire to stand facing him. Her cheeks glowed and her eyes sparkled. Her hair was braided up like Winfrith's and topped with a white lace cap. She wore her red woolen tunic and the silver belt he remembered seeing long ago. She was so beautiful that he felt suddenly awkward, unsure of what to say.

"Well, if you two will excuse me"—Winfrith laughed—"I have work to do. Don't forget, come to the kitchen and we can have breakfast in the morning, Branwen."

When the curtain had fallen behind Winfrith, he held out his arms to her. Lightly she ran to him across the rush-strewn floor. She raised her face.

"Well," he said after a time, lifting his lips from hers and taking a deep breath, "you seem warmer now."

"There was a time"—she laughed—"when I thought I would never be warm again."

"That was the hard part, Bran. The rest will be easier. We should never have been at sea but," he shrugged, "it couldn't be helped."

"It's all right," she said. "It's over now. Swein won't look for you here. We'll be safe for a while, won't we?"

"We can't stay, Bran, not for more than a week or two. Then we'll have to go." He rubbed his hand wearily over his face. "We've got to be back before spring. Once the good weather arrives. . . ."

"How far do we have to go, Thorkell?" she asked softly.

"Not too far. Eadric described a place near Lydney. . . ."

"Eadric!" Branwen turned away from him. "What does he know of all this?"

"Ah yes, I remember," he said slowly. "You were coming to London to join him."

"I was not! Never!"

"He mentioned it one night. 'This charming child from Wessex,' he called you—and laughed."

"He means nothing to me. I don't care what he calls me. He gave me the drugs I needed when father was so sick, there at the end. I'm grateful to him, that's all."

Thorkell laughed, a bitter laugh. "Tell Winfrith, why don't you."

"Why should I tell Winfrith?"

But he only shrugged and looked away. They sat in silence for a long while. Finally he said coldly, "He knows nothing of this. You don't have to worry."

She looked up at the despair in his heart and voice. "Oh Thorkell," she said, "I'm here—with you."

"I won't share you with any other man, Branwen, not Eadric, not anyone."

"Why?" she whispered. "Why?" But her voice was so low he didn't hear her. After a while she said, "How can there be anyone else? You are the only man whose heart speaks to mine. Isn't that enough?"

"Aye," he said, thoughtfully, looking at her, smiling finally, "it's enough—for now."

He lifted her and carried her over to the bed. He sat down, pulled her to him and kissed her, long and hard. She sighed softly and her body melted against his. He felt her hunger, and knew she hardly recognized what she felt. He knew he could give her such pleasure as she had never dreamed of. Tonight the unicorn would seem a small price to pay for their happiness. But tomorrow, he thought, what will happen to us if I take away her dream? It means so little to her now—I wonder if she would mind at all. Not this year perhaps, or even next, but the bitterness would grow. In ten years she would be all shrunken inside, hating herself, and me. She needs to find her answers. And all the pleasure in the world is not worth giving up a chance to find them.

And, thinking of Branwen's dream, he remembered his own, the dream he had had as a child, the one which had become part of him, and a darkness came over him as if a cloud had passed over the moon.

"What is it, Thorkell?"

"It's nothing."

"Tell me," she said softly.

"I was thinking of an old dream I had once." He laughed ruefully. "There's not much left of it now."

"Tell me," she said again.

He looked away and then began, self-consciously, "The first gift I remember getting was a wooden sword Sigvaldi gave me. I was barely able to walk but I already knew my half-brother was a famous warrior, that he had fought alongside Harald Bluetooth, that he had been given command at Jomsborg when the old king lay dying there. It wasn't until much later that I knew what Jomsborg was. Not just a village like the one my brother Hemming and I lived in but a great camp of warriors, where no women were permitted, with a harbor big enough for two hundred and fifty longboats. Hemming and I were sent to Jomsborg when our mother died. He was nine and I was five. Knut was there, too. But he came later. . . ."

He stopped, lost in thought, looking into the distance at scenes she could only imagine. After a while he looked down at the woman he held in his arms. "How patient you are, Bran." He laughed.

"Is that all you really wanted," she asked, "to be famous like your brother?"

"Hemming and I, and Knut, too, after he came, dreamed of being great Viking chieftains. We would be brave and daring, we'd never fear death, we'd laugh in the faces of our enemies. Well," he said slowly, dreamily, "for a while, I guess, it was true, but it's all over now." His voice was thick with emotion.

She was quiet, lost in thought for a moment, watching the fire crackling low in the fire pit. At last she said, "You are wrong, you know, about the dream. It wasn't about being a great Viking chieftain. It was about being a great man. And you found that greatness, you know, and no one can ever take it from you."

Their kisses and caresses that night held a sweetness sharpened by the restraints his will imposed. And Branwen was introduced to the beginning of love-making. After a while Thorkell, growing tired of children's games, rose and crossed to the fire. He added a log while she watched, warm and soft in the flickering light. He poured two cups from the pitcher of metheglin set on the side chest. She came and stood by his side, taking a cup from his hand.

"Here's to the unicorn," he said sardonically, raising his cup to hers. He emptied it and said, "Good night, Branwen."

She laughed dryly, "I think they will be surprised to find you sleeping in the hall."

"Aye," he chuckled, "that they will. And we'll keep them guessing a while longer. Winter can be so boring; they'll be glad to have something to talk about."

It was long after dawn when Branwen woke. She dressed quickly, grateful that her boots had dried during the night as they sat near the fire now greyed to ash. She pulled her cloak around her and hurried out to find the kitchen, Winfrith and some food, for she was very hungry.

As she stepped into the hall she searched for a familiar face. There was none. She started across the room and everywhere strangers turned to watch and a silence began to grow so that the door seemed miles away. By the time she reached it her face was the color of her jumper.

"Damn," she muttered, stamping her foot as the door closed behind her. "Damn, damn, damn!"

It wasn't hard to pick out the cook house. Smoke billowed from the roof and groups of men were clustered about the door. As she started reluctantly in that direction, a familiar voice behind her said, "Have you warmed up then, Lady Branwen?"

"Pym," she said, relieved. "Yes, I'm much better now."

They walked across to the kitchen talking of the pleasures of sleeping in a house again. When they got to the door and were confronted with the smells of new bread and roasting meat, Branwen suddenly felt as if she had not eaten in days. She heard a startled laugh.

"By God, Branwen's here and hungry, too."

Through the smoke she could see Thorkell sitting on a stool, talking to Winfrith.

Branwen smiled and walked across the room toward them.

"Good morning, my dear," Winfrith said. "I was just going to get you. Come, sit here. Let me get you something to eat."

"Good morning, my love," Thorkell said quietly when Winfrith had gone.

She smiled at him and asked, "Do you want to leave this morning, Thorkell?"

"Not today." He laughed. "We'll stay here for a few days. I've got to spend some time with the men working on the Raven's Wing. We're going to pull her up on the shingle later this morning."

"Oh," she said relieved, "I didn't know."

"Winfrith will keep you busy, Bran, don't worry," he said as the lady returned with a wooden bowl of stew and a thick crust of bread.

"It's good to have company, Branwen. It can get lonely here in the winter."

Thorkell left and Branwen and Winfrith sat together on the high stools, leaning against a large vat in which several salmon swam lazily. A continuous stream of men and women came in, had a cup of warmed wine and a slice of thickly buttered trencher loaf and left. There was a pot hanging over one of the fires which was full of rabbit stew, but very few dipped into it so early in the day.

The kitchen was much bigger than her own. Branwen counted four ovens set into the thick stone wall. There were fires burning in two hearths built in the center of the beaten earth floor, filling the room with smoke which eventually found its way out through holes in the thatch roof. Near where they sat a fire burned in an opening in the stone wall, and the smoke seemed to disappear behind the wall. Branwen wondered if it were a fireplace such as she had heard the Normans used. Between mouthfuls, she asked Winfrith, "Is all this yours?"

"Didn't they tell you?" she said. "Tottenness is Eadric's. He holds the whole Severn valley in liege from Ethelred himself."

"Does he come here often?" Branwen asked, concentrating on her bowl.

"Not often, praise be, and when he's not here," she said with a smile, "I am in charge."

"What's he like?"

"He's a bastard," Winfrith said, indulgently. "Shall I tell you a story?" She paused and Branwen nodded politely.

"Once there was a young girl who lived on a small country manor with her mother and father. When she was fifteen, she came here to this house for the Easter festival. Eadric, for some reason, singled her out for his attention. She was flattered but nothing more.

"And then her father had some difficulty with the money-lenders and stood to lose everything—his house, the stock, everything. Eadric came forward with the money and the sweet young thing, confusing gratitude with love, was suddenly his for the taking. But Eadric is crafty. He left the Severn valley without seeing the girl again. A whole year passed before he returned to collect his fee. By that time the young girl's imagination had created a hero in shining armor astride a white charger. She went eagerly, gratefully, to his bed and became mistress here and here she has stayed—his mistress for the Easter season.

"There, isn't that a good story? And do you know what?" she added, conspiratorially, "he has another at every one of his great houses."

No, not every one, thought Branwen.

"Oh, it's not a bad life, Branwen," Winfrith went on. "In fact, I like being mistress here and, of course, I am free to take any number of lovers as long as I keep the calendar free at Easter. His being in Normandy now may throw his scheduling off a bit."

Her voice caught and Branwen looked up at her.

Winfrith laughed and whispered, "Yes, my dear, I really do love the bastard. But don't tell anyone," she added, "it would ruin my reputation."

Branwen, her mind reeling, muttered a banality she hoped would pass as appropriate. In her confusion, she barely noticed the old woman shuffling up to the table, her lined face dark with fatigue and worry.

"The boy, my lady. It began again in the night."

"The fever again," Winfrith said softly. She rose to her feet wearily, all the freshness gone from the day. "Pray excuse me, Branwen, my son is ill. I must go to him."

"Let me come with you," Branwen said, feeling a surge of relief. Here, at least, was something she could understand.

The child was small, just turned four, his golden curls clinging to his sweaty forehead, his cheeks fever bright.

"Let me help, Winfrith. I am not without some skill. Thorkell will tell you. One of my bags has some herbs which will bring down his fever. Let me help, please."

"We've done everything we can but the fever only lessens. It never goes away. It's been a month and each time it leaves him weaker. Oh, Branwen, if you could. . . ."

Branwen stayed with the sick child all day. In the evening he was no worse. By morning the fever was gone. Gradually, over the next few days, he grew stronger. When it had been three days since he had had any fever, Branwen took her things and left the nursery.

She went back to Winfrith's room where she had slept that first night at Tottenness. Winfrith had insisted she come and share her room rather than move into the women's quarters.

"They all snore so. That one night when I thought you and Thorkell would. . . . I slept up there with those women and it was a long night, you may be sure. No, Branwen, you sleep with me while you are here."

"But what of your lovers?" Branwen asked, trying not to blush. She wanted so much to have Winfrith think of her as a woman, one who understood matters of this kind.

"My lovers?" said Winfrith, questioning. "Oh yes, my lovers. Well, they will have to wait. It will do them good."

Word spread of little Eadwig's recovery. A woodman came in one morning with a nasty cut that wouldn't heal. Then it was a cottar's wife whose stomach ached and no purgative seemed to help. When a man called Binney came in with a wracking cough and walked out quietly, she began to feel the change around her. No longer was she "the girl Thorkell brought in." She had become Branwen again. And she began to feel at home, sure of herself.

They had little chance to be alone together, she and Thorkell. The weather was bitterly cold. Snow blew in eddies across the courtyard, but was not enough to cover the ground. Two days after their arrival the Severn froze over. The rooms in the great hall were cold and drafty. Everyone gathered around the fires—huddling together for warmth. During the long evenings Winfrith's harper sang the traditional, complicated poems of historic battles and ill-fated lovers. One night he sang of Tristan and Iseult and the tragic love they tried to keep secret in the court of King Mark. "But love will not be hidden," he sang.

> "Every hour of every day
> It was there for all to see.
> In the way their eyes met,
> In the way they moved,
> They were never far apart.
> Like new wine working in a vat,
> Love o'erflowed and could not be hidden."

Sitting with the others, Branwen felt her face redden; embarrassed, she looked down at the floor. Thorkell grinned.

Late one afternoon, almost a week after they had arrived at Tottenness, Branwen had just finished treating a man with a painful boil on his neck. She washed her hands and took off the lovely, large, bleached linen apron, one of several Winfrith had given her, and hung it on a peg over the little dispensary chest in the corner of the cook house. She wrapped her cloak around her, pulling the hood over her hair which she now wore loosely twisted on her neck.

She walked thoughtfully down to the shingle beach, hoping to see Thorkell there. Disappointed, but not surprised, she saw that it was empty. The sun had gone down an hour ago and there was only an afterglow left in the sky. The longboat had been cleaned inside and then overturned on the beach. The bottom was scraped and refinished; gleaming, it awaited the coming of spring.

Where will you sail this spring? she wondered. Your captain and his men are hunted men, you know, here and in Denmark as well. They have no home left. Will they take you all the way to Byzantium? They say the streets are paved with gold there and the gardens grow all year long. I've heard there's work there for Vikings, in the mercenaries. A man could get rich, they say.

The thoughts made her feel sad and empty. Standing quietly in the growing darkness, she savored the cold, clean air which was a welcome relief after the smoke and reek of the kitchen. And then, suddenly, she knew Thorkell was there.

She turned and saw him, a dark shadow coming toward her across the rough stones. His long cloak swirled around his legs and his helmet gleamed faintly in the starlight. She felt a flush of pure happiness, just seeing him, knowing that he loved her, and not quite believing that it was possible to love a man as much as she loved him. She ran toward him and he caught her up into his strong arms, burying his face in the soft, dark cloud of her hair.

After a moment, Thorkell said, "We can leave tonight, Branwen. The work on the boat is finished. If you are ready, there is no reason to stay."

"Tonight?" she asked. She looked at him. There was no hint of the wildness which had possessed him. He seemed calm, happy.

"Yes," he said. "Is something the matter? Can't you be ready?"

"I can be ready," she said. "It's just . . ."

"What?"

"Nothing," she sighed. "I'll be ready. It will only take a few minutes."

He kissed her, and their hearts echoed emotions building to an intensity they were still learning to control, not yet realizing that it would never be controlled completely, never should be controlled, not yet realizing that the most precious part of their love was the magic between them.

After a while, he said, "We've got to get your things."

"I wonder what Winfrith will say," she smiled.

"He must be mad, setting out at night. What can he possibly be thinking of?" Winfrith said, horrified to see her packing. "And you, you're madder than he is to be going without question like this."

Branwen folded the last of her few clothes, which were all soft and clean again. "Please don't be angry, Winfrith," she said simply, placing her hand on the other's arm.

Winfrith shook off her hand and walked out of the room. Branwen sighed and looked around at the luxury she was leaving, Eadric's luxury. She might have had a room like this, its walls brightly painted, the wooden arches and beams deeply carved, the furniture spare but elegantly wrought, with rich fabrics covering the cushions. His bed was hung with beautifully worked crewel hangings. I wonder if Winfrith makes those, she said to herself, when time drags and the year seems endless without him. She felt no jealousy of Winfrith, only a kind of sisterhood which she had never shared with another.

When she got to the kitchen to pack her dwindling supply of herbs, they were gone, together with the little painted chest Winfrith had given her.

"Lady Winfrith ordered it carried out, my lady, not two minutes ago," said one of the kitchen maids.

Branwen went out into the deserted courtyard. The sounds of singing and laughter came from the great hall. There was a stiff breeze blowing, which cut through her woolen cloak. It would be a cold night. She pulled her cloak more closely around her and hurried toward the light coming from the half-open stable door.

"Oh, Thorkell," she exclaimed, seeing him there as she came through the door.

"Did you think I would let you freeze again?" he asked, obviously proud of the sturdy, little cart with high wheels.

There was a bay gelding hitched to the traces and a smaller dark mare was tied behind. The bottom of the cart was thickly laid with straw to keep out the cold from the frozen roadway. The seat was set lower than the sides so that the driver was protected somewhat from the wind.

"Here's something you may be able to use," he said, handing her a large, dark bundle.

She shook it out. Long and flowing, the dark wool was lined with the famous, thick fur of the silver northern squirrel.

"Is it all right?" he asked, trying to fill in the silent space as Branwen stood just staring at the cloak she held up in front of her.

"It's the most beautiful thing I've ever seen," she said, at last. "But how can I wear it? It's fit for a queen, not for me."

Thorkell laughed. "Of course you can wear it. In Denmark, all the chieftains' wives have winter clothes like this."

Her eyes were glistening as she looked at him. "Oh," she said, "I'd forgotten. I'm to be a chieftain's wife. I only wanted to be yours, Thorkell," she added quietly.

He said nothing. Taking the fur cloak from her hands, he unbuckled the plainer one and tossed it into the cart. He wrapped the new one around her, kissing her as he framed her face in the fur of the hood.

They left then, driving out of the empty courtyard. The sounds of their leaving were covered by the singing and the thumping of the dancers in the great hall. Only Winfrith and Pym stood in the lighted door to watch them go.

They burrowed under the fur rugs that seemed to fill the cart. Thorkell held the reins lightly with one hand; his other arm held her close against him. Although there was little danger, Thorkell's sword lay against the side of the cart within easy reach. His axe and spear, too, were upright in the corner, leaning on his round, black shield with the heavy gold boss in the center.

Branwen, wishing he would lay aside the hard leather armor which encased him like a turtle shell, asked, not unreasonably, "Where are we going, Thorkell?"

"Eadric once told me that the people near Lydney tell of an old woman who lives alone in a hut on the edge of a wood which no one dares enter. It is said that even in winter the smell of wildflowers comes from that wood. There are even rumors that the children have seen a unicorn feeding in the early evening under the trees. So we will follow this road along the river to Lydney and see this old woman and her enchanted forest."

Branwen wondered what would happen when they got there and found the wood as cold and barren as the forests around Tottenness. What would happen to Thorkell then? What would he do?

"How far is Lydney?" she asked.

"Not too far. By starting tonight we can let the bay follow the road himself. We can change horses at dawn and be in Lydney by evening."

It would have been a good plan, except for the wolves. They attacked shortly after midnight; six dark shapes hurtling out of the night. The horses screamed. The gelding bolted. With a wild cry, Thorkell leapt to his feet. Branwen woke from her warm sleep nestled among the furs. She was stunned by the sudden flood of fighting fury from the Viking at her side. Frantically, she struggled to clear her mind, smothering, gasping for a life of her own. But she could not free herself. The cart was too small; they were too close. She could only crouch low, erecting what walls she could to block his feelings.

The road was level here along the river, and the curves were gentle. The horse ran on and on. The wolves were there, always behind, waiting.

As the moments went by, Branwen strengthened her defenses and in the small secret places her own feelings began to grow. At first, she felt only a flicker of resentment against this wild man who would so brutally overwhelm her. The flicker grew into a flame of anger, fanned by the knowledge that she had seen him this way before and had accepted it, proud that he would show no fear in the face of his enemies. But this was different. The wolves were no threat. She had only to speak a word to them and they would go, disappearing into the night. But this great brutal warrior would not give her a chance. The very strength of his feelings blocked her.

Then the bay stumbled. It screamed wildly and resumed its frantic run, but it was clear the race was almost over.

Thorkell turned to her and she was revolted by the savage joy on his wild face. This was a stranger more terrifying than the wolves. Handing the reins to her, he secured the sword belt around his hips. "Rein in the bay," he commanded.

She struggled with the reins but the horse would not stop. It stumbled again, exhausted now, and in that brief instant, Thorkell leapt from the cart. She turned, as the cart continued its wild ride, to see him standing, bathed in moonlight, his battle axe raised in one hand, the other holding his gleaming sword.

Ten yards down the road his control over her mind began to weaken. Reaching out she spoke to the bay. He responded quickly to her voice in his ears and in his mind. He stopped while she was still speaking to the mare behind, calming her as well.

"Oh Thorkell, I hope I'm not too late," she cried as she jumped from the cart and ran back towards where she had left him moments ago.

As she came up from behind him, she raised her arms in that gesture of calming as old as womankind itself. The words she said were in a strange tongue, but the wolves understood. Four melted instantly into the darkness of the winter woods, one crawled away more slowly, and one would move no more.

Thorkell let his arm drop. Resting on the handle of the battle axe, he turned his head to look at her. "What took you so long?" he asked with a grin.

But Branwen had no response. She felt drained and terribly disappointed. What could she say to this Viking who had become a stranger to her?

Thorkell leaned down and wiped his blades on the back of the wolf he had killed. He sheathed the sword slowly and deliberately. He rested the axe across his shoulder like a woodman returning home. He felt her mood keenly and it angered him. He wanted to laugh and be glad that the wolves had not won, but she was spoiling their victory and he did not understand why. "Come along," he said stiffly, "we can't leave the horses standing after such a run."

Neither could sleep in the dark any more that night. They rode on, the cold growing from within.

The next day the sun rose dim behind low overhanging clouds. They stopped to change horses and eat some of the food they had brought with them, speaking those trivial things which needed to be said, no more. The day wore on and they drove through a cold mist which shut everything from sight and sound. They lost track of time. They seemed to be going nowhere; the horses just plodding wearily through the grey nothing. And Thorkell's anger gave way to sadness. He longed to break the silence but there seemed to be a thick wall between them and he didn't know how to break the barrier. Finally, he slept.

The stillness of the cart woke him. The horses stood quietly in the absolute greyness and he knew she was gone. "Branwen," he called. It was all he could say through a throat tight with tears.

She didn't answer.

"Branwen," he called again hopelessly.

Then he heard the sounds of footsteps approaching slowly through the mists. They were the footsteps of a stranger. He took his heavy battle axe once more and leapt down out of the wagon. He strode up to the mare's head and, holding the bridle in his hand, led her toward the approaching sound.

A figure emerged from the mist only a few feet away—ahead and to the left. It was clad in a long blue robe. The deep hood was pulled up, concealing the face entirely. As they stood there, he felt a peace stealing into his mind, replacing his anguish.

"Who are you?" he asked, realizing that this one was in his mind just as Branwen had been.

"Long have we waited for her who has gone on ahead," the figure said, in a voice which gave away neither age nor sex.

"Who are you?" he demanded again. But even as he spoke, the anger and resentment which tried to rise up in him were overpowered by the strength of the other's will, filling him with a feeling of calm and a sense that the world was finally to be put to right. And then he realized that the air was warm and there was heavy scent in the mist like lilacs.

"Come, Thorkell, we will tend to the horses."

With a beckoning gesture, the figure turned and started off, back the way it had come, and Thorkell followed, childlike, the battle axe hanging forgotten in his hand.

Chapter Eight

THE UNICORN APPEARED suddenly in the mist, the whorl of his horn gleaming softly.

Come with me, he commanded, beginning to move away, disappearing into the grey until only the warm glow of his horn remained. His voice was like none she had ever heard before, gentle, yet with such power she trembled as he called to her.

"Wait," Branwen called, "I'll come." She hurried to catch up with him, to touch his soft white hide.

Without quickening his stride, the unicorn stayed a step or two in front of her. She ran faster, anxious to touch him. But he stayed ahead of her, his stride unchanged, unhurried. She ran until her breath began to burn in her chest and still the unicorn stayed maddeningly just beyond her reach. On and on she ran, through the grey mist, ignoring the pain in her chest and in her legs, until suddenly, stumbling over a gnarled root which had stretched unseen across her path, she fell headlong on the frozen ground. Pain knifed through her. "Wait," she cried angrily, but he was gone. There was no sound, only an empty, cold, grey stillness.

"Please wait," she pleaded, "oh, please." And then, as

she spoke, a warm breeze blew over her carrying the scent of lilacs. She looked up. Just beyond her outstretched fingers, she saw a small white flower. The mist was thinning. A grove of rowan trees appeared, their leaves all pale and green and new. Little white mayflowers covered the ground between the fiddleheads of countless ferns. A thrush called. The unicorn stood beneath the trees watching her.

Then, deep within her, she heard the voice of the unicorn speaking to her. *You had only to ask*, he said, and then he lowered his head and began to graze.

Getting up, she walked slowly toward him. Her hand trembled as she reached out to touch him.

So, he said, *you've come at last. We've waited a long time.*

"Who are you?" Branwen asked, her voice hushed.

I am only a messenger, he said. *She it is you have come to see*. And there, beside a fountain, Branwen saw a woman, weaving. *Come, I will take you to Her*.

Branwen rested her hand on the unicorn's warm neck and they walked across the clearing. As they approached, the woman looked up.

"Mother," Branwen cried. She began to run toward her. Suddenly she stopped, confused, for the figure was her mother but not her mother.

"I am the Ancient One," the figure said simply.

The words, like an incantation, worked a strange magic on the young woman's soul, freeing her from the leaden chains, forged link by link from the responsibilities of adulthood. Branwen felt the weight slip off. The world was suddenly larger, brighter. Her Mother was here. Everything would be all right now.

"Come, child," the Mother said, holding out Her hands. Branwen knelt at Her feet. Gently the Goddess embraced her. The unicorn began to graze peacefully nearby.

"You were so young when your grandmother returned to her mothers. She was sorry for your loneliness. We could only hope you would remember her words and find your way here."

"Who are You?" Branwen asked softly.

"When the first child was born I was there. And when she died I was there as well. I am Birth and Life and Death and the First Answer to the mystery therein. Since the dawn of time women have served Me.

"It was I who taught them herbs to cure their illnesses and disease held no sway over them. I taught them to gather the fruit of the earth. I spoke to them of the movements of the moon so that they could know the changing of the seasons. Great was the wisdom of the ancients. For countless millennia they ruled the land, as a mother rules her children, in love.

"When the children of woman raised the great standing stones, it was in My honor, for the stones, rising up out of the ground, were a symbol to them of the new life springing up from the sacred earth each year. And the children of woman built mounds so that the shape of the flat earth became that of a fecund woman. There, within the mounds, were the dead returned to My womb in hope that they would be reborn again."

Branwen whispered, "Yet those places are old and forgotten today and no one knows the meaning of the standing stones."

"And I, too, my dear, am old and forgotten." The Goddess smiled. "But come, there is work to be done."

Branwen looked up, surprised.

"Have you not noticed the ground around you? Did you think I would send you back to the world of men empty-handed?"

"Send me back? Oh no, Mother, don't send me back!"

"Hush, child, you need not leave until you are ready."

"I'll never leave," Branwen vowed fervently.

"We shall see." The Goddess smiled with the infinite patience essential to motherhood. "Come, can you name the little plant growing by your right foot?"

Branwen looked down. "It looks like birthwort," she said, puzzled, "but I've never seen it so green, and its leaves so big!"

"That is because this is a land that knows no death, a place of eternal spring. The herbs here have power beyond the paler flowers that bloom and die."

They worked for a long time, Branwen gathering the herbs as the Goddess taught her their uses, and all that Branwen had learned from others seemed pale and weak beside this new lore. She gathered bitterbloom and eyebright, ladysmock, melissa, and whortleberry, dragon root, hellebore, and celandine, woad, elfdock, eglantine, and bryony, and spread them to dry in the shade of the oak, hung with mistletoe, at the edge of the clearing. Branwen knew no hunger, nor thirst, nor did she grow tired, and the light in the sky never changed.

Once, as they were working, Branwen sat back on her heels and asked, "What happened? Why have we forgotten You?"

"Oh, my dear"—the Goddess laughed—"man discovered the wonder of fatherhood." And, sitting there in that field of flowers, She explained, "You see, in the beginning, women bore children as a great mystery, a gift from the Goddess of Life, a blessing bestowed on women, and none understood the planting of the seed for what it was. The power of women to bring forth new life was a great mystery in which men had no share—not for a hundred thousand years," She added, almost wistfully.

"A hundred thousand years?" Branwen whispered.

"Not until men tamed the wild beasts and learned the ways of the herdsman did he come to suspect his role in creation. Not until then did he begin to wonder why, if it is the north wind which quickens life in a mare, does it never happen unless a stallion shares her field? So he saw what was true among his animals, and looked at the woman he knew and wondered about her sons."

"And before that, no one knew?" Branwen asked incredulously.

"It is not easily guessed, my dear. There is no obvious connection between an act of love and childbearing many months later. Indeed, a couple may make love many times, yet the woman does not bear a child for each act."

"But what difference did the knowing make?" Branwen insisted.

"Oh, knowing was not enough. Men coveted what women had. When a man came to know his son, he was no longer content to see the power he held pass to his sister's son as had always been the way. No longer was he happy to have the blood line traced from mother to daughter—his own role as nothing. But it was a great change he would have, a rending of the whole fabric of the heavens. Now he needed to possess a woman, to own her body, so that he could produce his sons without fear that another man would plant in his field. And women were taken by force and became men's property, and many who refused were killed.

"And it preyed on his mind," She continued, gazing into the distance, "that women should be the greater power, that all people should worship the Mother. Then men began to turn away from the Moon and worship the Sun. They called it the Great God and bowed down before Him. The Sun became the God of Power, and the Earth Mother, the Goddess of Love, was overshadowed; and power passed to the sons of fathers."

"But surely this was true when my mother and grandmother were still alive. Even the songs the singers sing of long ago tell only of the sons of chieftains."

"My child," the Mother said, smiling gently. "My power began to wane three thousand years ago. Few are the songs that are as old as I, and fewer the singers who know them still."

"Who am I?" Branwen whispered.

"You are the last of My priestesses," the Goddess said. "From the darkness within the earth, from the womb of ancient caves, there was born a race of women whose power was greater than all others because they opened their hearts to Me with joy. They were the wise women, the healers, the star gazers, the spinsters. They set out the great circles, gleaming white in the holy places, and led their people, worshipping Me as the Moon in the night sky."

"The last?"

"You will bear no daughter, my child. Man has turned away. Blinded by the glory of the Sun, he no longer recognizes the transcendent mystery that springs from the earth. But there will come a time when men and women will stand together on the level ground, acknowledging that only in love is power tolerable. Then they will realize that they, like the mighty oak, grow out of the earth, of which they are a part, up to the heavens. Only when their roots are strong in the heart of the earth will they grow tall enough to reach the Sun. So it will be that roots buried in love will support a mighty tree whose leaves will drink unscorched the light of power."

Branwen was silent. After a while the Mother held up a yellow four-petaled flower. "What plant is this?" She asked.

"That is shepherd's knot, Mother."

"And tell me how it may be used."

"It is a vulnerary and will heal wounds. When brewed in a tisane with water and wine, it will soothe a sore throat. Boiled in a stronger decoction, it will cure the flux."

"You have learned your lessons well, my child."

"Yet it is a curious thing, Mother. The very plants as they grow seem to teach me their uses."

The Goddess laughed. "Yes, Branwen, truly you are one of mine. This is as it was in the beginning."

They had worked their way around the field and stood near the loom once more.

"What are you weaving?" Branwen asked.

"Come closer and see."

Branwen looked on the tapestry stretched out on the loom and the flowers worked thereon were so real that the breeze seemed to stir the pollen dust on the anthers of a lemonlily.

"Can You teach me to weave like that?" the girl asked, her voice hushed and reverent.

"You must tell Me first, what is reality?"

Branwen was quiet for a while. "Many say reality is what we can see or hear or touch."

"And you, my dear, what do you say?"

"I think they are wrong. It is more than that."

"Yes, much more. To limit reality to the material, to deny imagination and faith, the magic of the shape-changer, the language of the birds and animals, is a great folly, for these are the riches of the earth's children. Pity the fool who denies such treasures."

And the Goddess taught Branwen to weave a millefleur pattern, and bees came and danced around the flowers they wove.

"Tell me of my grandmother," Branwen asked softly, as the shuttle moved through the warf.

"There were still three priestesses left when the slavers attacked during the midwinter dark of the Moon. The other two were killed but your grandmother was carried off, unconscious. It was many weeks before she was strong enough to break away from them. Your grandfather found her then, there on the south shore of this island. He was very kind to her and they loved each other, but still she returned to the shrine. It was destroyed. She buried the remains of her companions and cleared out the fountain. There was nothing else to be done. We spoke there, she and I. Hers it was to choose, as you must choose, whether to come with me, back to the lands of the great ones where your mothers await you, where there is no suffering and no growing old, where the tables are set with gold and the goblets are encrusted with jewels, or whether to remain here in this world to live out your days in the company of men who must suffer and grow old."

"And my grandmother chose to return to my grandfather," Branwen said. "What was he like, that she would give up the blessed isles to wait out her span of years with him?" But she knew the answer already. She remembered how she had loved once, a man whose heart spoke to her own. . . .

"Branwen, know this. There can never be a perfect blending of two souls. It is enough to stand alone together, taking joy from what can be shared—but allowing the other that part of his soul which is his alone. And thus, you must not be angry that Thorkell goes where you cannot reach. Would you give up those parts of your own soul which do not belong to him? Come here to the fountain. Look into the pool. Do you see?"

She did. There, in the still water, was the dark room of a small hut, lit with the flickering of a fire. A man sat hunched over near the fire. She walked around the fountain to the other side to see better. It was Thorkell, as she had known it must be. Tears streaked his face— the mighty Dane who had never shown pain, who laughed at death. She looked up at the Mother. The unicorn raised his head to gaze at her. Branwen's own eyes filled with tears.

"Branwen, I knew it must be so. Go now, and when your world has come to an end I will look for you here, in the meadow of eternal spring."

Then She was gone. The unicorn, too, had vanished, and Branwen was alone. The mists had cleared in the midday sun. Where the fountain had stood, a spring bubbled over tumbled blocks of stone, and at her feet a woven sack bulged with the harvest of another world.

Branwen gathered up the sack and started down from the hilltop. As she followed a path through the woods, the smell of spring faded, the trees became bare once more, and the song of the thrush died away. At the edge of the wood there was a small hut, a thin wisp of wood smoke rising through the roof. She opened the door. Thorkell looked up, and their eyes met.

"Branwen," he said hoarsely, "stay with me."

"I found the unicorn," she answered.

Chapter Nine

THE HOODED FIGURE who had led Thorkell to the little hut never returned. Villagers seldom ventured near the enchanted forest even in the light of midsummer. Thorkell and Branwen were alone on the edge of the woods for many days. They did not want for food—a sack of flour, new milled, stood in one corner. Outside a brook moved quickly under shelves of ice out of the forest and toward the river. Thorkell killed a deer and it kept well in the cold weather. Oddly, too, there were hay and grain in the lean-to beside the hut so the horses were well fed. The wood pile was well stacked with seasoned wood. It was as if they had been expected and everything had been made ready for them.

The hut itself was small but snugly built. The roof did not leak though it rained every day, a cold, wet, cheerless grey rain which isolated them in a world of warmth and firelight and soft fur rugs and sweet fresh straw. Theirs was the finest of wedding beds. The room was small and the fire burned high, throwing its warmth even into the corners.

There was little need now for layers of woolen clothing between them. Even in the quiet of completion they were not apart. And the very freshness of her pleasure heightened his own for, though he had known many women, he had never loved before.

Two weeks went by and they were neither bored nor anxious to leave, but began to look forward to coming back among their own. And they were idly curious as to how the fabric of their lives would change with this wonderful thing that had happened to them. And so, when the flour in the sack and the grain in the shed ran low, they made ready to go back along the road which had brought them here.

It was mid-February when they set out and the roads were still frozen. They left before dawn when the sky was still dark but had begun to lighten with the promise of day. Neither of them spoke of wolves but they pushed hard through the day and the early darkness to Tottenness, never seeing that the Viking longboat which should have been drawn up on the shingle beach was already prepared for departure.

When Thorkell threw open the door to the main hall, the draft drew every head around.

"Thorkell, by the right hand of Tyr, you've come back just in time." He was a great grizzled man, his voice booming through the great hall.

"Hemming, by Odin's eye," Thorkell replied in kind. "It's good to see you." They greeted each other with such shoulder clapping and bear hugging that Branwen was not surprised to hear him say, "Branwen, this is my brother."

"Well, well, so you're Branwen." The great bear eyed her critically. "There's been a good deal of talk about you, woman." He broke into a wide grin and added, "You might at least have been bigger."

"I do try, my lord," she said.

Even in the general laughter Branwen knew there was something askew, something hanging in the air and she waited warily, but not for long.

"He's dead, Thorkell. The old sot had a fit and died just after Christmas. He was still with Knut on the Trent. He just collapsed and no one could do anything more for him than see the ritual performed."

Who? Who died? Branwen wanted to shout but she did not dare. She slid her hand from Thorkell's where it had been forgotten, and moved through the shadows away from the fire to Winfrith's room. She stood outside the curtain and called out, "Winfrith, it's me, Branwen. May I come in?"

The curtain was swept aside. "Branwen, you're back! What happened? Where have you been?"

"Winfrith," she asked, "why is Hemming here? Who is dead?"

"That bastard Swein, of course. He's dead and no one knows what's happening. Thorkell will have to make his move now. Hemming knew he was here and brought the news. That's why the Raven's Wing is ready. They've been watching for him every day. Hemming's afraid Knut will take Thorkell's continued absence from the Trent as an indication of hostility."

Branwen paled and, even in the dim light of the small fire, Winfrith noticed. "What is it, dear Branwen?" she said quickly.

"I had not thought to lose him so soon, that's all."

"Oh Branwen, I'm sorry. I didn't realize. . . . But, of course, how stupid of me. Come in here. Warm yourself. Let me get you something to drink," she said and the curtain dropped behind them.

Branwen stood silently in the arch which opened into the main hall. Most of the men had gone back to their benches to sleep. Thorkell and Hemming sat near the fire, their heads close, their voices only a low murmur. Pym sat a little apart, listening. She stood watching them for some time before Thorkell became aware of her presence. He looked up, surprised to see her. She smiled at the look of small child guilt which rose over his face as he realized he had completely forgotten her. She turned back to the cold corridor, knowing he would come when he could.

And when he came at last, she asked, "We didn't have very long, did we, Thorkell?"

Holding her close, he said, "Come with me."

"We are on different sides now," she whispered, resting her head on the warm wool of his tunic.

"Come with me," he repeated. "There is little to keep you here."

"All my life I've grown up hating Danes. I can't change now."

"I am a Dane," he said softly.

"I know," she whispered. "But it's not the same. Swein was your enemy, too," she added.

"Swein was," he said slowly, "but not Knut. We grew up together, Bran. I cannot stay while he needs me."

"You can't stay . . . and I can't go."

"Where will you go?" he asked.

"To Thornbury."

"Branwen . . . will you wait for me?"

"I'll wait," she said.

"I thought I heard voices out here!" Winfrith appeared suddenly, and drew them both into the warmth of her room. "Come in, come in. I was just on my way to check . . ." she hesitated, her eyes sparkling with amusement as she fabricated an excuse, ". . . to check on the kitchen fires. You can have this room to yourselves for a while."

"Stay, Winfrith." Thorkell laughed, putting his hand out to her arm.

She smiled up at him, and walked over to the sideboard where she poured out mugs of warm wine for them all.

"We'll be leaving in the morning, Winfrith," Thorkell told her, "to join Knut."

Winfrith looked around inquiringly.

"I'll stay here with you for a while, if you'll have me," Branwen said.

"Of course, dear, stay as long as you like. You are good company—and a healer besides. Doubly welcome!"

"There's no way to tell what will happen next," Thorkell said thoughtfully. "Perhaps Knut will move to take up where his father left off, although I don't think he is strong enough yet to hold it."

"What of Ethelred?" Winfrith asked. "Will he return do you think?" And they knew she was thinking of Eadric, and the Easter season ahead.

"Who knows what Ethelred will do?" he said bitterly. "Or Edmund either for that matter. I only know that what I've hoped would happen, has. Now, at last, I will be sure of the man I serve."

They sat in silence for a few moments, watching the fire,

and then Thorkell spoke again. "When Branwen is ready to go home, she can go alone."

"Alone? You must be joking, Thorkell. Surely few men would travel alone and certainly not a young woman."

Thorkell laughed and Branwen said, "What Thorkell says is true, Winfrith. I am not only a healer." She paused, steeling herself, and continued, "I have also the art of the shape-changer and can speak to the birds and the animals. Wherever I go, nothing will harm me."

She called softly and a small, brown mouse ran lightly across the floor to her. She stroked its head gently and, with a word, sent it back to its hiding place under the chest.

Winfrith watched silently, her face thoughtful. "So, what the men say of you is true," she said at last. Her voice was cold and distant.

"It's all true," Branwen said with a sinking heart. "But all the arts in the world are not so much help to me as a friend. Oh Winfrith, I need a friend."

Thorkell watched the two women, his eyes bright as a hawk's in the firelight.

Winfrith sighed, and stood up from the fireplace, gathering the empty cups. "You need a night alone." It was a statement, rather than a question. "Eadwig's been having nightmares lately. I'll keep him company tonight and see if that helps."

She turned to go out but Thorkell had risen; taking Winfrith in his arms, he said quietly, "There is no evil in her."

"I know," she said. "It just takes time. In the morning. . . ." She hesitated, then turned away from him and went out.

They wasted many long hours that night talking together as they lay in each other's arms under the downy coverlets on Eadric's bed. They spoke of Branwen's little hut and the routine of the year so that when he was not there he would know what she was doing. And then, in his turn, he described the court in Denmark where he thought he and his men would return, at least for the time being.

Finally, very late at night, when they were truly satisfied with their love-making, he asked her again, as he had asked her so long before, to be his wife in name as well as fact.

"Come with me to Denmark," he said, "as my wife. It wouldn't be so bad, would it, Bran?"

"Not yet," she whispered, tracing a line with her fingertip down the center of his chest. "Don't ask me to. Not now. Not yet."

He sighed and leaned back among the pillows, resting one arm across his eyes. After a while, he said, "I wonder if you'll ever be ready, Bran."

"Someday. Someday I'll come sailing over the waves to Denmark—I'll send a raven on ahead as my messenger. 'Your wife approaches,' it will croak. Then perhaps I'll find that you've grown tired of waiting and taken a Danish wife and fathered children." She laughed sleepily, teasing him in a way that only women in the warmth of bed and the dark of night can tease a man.

But he held her fiercely and said, "Never, never will I have another to wife. And if I thought you meant it, if I thought you would come if I could not return. . . ."

"How could things change so that you could not return, oh great northern warrior?" But then she was asleep and he didn't know whether she had promised to come to him or not.

In the great hall Winfrith came up to her and hugged her warmly. "I am a fool, Branwen. We both—no, all three of us—are the kind of people who have to stand alone. When we find someone like ourselves, we should be careful not to lose each other. You are welcome to stay. I'm glad to have you for a friend."

"Thank you," Branwen said. She blinked back her tears and they walked together down to the river's edge where the men were preparing to leave.

Thorkell came over. "Take care of her for me, will you?"

"I will," Winfrith said.

"Safe journey, my love," Branwen said. "Come back soon."

"I'll be back," he said, running his hand over her dark hair. "Wait for me at Thornbury."

"I will wait," she whispered, watching his tall figure walk away from her.

"Oh Winfrith," she said as they started up toward the hall after the boat had passed from sight, "is this what you feel every year when Easter is over?"

"One gets used to it," Winfrith answered, but they both knew she was lying.

PART II

Chapter Ten

THE YEAR 1014 passed slowly for Branwen, creeping at a snail's pace from day to day. She had been late for planting. The roads in the Severn valley had stayed muddy until late in April and she had not gotten back to Sherborne until mid-May. By then she knew that Thorkell was gone. He had sailed back to Denmark with Knut, whose older brother, Harald, was now the king there. But why or for how long he had gone, no one could say for sure. Many people laughed and said Knut was too weak, too afraid, to seize his father's spoils. Others, listening to them, frowned, drained their ale cups, and went back to their homes, unconvinced.

Ethelred had been called back from Normandy. Eadric Streona, the king's most trusted advisor, called the Grasper by many who hated him, returned with him.

Although Eadric held great tracts of land, countless residences, fiefs, forests, towns, and the vast income they produced—from the Severn valley in the west, north through Gloucestershire, east through Mercia, across the island to the borders of the Five Boroughs of the Danelaw—he was not satisfied. Although his fyrd strength, the number of men who served his standard in time of war, was second only to the king's, he was not satisfied. Always lusting for more lands, he had persuaded Ethelred on his return to power to punish the noblemen of the Danelaw who had surrendered so readily to Swein the year before. Then, surprising no one, the holdings of Sigefirth and Monkere, executed as traitors, were awarded to him by the king. This completed his holdings, which now stretched in an unbroken belt from the Irish Sea to the Channel.

And Edmund, finally, made his move.

She smiled to herself, remembering just how neatly Edmund had pulled it off. How much of it had been her brother's idea, she wondered, or Leofric's? The two of them were close to Edmund now, three young adventurers, with not very much to lose and a kingdom to gain if they were lucky. Edmund had married Monkere's widow, who, conveniently enough, was young and attractive, too attractive to remain for long in the nunnery where Ethelred had sent her. As her husband, Edmund had claimed her rights to her dead husband's lands and Edmund's claim had been accepted by the neighboring nobles.

But Branwen's smile faded quickly, as all her smiles did now. There had been no word from Denmark. By fall the events of that February seemed dim and by midwinter almost dreamlike.

At the end of the year, she stopped waiting for word to come. She went quietly through the motions of living, finding what pleasure she could helping out where she was needed.

Branwen stood up. There was nothing more she could do here. She added a stick to the fire burning low in the dark room and watched the flames reach up to welcome it.

Thank you again, Mother, she prayed in her heart. The child would have died without Your help. She frowned a little, thoughtful, staring at the fire, wondering as she had four times that year whether there would ever be a time when she could replace the sacred herbs she used so sparingly.

She sighed, trying to shake off the melancholy which had settled on her during the long, cold night while she had worked to save the infant. He was very small, born too soon of a mother too young. He had needed more strength than this world could offer to keep his tiny chest rising and falling. But he had struggled to live and she had helped him. Outside a freezing rain had fallen steadily through the night, but the air in the small cottage was warm and smelled of spring. After a while, when the baby began to suckle, Branwen had smiled at Huda. "He'll be all right, I think," she'd said.

They were both asleep now. Branwen picked up her cloak and went out through the low doorway into the rain. Icy mud crusted up around her boots. She laid her hand on the young man's arm as he stood, smiling proudly, holding her stallion.

"She's very weak, Wade, and must be cared for carefully if she is to have enough milk for the child," she said warmly. "Will you let them come and stay with me awhile? Aelle will be glad for the company. She complains that the house is too quiet now with Elin and the little ones gone."

"I'd miss her sore here, my lady," he said, looking down at the mud of the cartway.

"But there's no need, Wade. It's only February, still a month before the ground can be worked. Stay with us for the next four weeks. You can add a room onto the infirmary while you're there. It's work I've wanted to have done for a long time. What do you say? Will you come? It would be so good for Huda—and for your son," she added.

"It's very kind of you, lady. We'd be much obliged," he said slowly, reluctantly.

"It's settled then," she said, smiling at the man who had spent lazy summer afternoons fishing along the banks of the Coombe with her in the long ago when they were young enough to be just friends. "I'll send Tom with the cart in a day or two—when she is stronger. Meanwhile, the pot is full with Aelle's good stew. See that she eats some when she wakes up, will you?"

She rode home between the hedgerows, her head bowed in her hood, hidden from the rain. The gloom of the day only exaggerated her loneliness. The year that had passed since those weeks at Lydney had been filled with births and deaths, with endings and beginnings—but not for her. For almost twelve months now she had gone through the motions required of her as mistress of Thornbury and thegn of Sherborne, but they were duties she took no pleasure in, happy to have Dyffed act in her place whenever possible.

More and more her days were spent tending the sick who came to her. At first only the villagers she knew and had grown up among knocked on the door of her little hut, but then others came from farther off, simple folk she did not know. Often they were frightened, for they had heard strange tales of the power of her healing. Many she was able to help, but there were others for whom she could do little. It was work she felt comfortable with now, more sure of herself than she had ever been, knowing her gift for what it was, learning to rely on it, use it. It seldom bothered her that she was different from other women. There were still unanswered questions, still pieces missing, but she had learned the most important part and had willingly accepted what she had learned. Only sometimes it was not enough.

What if Thorkell never returns? she wondered as she rode home that morning. Did I really promise to leave Thornbury, to join him in Denmark? What a fool I was. Denmark.

Lost in the hopelessness of her own thoughts, she never noticed the armed man who waited quietly at the side of the road. Not until they had gone some way did she realize that he rode behind her on the narrow track between the hedgerows. She reined up and turned in the saddle, her hood falling back.

The man was fully armed and wrapped in a thick woolen cloak. His face was hidden by the nose piece on his helmet. He sat easily, watching her for a moment, and then he said, "Lady Branwen, Thorkell sends his greetings."

"Pym?" she asked, her heart racing, "Pym, is it really you?"

"Aye, lady."

"Oh Pym, it's so good to see you. But how did you get here?" she asked, suddenly concerned, her eyes scanning the roads and fields empty in the early hour. "The roads are watched. It isn't safe. If you were seen, you'd be killed. Come, quickly."

She did not wait for an answer, but urged Beornwig into a quick trot, splashing freezing mud onto the low branches of the hedges on either side of the track. They rode through the half open gate at Thornbury and into the stable. Tom was alone.

"I met a sick man on the road, Tom. He's going to stay for a while. See that we're not disturbed."

Tom looked steadily at her and at the strong, armored man standing at her side. "Aye, my lady," he said deliberately. "Will there be more as suffers from the same sickness?"

Branwen looked at Pym and he said quietly, "Perhaps."

Joy flooded through her so that she had to lean against the stable to steady herself.

"You all right, my lady?" Tom asked, missing little.

"Yes, of course," she said. "But not a word to anyone. You understand, don't you?"

"Aye," he said, "I'll not breathe a word to no one."

She nodded. "This way, then," she said to Pym.

Taking his saddle bags with him, he followed her across the courtyard and into the great hall where a fire burned high, banishing the cold, damp air to the farthest corners of the room. They hung their wet cloaks on two pegs.

Turning to him, she asked, "Will you disarm, Pym? Do you want me to help with the buckles?"

He looked at her steadily. "Not yet, if it please you, my lady."

"Very well," she said with a smile. "You can keep watch while I go and get some hot food for us both. Then we can talk."

She was not gone long. When she returned with the heavy iron kettle filled with thick stew, he was staring intently at the work spanned on her loom.

"I'm afraid it's only rabbit left from yesterday," she said, "but Aelle's just starting work on today's dinner."

They sat on low stools on either side of the three-legged pot, dipping the dark crusts of trencher into the thick stew, feeling better and warmer with each bite. Branwen spoke rapidly between mouthfuls, anxious to reassure him.

"My brother's with Edmund. He's seldom here anymore. I haven't seen him since early December.

Thornbury is mine and I keep only the small staff who I've known all my life. Thorkell," she continued, happy to say his name aloud again, "is always safe here."

"And if Edmund should learn that you sheltered his enemy, what of you then, Lady Branwen? He would know what danger his coming puts you in."

He was startled by her laughter. "Tell Thorkell, there is no danger." Then, seeing the bewilderment on his face, she added, "You and he will have to trust me, Pym."

They ate silently for a few moments and then, emptying his cup, he settled back and said, "He is well. We joined Knut last spring before he left the Trent. As a matter of fact, it took a great deal of persuasion from Thorkell and Hemming to convince Knut that it was folly to stay last year. He is young and wanted what was his, but. . . ."

"He mutilated the hostages he held," she shuddered.

"He released them, though he might have had them killed."

"There was no cause," she said angrily.

" 'Twere well the might of the Dane be remembered, lady," he said gently.

"I'm sorry, Pym," she said stiffly.

"Aye, lady, it isn't easy."

They refilled their cups with wine and he continued. "We spent the year in Denmark. For my part it was good to be home. My children did not know me, but my wife did, and it was a warmer winter than I had been used to, this last one. Though Thorkell found little comfort, I daresay." And he smiled at her.

She laughed. "I thank you for that," she said.

She spread the cloaks to dry more quickly over the stools by the fire before turning back to him again. "When will he be here, Pym?"

"I cannot say, my lady, but he is not far off. I'll be back in camp before dark. Ye best leave the gate unlocked."

Pym left shortly afterwards, his cloak still damp. Branwen built up the fire in the sleeping room and, wrapping herself in the quilts, slept all morning, waking only when Aelle came to fetch her for dinner.

She slept in the main house now that it was empty. She

had given Elin and Dyffed a holding at Nettleden which had fallen vacant. Dyffed still served as steward at Thornbury, seeing to it that the work was done as it should be, and Elin came when she was needed. Cobbe and his younger brother had moved into the stable with Snel. They had been orphaned the previous winter and had come to Thornbury to help Tom with the chores.

Tom and Aelle, she thought, they go on, unchanged by the years. Whatever will happen to Thornbury when they are gone?

The afternoon dragged slowly. Branwen knew she was foolish to think Thorkell would come so soon. She settled herself on a little cross-legged bench to work at the loom which stood near the window in the hall. She was nearing the end of the pattern now and, as she looked lovingly over the finished work, she saw that, although it would never fool the bees, yet there was some magic in it. And all the herbs were there, all the ones she had learned in the sun and the rain through the seasons with Ansgar. She worked steadily, passing the shuttle back and forth, the soft colors of the woolen woof giving her pleasure as they passed through her fingers. When it grew dark, she lit the tallow candles. The rain began again. The hours passed and the candles burned down so that she knew it must be nearing midnight.

"What a foolish child I am," she murmured as the abbey bell tolled for compline. Her shoulders ached from sitting in one position for so long. She set aside the shuttle and stood up. Though determined to sleep, she reached instead for her cloak and walked to the great gate. The night was very dark. Everywhere there was unbroken quiet and she turned back, disappointed.

Branwen put out the candles, guttering in pools of tallow, and undressed by the light of the fire. She added another log to the coals in the back room and lay down across the bed.

I'm too excited to sleep, she said to herself, watching the flames dancing in the dark room. Moments later her eyes closed. She never heard the single rider enter the courtyard.

His bulk filled the doorway as he watched her sleeping. Finally, Thorkell turned to the outer hall where he hung his wet clothes over the bench to dry. He pulled off his sodden boots and stood them by the fire. Barefoot, dressed only in his loose-fitting riding pants, he padded around the room, tearing at the bread and cheese he found on the sideboard. Gently he touched her tapestry and then he saw the hardening pools of tallow where the tapers had burned down.

You did wait for me, didn't you?

He didn't speak aloud but she heard him in her dreams and even as she slept her mind was filled with the joy of his coming. If he had any doubts about what welcome would be waiting for him after a year's absence, they were instantly removed by the strength of emotion which flooded his mind from the still, sleeping woman. He emptied his goblet and went into the room where she slept. The strength of his desire wakened her.

"Oh, Thorkell, thank God you've come." She held out her arms to him.

There was an urgency in him that would not wait and he took her quickly.

"I do love you so," she said when he lay back.

He grunted ruefully, angry with himself for leaving her still unsatisfied.

"It would seem you are somewhat out of practice," she said, raising up on one elbow, "and I am very glad."

"Next time," he promised as her fingers traced half forgotten paths over his skin.

But the dawn came early and he left her.

"Only for a few hours," he said, "I will be back before nightfall."

"I'll keep supper warm for you, my love. Be careful, the roads are watched."

He had been gone only an hour. She was standing in the kitchen with a goblet of mulled cider, going over the day's work with Dyffed, when a rider came through the great gate. She didn't recognize the man but he wore the blue and silver of Edmund's livery.

"Regards from Prince Edmund and your brother, my

lady," he said, bowing to her. "If it please you, they are
hunting in the area and desire to have dinner here."

"It never rains but it pours, child," said Aelle, standing
behind her.

"Hush," Branwen warned, frightened. "Will Edmund
and my brother stay the night at Thornbury?" she asked
the messenger, her voice carefully controlled.

"Oh no, my lady. They hope to get in some hours of
hunting after dinner and return to Holcombe before nightfall. Edmund is anxious to visit with his gentle grandmother, the Lady Aelfthryth."

"How many ride with the prince?"

"There are twenty men-at-arms, my lady. They are
sending a goodly hind to ease the burden of their sudden
presence."

"I would be obliged if you would convey to the prince
and my brother that Thornbury is eager for their arrival and
promises a feast worthy of a king. After you have refreshed
yourself, that is," she added, noting his crestfallen face.

All that morning the household fell to. Wiggs, Cobbe's
younger brother, was sent to fetch Elin. Loaves of fine,
white wastel were kneaded and set out to rise. The venison
was butchered to go into deep clay pie pans as well as onto
spits over the fire. There was good wine from Father
Anselm's vineyard which had to be decanted and allowed
to breathe in the main hall. The fires were built up. Cobbe
and Wiggs were set to work polishing the silver with wood
ash and vinegar. Snel began to turn the spitted venison.
The beeswax tapers were set out. Tom and Dyffed hung
the tapestries from their special hooks between the rafters
covering the smoke stained walls. By midmorning, when
the abbey bells rang out for sext, everything was ready.

Branwen went into the sleeping room where she kept her
chest of good clothing. She plaited her hair loosely in a
single braid which hung down her back. She pulled on the
dark green tunic which she had made this year, dyeing the
wool with larkspur. She fingered the embroidered ribbons
which trimmed it. I wonder if Godwin will remember
these, she asked herself. He had brought them back from
Coventry last summer.

Horns sounded. The dogs barked. She went out into the courtyard, her squirrel cloak thrown open in the feeble, midday sun to watch the men ride in.

She held Edmund's bridle as he dismounted. Standing in the muddy courtyard, with his hands on his hips, he accepted her graceful, deep curtsey before sweeping her up into his arms.

"Welcome to Thornbury, Edmund," she said warmly.

"It's good to see you again, Bran," he replied.

"And Godwin, welcome home."

"You're absolutely blooming, sister. The quiet country life certainly agrees with you."

She laughed and hugged him.

"God's blood, girl, we're hungry. I hope Aelle's had time to get dinner ready."

They went into the hall where the fire crackled with the dripping of the venison spitted above it. As they stood warming around the fire, she handed the jeweled goblets filled with wine first to Edmund, and then to her brother and the rest of Edmund's friends who rode with him. She took care to see that her own goblet was well watered.

"Now tell me, Edmund," she said as they settled down, "how is your wife, Ealdgyth? Is she at Holcombe with you?"

"She's fine or was when we saw her last. We left her behind at Thetford; she's pregnant, you know?"

"Oh Edmund, that's wonderful! I hope she will give you a son who will reign after you."

Edmund laughed.

"And you're looking well, brother," she said, turning to Godwin.

"I can't complain, sister dear, though Edmund sets a fast pace and woe to him who falls behind."

"Have you made plans yet to follow him to the altar as well as into the fields?"

"If I could gain half a kingdom by marrying a woman as comely as Ealdgyth, I'd consider it."

"Not everyone marries for political gain, Godwin dear," she said laughing.

"What's the point otherwise," he answered with a grin.

When the meal was almost over, Godwin asked, "We heard that Eadric's been at Cray. Have you seen him?"

"He was here last fall, just before Christmas," Branwen said, getting up and walking over to the sideboard for the pitcher of wine. "He sold Cray back to the abbey, you know. He swears he will never return."

"Ha! Good!" Edmund said. Eadric had, for Edmund, become the very embodiment of everything hateful about his father. "Here, fill up my goblet," he said. "Now, tell me what happened."

"We were all invited," she began slowly, "for dinner on the feast of St. Michael. Everyone was there; they all know Eadric never stints on food or drink. There were a lot of aching heads the next day." She laughed. "Eadric hardly spoke to me at the party but a few days later he came here. I was working at the dispensary. Our woodman had cut his leg badly that morning and had only just come in. Eadric stood quietly," she said, remembering how he had looked at her, watching her work, "while I dressed Brun's leg. We came in here for dinner afterward and he said how he had been to hear of father's death. I told him that we were very much in his debt for making father's last days peaceful and he laughed bitterly—I can still hear his laugh, Godwin—saying that my brother didn't think it was much of a debt. He blames you as much as Edmund for snatching that land from him. He thinks Edmund's marriage was your idea."

"He's a fool," muttered Edmund, his voice hard. "How did he plan to cash in on your 'debt,' Bran? He must have had something in mind; he's not given to acts of generosity and unselfishness."

"Now, Edmund, don't you think my lovely sister," Godwin paused, refilling his cup, "would have graced Cray?"

"By God, he wouldn't dare."

Branwen laughed, covering the ache she felt in her heart. "He never had a chance to ask, Edmund. I told him I'd been to Tottenness, and I asked if he'd been able to get to see Winfrith last Easter."

"What did he say?"

"He just froze over," she lied. "He left soon after. The next day Father Anselm told me Cray was being returned to the Church."

"So in a year we do him out of his foothold in the Danelaw and a holding in the west as well. I wonder how he plans to make up his losses. Perhaps he will throw his lot in with Knut," Edmund said with a laugh, "if and when the Dane returns. Too bad for Knut, if he does."

The conversation turned to talk of war and Branwen's thoughts drifted back to that other afternoon when Eadric had come to Thornbury to collect a debt. . . .

He had come alone, she remembered, with not even a groomsman. He must have been riding hard because his horse was lathered with sweat, and he had asked Tom to walk the animal until it had cooled. His clothes were dark, black with silver, and perfectly fitted to the tight muscles of his legs and shoulders. Branwen remembered how her body had burst into flame when he touched her. We were standing over there, she thought, by the window, looking out at the river, when he kissed me.

He had kissed her and incredibly she had been glad, melting against him, hungry, thrilling in the desire which consumed her. How long had they stood there, she wondered, locked together with a blinding intensity, before the torrent eased and their straining bodies had softened to each other? She remembered the sweetness she had tasted, anticipating a climax which seemed to be inevitable. He had held her in his arms and her head rested easily on his shoulder against the warmth of his neck.

And then he had spoken to her, his voice thick with desire, "Come with me," he had said, "come with me, to Cray."

She could smile now, months later, remembering how the words had chilled her, turned her blood to ice, all in a moment. Like blowing out the last candle in the dark of night, the flame of her passion was snuffed out, leaving a dark chill behind.

"Shall I go with you to Cray?" she had asked. "Shall I be your mistress for the harvest season . . . as Winfrith is at Easter?"

He had grown angry then, releasing her, his eyes

challenging. "Would it be so bad? Or is it true you sleep only with Vikings?"

"I sleep with whomever I please," she said icily, refusing to yield to the desire to strike him. "But I will tell you this, Lord Eadric: I belong to no man. Never will I be your property, to decorate a house you visit only occasionally."

Her anger had amused him and he had asked, "Would you rather another woman came to Cray?"

She had looked up startled, unable to mask the quick flash of jealousy she felt at the thought.

"No." He laughed. "I thought not."

Then she knew he would only destroy her if she yielded. He would demand a surrender she would never make. He would never let her go. She would be his to possess, to pick up and put down. Branwen had shivered with abhorrence and walked over to the sideboard. She poured two goblets of wine, allowing the silence to build. Holding out one goblet to him, she had asked, coolly, "Why did Monkere and Sigefirth die, Eadric?"

"Ah yes," he had said, relaxed and smiling. "Your brother and his friends must be pretty smug about that little coup."

"Why did they die, Eadric?" she persisted.

"Do you know what will happen when Knut's forces land next spring?"

"How do you know they will come?"

"They will come, never fear. Your lover," he sneered, "will be back. They couldn't stay away if they wanted to. But, if I held the lands that fool Edmund grabbed, there would be no need for death and destruction. Anyone holding the lands I would have held, stretching from east to west across the Midlands, could have reached an agreement with Knut and saved a lot of needless bloodshed and expense."

"What kind of 'arrangement'? What kind of deal would you make with a Danish king?"

"Is Ethelred such a great king? Do we have to sacrifice ourselves to defend him?"

"He's *our* king, Eadric, and Edmund is his only rightful successor."

"That is pure drivel, Branwen. Don't you ever think for

yourself? Your brother has thrown his support behind Edmund because he thinks it's there he stands his best chance of gaining power. Don't let him fool you. Did it ever occur to you that Godwin permits you to remain unwed, entertaining a Viking chieftain, as his ace of trumps in case Edmund fails?"

"That's not true," she said fiercely, realizing suddenly that it was.

"Are you sure? But it matters little. Godwin answers only for himself, while I have a responsibility to the people of Gloucestershire and Warwickshire."

Branwen laughed.

"You're right," he laughed easily. "But I will do whatever is necessary to keep the men of my command from being killed, for it is in that quite impressive number of men that my power lies now. I won't throw them away in a losing cause. But we talk too much of war, my love," he said, touching the back of her neck lightly with his finger tips. "We live for such a short span of years. What fools we are to waste a moment of pleasure."

He drew her into his arms. She was very tired and rested in that circle. "Branwen, Branwen, there are years of war ahead now that could have been avoided if I had had control of that land. How many will die so Edmund can go on struggling for a crown which he cannot really hope to win? There are some things which have to be faced no matter how unpleasant, and Edmund's helplessness while his father and older brother live is one of those things. Come with me. Oh, not to Cray, if that is offensive to you. No, ride with me. We can cement together a power which need bow to no man, neither Knut nor Edmund."

"I'm sorry for you, Eadric, I really am," she said softly, "but I won't crowd the pinnacle on which you stand."

He turned away and his voice was bitter when he asked, "Which side will you be on this year, Branwen?"

"I won't take sides at all."

"You are a fool if you believe that. When Thorkell and Godwin face each other across a sea of blood; when they raise their swords and close to strike, what will you do?"

"I pray it will never come to that."

"You pray? To whom do you pray? What god has ever

answered a prayer?" he asked angrily. "But it grows late and I detest riding after dark. Farewell, my lady. Someday I will find out what side you are on—and for whom your heart pounds."

He had bowed, and placing his goblet on the sideboard, was gone. She had heard nothing from him since then.

Edmund rested his hand on her arm as it lay on the table. "We've had reports that Thorkell landed a few days ago somewhere to the southeast. We think he's scouting for the larger invasion force. He may stop here."

"And if he does?"

"The roads are watched. If he comes, we'll kill him."

"Here at Thornbury?"

"Not here. We owe you that."

"He won't come here, Edmund. He's no fool," Godwin said. "He must know we'll be looking for him here."

They stood up and got ready to leave.

"What are you going to do, Bran, if and when war does come? Do you still insist in joining us in the field?"

"I can help in the hospital train; you know I can, Godwin. They always need skilled help. You said so yourself. And how can I sit here, not knowing what's happening until weeks after it is all over?"

"Never mind, Bran, it may not come to that." He gave her a brotherly kiss and a hug and left, with a promise to see her soon.

It was raining again by nightfall. The raindrops coming through the smoke hole in the thatch hissed on the fire. Branwen sat working at the loom, refusing to allow her fears to surface.

And then he was there, cold and wet. "Branwen, Branwen," he said, "we should never have left Lydney."

She smiled, remembering, and said, "You needed more space than we had there, my love."

He did not smile. "I want to wash the blood off my hands," he said, watching her.

She paled. "Are you hurt?"

"No," he said, "but tell Edmund not to send boys against me."

"They were here this afternoon."

"I know. I don't think your brother or Edmund are fools and they shouldn't think I'm one."

Later in the evening, when the stains of violence were washed from his hands and buried in his heart, they sat near the fire, wrapped in each other's arms on the furs he had brought as a gift to her that night. Branwen was happy to have him back, especially since he was once more the Thorkell she had first known, at peace with himself, clearly focused again. The wildness that had swept her along to Lydney was gone. He had come back to her a man who was sure of his direction, of his life and its meaning.

But it was not the kind of thing they could talk about, not yet, not with so little time together. They talked of easier things. And she didn't worry about Edmund's secrets. What she told Thorkell he could hear in any tavern. They talked of Edmund. She told him of the prince's sudden great popularity in the countryside, knowing he would take the news to Knut. She explained how Ethelred had ordered the noblemen of the Danelaw punished for surrendering to Swein the previous year.

"They were staying with Leofric at Coventry when word came that Sigefirth and Monkere had been executed, their extensive holdings to be given to Eadric. Edmund was so angry he would have armed in rebellion, I think," she said, "but Leofric knew Sigefirth's widow. He said she was young and fair and wasted in the nunnery at Malmesbury where Ethelred had sent her. He proposed that Edmund ride to her rescue. And that is what they did, with banners flying. Before Ethelred or Eadric got wind of what was happening, Edmund had reined up in front of the nunnery, humbled himself to the abbess, and begged a word with the bereaved widow. They were married the next day in the convent chapel. Then they rode off to the Danelaw to avenge the lady and secure her great estates for Edmund. Oh Thorkell," she said, with eyes shining, "the people cheer when he rides down the road. They will follow him this year. There will be an army in the field. Knut will not sweep across the land the way his father did."

"We'd heard as much," Thorkell said thoughtfully. "And you? What will become of you in the middle of all this warring?"

Branwen hesitated, filling their cups, before replying. "I will go into the field with Edmund's hospital train," she said finally.

"By the Holy Mothers," he said softly, "you won't!"

"It's something I have to do, Thorkell," she said, handing him a cup. "Don't you see? All summer long you and Knut will fight Edmund and my brother. How can I stay behind, waiting for news, when any news will be bad?"

"Branwen, you've no idea what you are going to see. It takes a callousness which deadens the heart. How did Godwin ever agree?" When she did not answer, he went on angrily. "Have they told you what it's like on the battlefield after we are through hacking at each other all day?"

She shook her head.

"Well, lady, neither will I, but . . . take a sharp dagger. It's the best medicine for many who lie wounded on the field, the only help you'll be able to give."

"I'll do what I have to," she said, her chin up.

Seeing the color drain out of her face, he took her into his arms and held her close for a long time. She could feel his anger, diffuse now, no longer directed just at her as it had been moments before. Now he was angry with Godwin, too, and then with the whole idea of war, with its maiming and death.

"I'll come through the lines to you, Thorkell," she said after a while.

"No," he said, holding her fiercely, "I don't want to see you there."

"Don't be angry with me," she whispered. "We're both only doing what we have to do."

"You know that I'll be lost if anything happens to you?" he demanded angrily.

She looked up at the great warrior who struck dread into the hearts of those who heard his name. She knew that what he said was true and that she felt it just as strongly as he did. She told him so and their conversation of war ended for the evening.

In the morning, when he had finished dressing, he turned to her and said, "Stay here, Branwen. Wait for me here."

"I can't, my love. Don't ask me to."

"Can't or won't?" he asked angrily. When she did not answer, he turned and left her.

Chapter Eleven

KNUT ARRIVED AFTER the April storms were over. The Viking fleet anchored off the south coast and the sea from the shore to the horizon was thick with longboats. And then they came ashore at Wareham.

Now the mockery of Knut was bitter in the mouths of the Dorsetmen, for here was no fledgling child, afraid to grasp the heritage left him by a conquering father. Well had he spent the last year in the north, for swelling the ranks of his invading army were men who followed the standard of Harald, king of Denmark, side by side with the army of Eric, ruler of the vast northern waste called Norway. Combined they meant limitless supplies of men and arms. Darkness fell over the hopes of the island-born.

When word of the invasion reached Thornbury, Branwen finished seeding the row of cabbages and then stood up.

"Wiggs," she said to the small boy who was helping her, "find your brother and tell him to saddle my stallion."

She walked through the alley between the kitchen and the laundry and drew a bucket of cold well water. She washed the gobbets of dirt from her hands, noting absently how it clung under her nails. Oh well, it can't be helped, she thought. Perhaps the old lady will not notice. She had changed her tunic and boots by the time Cobbe led the horse out into the courtyard.

"Tell Aelle I won't be back tonight," she told him as she stepped off the mounting block into the saddle.

The sun was warm as she rode through the meadow toward the Coombe, which was still swollen with the spring rains. The fiddleheads were tall in the shady places under the alders. She was glad they had picked their fill earlier in the week, for the ferns were beginning to open.

She smiled to see the great raven, lazily preening himself in the sun amid the soft, green leaves of the old oak.

"Well, your kingship," she said, reining up, "it's been a long time. Have you been away?"

You missed us then? Blaec asked royally.

"Aye, and when I asked your lady wife where you were, she did not know. You really do treat her shamefully, you know."

I was about kingly business. It was not for her to know.

"And your business went well?"

I am still king, he said, with bird-like mystery.

"And may you reign with great length of days."

She waited.

There will be some difficulties among those who do not fly this summer, he announced with his eye bright. *A great army has landed.*

"I'd heard as much, Blaec," she said gravely. "They may come here."

There is none to stop them.

"Perhaps not, Blaec, but still I should like to know when they come near and how many."

He was silent.

"We worked well together once, Blaec," she said quietly, sadly.

Not well enough, it seemed.

"I couldn't stay."

Why? he croaked. *Why walk when you can fly?*

She did not answer him but leaned forward, running her hand over the horse's neck, thoughtfully. After a moment she looked up again at the bird above her.

"Have you ever seen your reflection in the stream, Blaec?" she asked.

On occasion, he answered.

"Let's look now," she said, sliding down from Beornwig's back. She walked across the meadow to the stream bank. The bird flew ahead, perched above the stream on an alder branch and waited.

"What do you see, Blaec?"

A raven. I see my own reflection, of course, he said impatiently, watching her now, not the stream.

"Look again," she said.

There was silence then for many moments, for what the great black bird saw was a young man with long black hair and intense red eyes.

"Who are you, Blaec?" she said as the man/raven looked at his own arms and body.

I am Blaec, he said. *What have you done to me*?

"It's nothing, my friend, only an illusion. You are really as you always were. You only look like a man. Do you like it?"

It is interesting, he said.

"Would you like to stay this way . . . forever?"

Ah, he said slowly, understanding now. *And so it was with you. What is interesting and perhaps useful would all too soon become unbearable if it were forever*.

"We can fight together again, if you wish," she said to the raven above the stream.

How will you fight an army which blackens the field from one edge of the world to another?

"Not here. Not alone. I'm going to join Godwin and Edmund when the time is right—a week or two. Come with me then."

I will come, he said, *and you will know when the army approaches this valley*.

"Good," she said with a warm smile.

Branwen continued along the cartway until she reached Dyffed's holding. She sat at the gap in the hedgerow watching him turn the oxen at the end of his furrow and start back toward her. He saw her but was too busy with the plow to wave. As he reached the gate she dismounted and began to walk the next furrow at his side. She knew how vital every moment was for him. Today it was his turn to use the village team, plowing his own strip.

"You've heard the news, no doubt."

"Aye. How long until they are here, do ye suppose?"

"Who knows. Perhaps two weeks. What do you think?"

"Probably less. They're meeting no resistance, what I hear."

"Call the fyrd together, Dyffed. Right away."

"Begging your pardon, Branwen, but ye must be daft. The men won't come. Why should they? Who is Ethelred to them? If Knut conquers the land as his father did before him, how will our lives change? But if we miss this planting season, there's many will starve. They won't fight, Branwen. It's wrong to ask them."

"Is Edmund, too, nothing to them?"

"Why do you ask?" he said wearily. "You know the villagers. They're your neighbors; you grew up among them. You know they care little what goes on beyond the hills. All they want is food on the table and a warm woolen cloak against the winter chill. What happens in Essex or the Midlands, in Yorkshire or the Danelaw touches us not at all. Let the Dane have the crown, Branwen. What difference does it make to us?"

"Call the fyrd, Dyffed," she said, her voice firm. "I don't mean to fight but neither do I mean to give the invaders any more than I can help. We'll get a supply train and send it north. We'll keep only what we need to survive until harvest; the rest will go to Edmund."

"And when the Danes come and take what we have left, what then?"

"Dyffed, Dyffed, I am thegn here. This much I can promise the people who owe me service as I owe them protection: they will not go as hungry as many in the year ahead. They will trust me if you do. We'll stand by Edmund in this," she said, her black eyes burning into his. "He's Alfred's seed and should be king."

Dyffed did not answer her and they walked on in silence behind the plodding oxen.

"It's a good plow, Dyffed. The oxen are young and strong."

"Aye, there's not many better. The men know who to thank for it, too, my lady. No doubt there's many owes you much." He was thoughtful for a moment and then said, "I'll call out the fyrd tonight. We'll send out the wagons."

They reached the end of the furlong and he halted the oxen. "Branwen," he asked, "are you sure you want to do this? If the bairns go hungry, the village will hold you to account."

"We all do what we have to, Dyffed," she said. "If you need me I will be at Holcombe."

She turned and walked back to Beornwig across the fallow.

She found Edmund's gentle grandmother sitting in the apple orchard, her needlework on her lap.

"Lady Aelfthryth, I beg pardon for disturbing you. . . ."

"Not at all, my dear child, how nice to see you. I was just sitting here letting the sight and smell of these blossoms chase the last chill of winter from my old bones."

"And you look like an apple blossom, all pink and white, grandmother," she said, bending down to give her a kiss.

"Not likely, Branwen, more like a wrinkled, old apple doll that little girls play with." She laughed but Branwen did not. "Ah well, I can see you have serious business on your mind, my dear. Well, out with it, what has my grandson done now?"

"No news from Edmund yet." She turned away and looked off through the orchard. "It's Knut," she continued. "The Viking has returned with his army. We have word that he is sweeping through Wessex and will be here within a fortnight."

"I pray to the Holy Virgin you are wrong."

"As do we all, my lady."

"What are we to do, Branwen? Will you call out the fyrd?"

"I will not ask them to fight."

"But then all will be lost!"

"No, not all. We will send everything we can north to Edmund at Uhtred's in Bernicia. Those roads will still be open. All the foodstuff which can be shipped and what livestock we can spare must go within the week. We will strip

Holcombe clean and when Knut takes it he will get only the four walls."

"Ha! The four walls and one old lady! You cannot ship me off, Branwen. I would not ship well or far."

"Oh, my lady, I don't want to send you away but, like all the beautiful things here, you must be saved for Edmund when he returns—as he must. I'll help you pack your things. Let the good nuns grant you asylum until the Vikings are gone at last."

"I had given some thought to entering the convent when I should grow old and feeble. I hadn't thought the time to come so soon." She stood up and said, "Tell my grandson to make haste for I would not wait the seasons round before I return to this orchard."

And they made their way slowly back to the manor house.

So it was that a few days later, when Elfheah rode in through the fallen petals of the apple blossoms, he found the stockade open and the walls empty and bare. He rode silently on to Thornbury, for it was there he had been sent, bearing a letter sealed with a great node of wax.

Branwen heard the rider come in. She was in the hall talking with a crippled girl who was perched high on a ladder decorating the dark cross beams with bright ribbons, intertwining fantasies of flowers and birds and small animals.

"You'll have worked off your debt in another day, Wylla," she said, "and then I'll have to send you back home with my hall unfinished."

"I don't want to leave before I've done, my lady, and my family is glad there's one less to feed, especially one as useless as I am."

Branwen frowned. "Well then, perhaps you can stay. I'll speak to your father in the morning," she said over her shoulder as she went to the door. "You can make Thornbury glow from one end to another."

She smiled warmly as she greeted the man who had ridden in. "Elfheah," she said, holding her hands out to him, "welcome to Thornbury."

"Lady Branwen," he said coldly, bowing slightly, ignoring her outstretched hands.

Chilled, Branwen let them drop. She curtseyed correctly and, matching his tone, said, "Won't you come in, my lord? Have you ridden far?"

"Far enough, my lady. My brother sends you this," he said, handing her the letter.

Cobbe came in just then. He stood staring from the doorway as she took the letter from him.

"Help Prince Elfheah to disarm, Cobbe," she said.

While they were busy with the buckles she moved to the light by the window. The shutters were open. The breeze tugged at her loose braids. She broke the seal and opened the letter. It was brief, giving little news and asking that she allow Elfheah to remain at Thornbury, disguised as a singer. She folded the page and turned back toward the man who stood, disarmed now, dressed in a fine sandal tunic caught up on the shoulders with heavy gold pins. The newly grown beard really hid little of the strange beauty of Edmund's younger brother. And Elfheah intrigued her. Why wouldn't he smile at her, she wondered? Why was there always a barrier between them?

"You may go, Cobbe," she said. "But don't tell anyone the prince is here." She had never seen him so dull-witted. Turning to Elfheah she asked, "What does the letter mean, my lord?"

His voice was low, clear and firm. He looked at her steadily as he explained, "My brother feels Thornbury will be near the center of the invading forces shortly and he wants me to find out what I can of their strengths and movements."

"To spy."

"He does not ask you to spy," he said coldly.

"It is enough to let you stay," she answered him quietly. "And you will play the minstrel and none will suspect you."

"I will not embarrass you."

"I remember your singing well, my lord. Any other time I would be proud to have you sing in my hall."

She sighed and shook off the feeling of sadness. Then she said, "Your grandmother, the Lady Aelfthryth, is well, safe at the abbey convent. Perhaps after you have refreshed yourself you would like a horse saddled."

"Thank you," was all he said.

A week later, when the air was mild, full of the scent of new mown hay, Branwen stood quietly in the shelter of the dark oak doorway waiting for the Vikings to dismount and the noisy confusion of dogs and horses to settle. She watched Thorkell dismount and come across the yard toward her.

"Well, Bran," he said, smiling, "it looks like you were expecting us."

"You and your friends do not travel inconspicuously, my lord," she said softly.

"Well, come and meet 'my friends.' I promised them they would be welcome here."

"As they are your friends, they are welcome at Thornbury."

She crossed the yard at his side, seeing for the first time the man called Knut. He stood easily among his men, although the chain mail shirt which reached almost to his knees might have bowed a lesser man. The well-worn scabbard hanging low on his hips gave mute testimony that the sword within belonged to a man who used it often. She knew he was no older than her own nineteen years but his face, clean shaven and tanned, was already hardened into the planes and angles of manhood. His hair was gold, thick and disheveled from the morning's ride. His eyes were a clear northern blue, cold and intense. He would see everything, she thought, and seeing, take whatever he wanted. The power of the man was undeniable. He frightened her, for she knew that here was the enemy she had dared to challenge within the gates of Holcombe.

"Lady Branwen—my liege, Knut," Thorkell said.

She curtseyed deeply as she had so often for a different prince. "It is a great honor you pay us, Lord Knut," she began honestly enough.

"On the contrary, Lady Branwen, we have found hospitality somewhat forced of late, and Thorkell spoke highly of Thornbury and the woman who is mistress here."

"Well, my lord, I trust you will not find our hospitality forced. We live very simply but I hope we can make your stay a not unpleasant one."

"Welcome, Hemming," she added, recognizing the big man standing to one side.

"So you remembered, did you, Lady Branwen? It seems a long time since we met at Tottenness."

"Not so long, my lord, as to forget you," she said, smiling at him.

He laughed and answered, "Thorkell was right, Knut. We'll have a most enjoyable visit here." He took her by the hand and said, "Let me introduce my second-in-command, Eilaf and his brother, Ulf."

The brothers were very different, one taut and dark, the other fat and blond. Perhaps they are only half brothers, she thought.

"Lady Branwen," the dark one said, with a bow.

He's laughing, she thought. Something is amusing him. Whatever can it be?

The other man said nothing.

"There are others coming later, my dear," Hemming added. "Toki and his men have gone on to Holcombe."

Branwen drew water for her guests at the well. When they had washed they followed her into the rose garden where the ale was cold and plentiful.

As they stood, out of place, admiring the early roses, Ulf said, "Well, Lady Branwen, what do you think of your king now?"

"I beg your pardon, my lord, but I have had no news of the king for some weeks now," she said. She paused and then added lightly, "Your army has somewhat isolated us here in the southwest this spring."

The others laughed but Ulf, with the tact of a soldier unused to gentle company, plowed on. "I guess we have. Well, perhaps I can fill you in somewhat. Ethelred, the Unraed, is ill and has been since our arrival a month ago. Too ill, it seems, to leave Portsmouth. Certainly too ill to support his over-bold son, Edmund, in the field."

Branwen's heart froze at his words. Again, she thought, again Edmund is to be betrayed by his father. Is everything lost so soon? Her voice, only lightly curious, betrayed none of her anguish when she asked, "And Edmund, my lord; what of Edmund?"

"Edmund has something of an army with him," Knut

said with no trace of mockery. "We take the field against him shortly."

"What did you make of the messages from Sigvaldi that came in this morning?" Thorkell interrupted, changing the subject. And for a while the Danes talked among themselves. Branwen listened politely, trying to follow their discussion until her smile grew stale. She was relieved when Elin signaled to her that dinner was ready.

They had only just taken their seats in the hall when Toki rode in.

"Stripped," he said, pouring himself a cup of ale, "to the bone." He sat down at the end of the table. Breaking a piece of wastel, he stuffed it into his mouth.

"What of the old lady?" Knut asked calmly.

"No trace."

"A pity. I've heard she's a remarkable woman. I'd hoped to meet her."

"Well, she's not there. Only the bare walls are left. Even the hearth has been cleaned out, swept clean, the barns, forges, root cellar, everything."

"The fields?"

"Barren."

"Interesting. I wonder at whose command this little piece of work was done. Perhaps you will be kind enough to tell us, lady." There was no trace of humor around his eyes now.

Branwen broke the bread in her hand into two pieces and laid them carefully on the table. She looked up at the conqueror sitting next to her and said, "What was Edmund's has been sent to him."

"At whose command?"

"I am thegn in this village." She kept her voice even, neither challenging him nor yielding to him.

"So, thegn, is it?" he said, laughing.

She sat unmoving, waiting for the laughter to stop. Thorkell watched quietly and Dyffed, too, waited standing in the doorway.

After a few moments Knut said, "Thorkell, you were right."

"How's that, Knut?"

"You told us that there was a lady in these parts who was

extraordinary. I thought you were exaggerating, but I was wrong." He turned back to her and said thoughtfully, "You are indeed an extraordinary woman. What shall we do with you?"

"There is no need to do anything. There is little I can do to interest you further, my lord," she said, and whatever her thoughts and feelings were, there was no hint in her tone or manner.

"Perhaps," he said.

Course followed course through the meal. When Elin brought in a golden glazed roast piglet, Elfheah, sitting unnoticed in the far corner of the room, picked up his intricately worked harp and began to tune it softly with a key.

"Ho, what's this?" called Hemming, his knife cutting into the roast.

And then she felt Thorkell's amusement. He had recognized Elfheah; he saw through their plotting and was laughing at them, as one would laugh at children playing games. She looked at him and smiled, trying to tell him that she was glad, that she had wanted no part of this game anyway. He grinned back.

"If it please your graces," Elfheah was saying, "a song to while away the heat of the day." He picked out a chord and they settled back, not at all reluctant to remain in the pleasant, airy room whose walls gleamed white while squirrels chased rabbits through small flowers traced along the arches.

Then he began to sing the ballad of the Battle of Maldon. Branwen was pleased with the choice. She knew the Danes would be unfamiliar with the song, although not the battle, which had been won by the Norsemen fifteen years ago. The song told of the superb courage of Byrthnoth's men who, after the fall of their chief, and knowing the battle was lost, deliberately chose to fight to the death against overwhelming odds, thus avenging their slain chieftain.

When Elfheah finished, there was much praise for his song and his singing.

"When you are tired of Thornbury, you must come to us and try your luck at courtly entertaining, minstrel," said Knut, tossing him a gold coin.

This time Thorkell laughed out loud but no one seemed to notice.

It was late afternoon when they finished but the sun was still high. As the men rose to leave, Knut turned to Branwen and said, "I haven't spent such a pleasant afternoon in a long time. Our thanks to you and our pardon for your action at Holcombe. We will be leaving a garrison, however, to see that the fields are worked now and the barns filled. Thorkell will see to it."

And so they rode out and she watched them go, relieved and disappointed that there had been no time for a word alone with him, no touch, no sign. But she knew his protection was all around her. She knew that the invading army which was camped to the south and east would not descend on her small village. He had seen they were spared that. Whoever was in charge of the garrison at Holcombe, she was sure there would be no trouble.

"Elfheah," she said, as Tom swung the gate closed, "Thorkell recognized you."

"Yes, I was afraid of that. We met briefly last year. We hoped he wouldn't remember."

They walked back into the hall where Dyffed was helping Elin clear away the debris.

"Dyffed," she said, going over to the window, "will you stay and see that the work is done?"

"You're leaving then?"

"There's no reason for me to stay."

Dyffed kicked a discarded bone under the table and waited for her to go on.

"I want to join Godwin. I told him I would."

"What will your brother say if I let you ride out alone?"

"He won't blame you. He knows I often ride alone."

"Aye, but not so far and not in time of war."

"I'll ride with the Lady Branwen. There's nothing I can do here," Elfheah said.

Ignoring him, Dyffed went on, "And how are we supposed to put away the harvest for Edmund, with Knut's men billeted among us?"

"Do what you can, Dyffed. It's all anyone can expect."

Elin left the hall carrying the heavy crockery, humming.

Chapter Twelve

SHE WAS GLAD Blaec had come with them. The glade he had found along the banks of a wide brook was infinitely to be preferred to the flea-ridden hospitality they had endured the night before. She leaned back against the tree, full of the goodness of fresh fish, bread, and cheese, listening to Elfheah pluck softly on his harp.

After a while he began to sing.

"Tell him to find me an acre of land,
Parsley, sage, rosemary and thyme,
Betwixt the salt water and the sea-sand,
And he shall be a true love of mine.

"Tell him to plough it with an old ram's horn,
Parsley, sage, rosemary and thyme,
And sow it all over with one peppercorn,
And he shall be a true love of mine."

It was a familiar old tune but tonight it seemed to have a poignancy Branwen had never heard before. Cobbe had come back from washing the pan in the stream and stood listening, the pan hanging forgotten from one hand. Then, softly, he began to sing the refrain. Elfheah looked up, neither frowning nor smiling but adjusting his own voice ever so slightly to match the clear untrained sounds from the boy. When the song was done, Cobbe turned toward the fire and set down the pan. Elfheah began again, tentatively, to sing another ballad. Cobbe sat silently, his back to them, watching the fire, listening. Branwen pulled her blanket up around her against the coolness rising from the water and slept.

The next day the wind blowing over the fields wafted the scent of wet grass growing into hay. A bright sun rose, bleaching their worries, sparkling on the morning dew. The barriers between them faded as they rode north. By the time they reached the outskirts of Chippenham they were singing together without a thought for the stares of the men who were working in the fields.

Chippenham was a goodly town and Elfheah knew a tavern where the meat was fresh killed and the bread new baked.

Leaving Cobbe to tend the horses, they went into the cool dimness of the thick-walled tavern. Their eyes adjusted quickly, for the shutters were open and the room was not dark. The aroma of roast pig spitted over the fire, dripping fat into the flames, was overpowering. Branwen suddenly realized how hungry she was. The hour was late, and the room was crowded with men who had come into town on business and were ready for their dinner. Elfheah and Branwen found a place in the back at a dark oak table, its thickness scarred and worn. The tavern keeper, noting their fine clothes, hurried over to them. When Cobbe came in, the horses watered and turned onto the common to graze, the jug of cold ale was already dripping on the table.

"Will we make the Thames tomorrow?" Branwen asked.

"Perhaps, if we keep pushing," Elfheah said.

Neither of them noticed a man standing nearby, listening.

When they left, their saddle bags bulging with fresh loaves, cheese, and a crock of butter, they paid the innkeeper with a silver coin. Sleepy with food and ale they rode out through the city gate and into the sunshine that still filled the lanes between the hedgerows.

The sun was lower in the west by the time they reached a wide meadow where the air was heavy with the humming of bees and the smell of wild strawberries.

"Let's rest the horses here," Branwen called ahead to Elfheah who was leading the way.

"If you wish," he answered, turning back.

Blaec had already settled on the field, his beak dripping red juice, when they led the horses to drink at the tiny stream which ran through the bottom of the meadow. Their minds were full of the pleasure of the ripe red fruit and they never saw the tracks which led through the wet earth along the road north. The strawberries were good, ripe, and sweet, and full of warm juice. In no time their faces and fingers were stained. After they had eaten their fill, Branwen and Cobbe filled a napkin with more for supper.

Just as they were getting ready to ride on, Blaec flew down to the pommel of her saddle.

"Tired already?" Branwen asked with a smile.

Are you so tired of life then that you ride with never a care through strange fields?

"I trust you, Blaec. If there were any danger, you'd warn us," she said. Suddenly, realizing the meaning of the bird's message, she straightened. "Have you seen something? Is there trouble ahead?"

Over the next hill, there is a grove of ancient oaks. In their leafy darkness six armed men wait.

"Six? They must think we carry more coin than the king!"

She was thoughtful for a moment, weighing the possibilities. Elfheah knew she talked to the great rook. She had often seen him watching her with the bird, frowning. She thought perhaps he envied her voice which could do things his own could not, so she seldom spoke to Blaec in his presence any more, and he had frowned at her less often. And today, finally, he had seemed more relaxed. She had even begun to think they could be friends. What would he think now?

Six armed men—too many to fight. They had no idea how to go around the wood. If they just struck off at an angle to the trail it might take hours longer and the robbers could fall upon them anywhere, knowing the land here as she and Elfheah did not.

If they weren't going to be forced to turn back, they would have to ride through the woods hidden by the magic of the shape-changer. She would have to explain to Elfheah and Cobbe. They would see themselves as she willed for she did not have the skill to leave their eyes untouched by the illusions she wove. Not yet.

"Elfheah," she called, "there's trouble ahead." Quickly she explained what Blaec had seen and what they must do. "All they'll see is three monks leading scrawny mules. Hardly worth their attention, especially when they are waiting for richer game."

Elfheah said nothing, nodding tight-lipped. Cobbe's eyes were round with disbelief. They began to walk the horses over the top of the hill and into the copse on the other side.

It was dark under the trees, for the branches were laced thickly overhead. The path was narrow, and tall bracken on either side hemmed them in. They walked along slowly, single file, hushed by the cool stillness of the trees in the late afternoon calm. There was no sound other than the soft clopping of their horses' hoofs on the mossy trail. They heard a twig snap, off to the side, where the shadows were darkest. Branwen tightened her control, frowning with concentration, refusing to let panic shatter the illusion. She knew she could hold it, had to hold it, would hold it. Only a little further now. Around the corner the bend in the trail would hide them from the men who lay hidden, behind them now.

It was not a big wood. Less than fifteen minutes had passed when they emerged on the other side where the ground was worked and the smoke from evening fires rose from nearby cottages.

"Now," Elfheah said, "end it."

She looked around at the bitterness in his voice. "It's gone," she said.

"Good," he snapped. Mounting his horse, he kicked it into a quick trot, leaving Cobbe and Branwen no choice but to follow.

The sun lingered late in the summer sky and they rode for many miles before making camp well back from the trail along a little rivulet rushing between walls of cattails.

Only the frogs sang that night. There was an otter, too, hidden in the weeds. She spoke with him briefly and then, wrapped in her blanket, went to sleep, confident that he would warn her if strangers approached during the night. Cobbe fell asleep quickly, strawberry juice still on his hands and bread crumbs in his lap. Elfheah sat for a long time, staring moodily through the night darkness at the sleeping boy.

They crossed the Thames and continued north, but the camaraderie which they had shared, riding through the sun up to the stockade around Chippenham, never returned. More and more Branwen felt isolated. Elfheah, feeding on the boy's open admiration, began to teach him the long verses of the Gododdin, the ancient bardic tradition.

Men launched the assault, moving as one.
Short were their lives, made drunk by pure mead,
Mynyddawg's band, renowned in battle . . .

The boy learned quickly, the old words halting at first, then flowing easily. In a small village outside of Warwick, Elfheah found a crude three-stringed dulcimer, hanging dusty on the wall of a carpenter's shop. That night he sat up late, teaching Cobbe to play. The boy, eager, his eyes shining bright in the firelight, searched for the music which was still hidden from his fingers. Branwen watched quietly, alone, as the boy struggled to learn, his work-soiled hands contrasting with the pale elegance of Elfheah's.

Cobbe must have noticed it, too, for early the next morning Branwen woke to the sounds of splashing from the river's edge. The morning was already warm. She rummaged through her saddle bag looking for a clean undergarment and then picked her way upstream a little way. Shedding her travel stained clothes she slipped into the cold water.

"I wish I'd thought to bring a piece of soap," she said to Blaec, watching from a branch overhead. Lacking the luxuries, she picked up a handful of river sand and rubbed enthusiastically, feeling her skin come alive under the rough treatment.

When she walked back into the little clearing where they had slept, she found the horses saddled and Elfheah ready to leave. Cobbe had washed his only shirt and pants in the river and stood there dripping, holding the bridles in his hand.

"I'm glad for your sake the sun is hot this morning, Cobbe," she said smiling, taking Beornwig's bridle from him.

"You might at least have given the boy a change of clothes," Elfheah said.

"We left in a hurry, or don't you remember? There was hardly time to make the boy new clothes," she snapped.

Eadric Streona, despised, feared, and called The Grasper, was ealdorman of Warwickshire. Sixty-three thegns owed him service. Each thegn saw to it that local justice was administered, taxes collected, roads and bridges maintained and a fyrd raised, fully equipped for battle, when Eadric called. Seven hundred freemen—geneats, cottars, woodsmen, swineherds, craftsmen—swelled the fyrd from Warwickshire.

Eadric's control over the villages of Warwickshire, however, was only part of his powerbase. All the villages around Gloucester, and the whole of Herefordshire north to include most of Worcestershire, answered his summons as well. From the Welsh border, across the Severn, east to Warwick, Eadric controlled the land, and he had complete support from the king whose daughter he had married. Eadric's scorn for the other noblemen, for Leofwine in Coventry, for Uhtred in Bernicia, for the dead Monkere and Sigefirth in the five boroughs of the Danelaw, was monumental. Eadric was a power in the land who had no equal.

The system would, within the next century, solidify into Norman feudalism, but in 1015 thegn and fyrdsman alike served freely, albeit sometimes grudgingly, for as many as fifty-seven days a year. Thegn and ealdorman differed only in the extent of their holdings. There was considerable up and down movement between the two levels through marriage, warfare, and financial or political successes. Many parts of the country, like Wessex, where Branwen had inherited the thegnship of Sherborne when she inherited Thornbury, had no ealdorman and fealty was directly to the king.

The land was far from unified. Even the laws differed from place to place. No one considered himself an Englishman—rather, each was a Saxon, a Dane, a Celt; or perhaps a man from Kent or Yorkshire. The English nation was still some centuries in the future. It was just this fragmentation of loyalty which made Knut's job of conquest easy, just as his father's had been two years before. Unified resistance was impossible unless a charismatic leader stepped forward. Men who could not yet conceive of giving up their lives for England would fight to the death for a leader they believed in. Edmund was trying to become that leader, but he was young and unproved. He had yet to win a battle. His claim to the throne was muddied by a sickly older brother still clinging to life in a cloister in Oxford. Also, Ethelred's second wife, Emma, a young and powerful queen, had two sons of her own by Ethelred. It was by no means clear that Edmund had the right to stand for the crown against the Dane.

Technically, the thegns of the Danelaw owed him service because of his recent marriage to Sigefirth's widow. But he had had no time to cement their loyalty, nor had he any great personal wealth to bestow on his men. There was no way he could force them to serve in his army. If, somehow, he were victorious, he would then be in a position to punish those who had refused to answer his summons, but chances of his victory seemed poor. So it was that his army numbered less than the companies Eadric was assembling as Branwen, Elfheah, and Cobbe rode into Warwick on a warm afternoon in late June.

Travel-wearied, they made their way through the crowded streets to a rambling public house near the cathedral.

There, in the shady courtyard, they met one of Eadric's thegns who was ticking off his men as they reported in for service. It was apparently thirsty work, for an almost empty ale jug sat on the bench next to him.

"Ah, Prince Elfheah," he said, getting up, "how fortunate for us. Are you riding north?"

Elfheah, every inch a prince now, looked slowly around the courtyard, noting every crude stool and uneven cobble. The fat, greasy landholder shuffled his feet uneasily.

"Aye," Elfheah said disdainfully.

"Perhaps you will join us. We leave on the morrow. We would be honored."

Branwen went over to a bench along the side of the building and sat down, deliberately delicate, arranging the folds of her soiled skirt.

Finally Elfheah nodded to the man. "You'll make Coventry before dark tomorrow?" It was only barely a question.

"Yes, my lord, with luck and a goodly pace we'll make Coventry easy."

"Then we'll ride with you. Watch the woman," he said coolly, "I've other business."

Branwen looked up, astonished at his words. It was seconds before she started to laugh. By then he had gone out of the yard and she couldn't be sure he heard.

"I'm afraid a week's hard riding with the prince has not improved our friendship," she said, wiping her eyes. "I am Branwen, Wulfnoth's daughter, thegn of Sherborne."

"Oh, my lady, we are honored to have you join us. I am Osborn, thegn of Reditch. Perhaps your brother is travelling with you as well?"

"No," she smiled, "I expect to see my brother tomorrow when we join Edmund."

"Ah, then it shall be my pleasant duty to deliver you safely to him. How many of your men rode with you through Wessex?"

"I came alone with Elfheah and a boy."

"But, my dear, the country south of here is filled with Vikings."

"We saw none," she said simply.

* * *

Cobbe rode proudly into Coventry wearing a new, green tunic over his homespun pants. His hair had been cut to his shoulders, no longer tied with a thong in the back. Although Branwen said nothing, she wondered why Elfheah should take such an interest in the boy.

Leofwine's house was the grandest Branwen had ever seen. No long, low, rambling collection of thatched buildings here—a great, timbered hall rose high above the one-story shops and inns along the street. The timber cross bracings shone darkly against the fresh whitewash of the plaster. The windows on the lower floor, their heavy shutters thrown open, were all glassed. There was a stream of traffic in and out of the massive, carved oak door which faced the street. A cobbled alleyway along one side led to the barns and stables. Dismounting, they handed the reins to Cobbe and went in.

"My lord Elfheah, welcome back." A liveried attendant hurried over to them. "Your brother has just this hour returned from hawking."

Elfheah glowered at the man. "Show me in to him," he said.

Bowing, the man turned and led the prince up the stairs. Branwen was left standing in the gloom of the inner hall. She sighed, relieved that the trip was over. "God's blood, Elfheah," she swore wearily under her breath, "never again."

Following the reek of cooking venison, she walked through the house into the back courtyard where smoke issued from the enormous cook house. That must be the laundry, she thought, noting the somewhat smaller building set into the courtyard wall.

She had washed the travel stains from her hands and face and combed the tangles from her hair when she heard a voice bellowing in the courtyard outside.

"Branwen, Branwen, where the hell are you?"

Smoothing down her pleats she went out into the last rays of the afternoon sun and walked over to where her brother was standing with his back toward her.

"You called, my lord?"

He whirled and caught her up into his arms. "You made it. Where have you been? Why didn't you come up with Elfheah?"

"Don't ask," she said.

"Well, never mind. Edmund wants to see you right away."

As they walked toward the hall together, she glanced around the busy yard. Blaec had settled, alert, on the corner of the ridge of the barn, ready for any challenger. Cobbe was making his way out of the stable, his dulcimer tucked under his arm just exactly the way she had seen Elfheah carry his harp. And then they went in through the doorway, into the cool darkness and up the stairs.

"Branwen!" Edmund shouted as she walked into the big, sunny room. He crossed over to her and hugged her. "I'm glad you've come. You're just what we need."

Branwen curtseyed, first to the prince, then to Leofwine, ealdorman of Coventry, her father's old friend, and then to his son, Leofric, standing to one side.

"Eadric is due any minute," Edmund said. "We were just discussing the best way to handle him. Now that you're here, it's easy."

"Easy, my lord?"

"Leofwine will take these hot-blooded, outspoken friends of mine downstairs to the great hall while you and I shall receive Eadric alone up here. You will be my hostess. I know I can trust you to be charming, delightful company."

"You forget, Edmund—Eadric and I are not . . . the best of friends."

"You forget, Branwen," he said, the laughter narrowing out of his eyes, "Eadric has no better friend here than you. You'll have to do. Leofric, see if you can find her some suitable clothes and, for God's sake, be quick about it."

"Of course, my lord," Leofric said. "Come on, Bran, you can take your pick."

She was still dressing when a clamor in the courtyard below her window indicated Eadric's arrival. Quickly she slipped her feet into the dainty brocade sandals Leofric had produced to replace her riding boots and left the room.

Edmund was alone, looking out the open window when she swished in, all starched linen and pale blue damask.

"You know how important this meeting is, don't you?" Edmund asked, not turning from the window. "I *must* have his help. I don't have enough men without the fyrds from Herefordshire and Gloucester."

"He won't serve under you, Edmund," she said quietly. "He's the most powerful man in the kingdom. He won't yield to you, especially while the aetheling still lives. You need him, but he would be better off without you. As long as no one man rules the land, his power grows."

"Do you think I don't know that?" Edmund snapped. "But one day I will be king. Eadric must serve under me."

"And if he will not? What then?"

"You will see that he does," he said slowly, deliberately. "I understand you can do it. Godwin says. . . ."

"Never put your confidence in a drinking man," Branwen said, turning to the side table where the fine royal wines had been decanted and stood ready. "What exactly has my brother told you?" she asked, trying to buy time, time to think of what to say.

"That you can bend others to your will, make a man do what you want him to do. Is it true?"

"To some extent," she hedged.

"Never mind 'to some extent,' woman. Is it true? Can you make him promise what you want or not?"

"Yes," she said wearily, "while he's here, in this room, I can make him agree to anything. But, Edmund," she said, turning to him, her brow creased, "I can't make him stand by what he promises here. Once he has gone, the power fades. . . ."

"Nonsense. He is well born. He will honor his word once given."

When Eadric had gone, Edmund slipped a heavy gold ring off his finger and handed it to her. "You did very well, Lady Branwen," he said coldly. "I did not believe your brother at first, but. . . ." He shrugged.

She fingered the thick, gold ring, intricately worked around a glowing amythyst. It was a warm ring, the edges of the casting worn with years. Who had had it made? she wondered idly. After a moment she held it out to Edmund.

"Take it, my lord," she said slowly. "I am no trickster to be hired and then paid, even with such a jewel. What I did, I did because you asked, because you will be my king."

Edmund eyed her narrowly. "Well, I suppose Arthur had his Merlin."

"Merlin is a fantasy of the bards, Edmund. But even so, the help he gave Arthur was often two-edged. And that's the way it is with this promise of Eadric's. You can't believe it. He won't keep his word. Honor doesn't exist for him."

"It must, Branwen. Without him and his men, we have no hope of overcoming the Dane this year."

"Then give it up."

"No, damn it, girl. We will go into battle within the week. Eadric will keep his word."

"I hope so," she said. "I hope so for all our sakes."

I hope so, she thought, ten days later as she picked her way over the field which lay between Edmund's camp and Eadric's on the Wiltshire plain. Edmund may believe you're going to lead your army along his right flank when the sun rises tomorrow, Eadric, but I'm not so sure. She passed unnoticed through his picket lines, prowling between fires lit under the cookpots, until she reached Eadric's tent. She stood quietly there, a large, grey cat, half hidden by the roots of an old rowan. He paced back and forth, his thin face framed by a narrow beard. His court clothes put aside, he wore the plain browns of a fighting man but his boots were tall and soft, unscarred by wear. His eyes were dark and brooding; she wondered what thoughts were hidden behind them. The illusion she had woven wavered as her body warmed to his nearness. She laughed at herself for being a fool and tightened her control. She sat down between the gnarled roots and began to lick her paws, rubbing her face. She had finished her bathing and lay curled around, her eyes merely yellow slits, when she heard what she had come to hear.

"What did he say?" Eadric asked as a young man approached through the darkness.

"He accepts your token."

"Good. I knew he would. And that bastard Thorkell will owe me one. Ha! Now we can get rid of Edmund once and for all."

Stretching up on her hind legs, she raked the tree with her claws and then stalked back the way she had come.

Edmund was not asleep when she got back. Standing with her brother just outside his tent, she told them both what she had heard.

"Damn Eadric to hell," he said, tears of frustration in his eyes. After a moment he looked at Godwin and said, "Dismiss the men. But do it quietly," he added. "If they value their hides they'll disappear into the darkness leaving not a trace."

Godwin turned and walked away from their fire. There was nothing to be said.

"How many hours to dawn, would you say?"

"Two perhaps, Edmund," she answered. "The summer night is short."

"Hmph," he snorted. "Hardly time to pack up camp and be far gone. Seems a shame to lose these good tents though. Leofwine will be annoyed. You don't suppose you could. . . ."

Branwen sighed. "I am not your personal wizard, Edmund."

"Well perhaps, but I can hardly stay around to pack, Bran."

"No," she said, knowing that the lightness of his words was like skim ice over the depths of his despair. She smiled. "It's only just. . . ."

"I'll leave some men to help you."

"Not Elfheah!"

He laughed. "Bring the wagon to Thetford. I'll try to meet you there," he said, buckling on his sword and moving off in the direction of the tethered horses.

"Oh Mother, it's all your fau·lt," she muttered, pushing up her sleeve.

She had gotten as far as Oxford when Thorkell found her. It was mid-summer now, late in the haying season and no one remarked at the heavily laden hay wagon moving slowly over the roads toward the bridge over the Thames. They were an hour short of the crossing when the Viking army overtook them.

"Off the road, you peasant oafs," they shouted.

There was nothing to be done but pull into a new mown field and watch the conquering army move down the road. The four men who had stayed to drive the wagons lay in the shade, no longer surprised that they went unnoticed. Branwen sat close by, worried. She dared not move too far off or she would lose control over the illusion. Although the wagon had been disguised with a covering of hay, still the wheels and traces were too fine to belong to a genuine hay rick. Only the illusion she wove persuaded those who noticed them drive by. She watched the troops pass, hardly daring to breathe, as if that would stop the voice of her heart.

There was a fluttering of pennants, and then he was there, sitting easily on a great grey war horse, one knee drawn up over the pommel as he laughed with Hemming, who rode beside him. His helmet was off and his hair was longer than she remembered, golden in the sun. He came even with them and she began to hope he would pass by them after all. Suddenly he reined up, looking around curiously.

He knows, she thought. Now what?

He dismounted and walked over to the men lying in the shade of the wagon. They jumped up, panic-stricken.

"Take it easy, fools," he growled. "Tell the Lady Branwen I want to see her, alone, after dark, at the Sign of the Dove, across the bridge." Without waiting for an answer, he turned and strode back to the line of march, where Hemming waited, holding the bridle of his horse.

They watched the northmen pass by all afternoon until the sun was setting. When the last of them had gone, they drove the wagon back the way they had come until they came to a narrow lane. There they made camp, hidden until morning. Branwen scrubbed at the imbedded grime, without much avail. Even her cleaner clothes were worn and soiled. Her boots had holes in them. She braided her hair softly and buckled on her Celtic belt. It was black with tarnish. She tried unsuccessfully to rub it off. Well, she thought, it's the best I can do. Mounting Beornwig, she bid the nervous men goodnight and rode toward the Oxford bridge.

Once in the city, she was caught up in the crowds of soldiery milling in the streets on the warm summer night. Her face flushed as men turned to stare. Lost, she had no idea which direction she should turn. One group, more drunk than the rest perhaps, began to move toward her, egging each other on.

Suddenly Beornwig neighed and lashed out with his front hoof at a man who had seized hold of his bridle.

"Tell him it's a friend, my lady," the man said quickly, turning to her.

"Pym, thank God," she said. "I've come to find Thorkell, but I don't know which way to go."

Pym did not answer. His attention was on the group of men moving in on them. He braced the butt of his spear against his foot, the tip pointing outward. He said, his voice cold with command, "The lady's meant for better than you, scum."

"Oh, is that so? And who might that be? Yourself, perhaps?"

"She's come to speak with the Lord Thorkell, and God help any that touches her."

"Thorkell, is it? He's not one for the ladies," the man said, snorting. "Unless," his eyes narrowed as he tried to focus his drink-blurred mind, "unless she be the Lady of the Ravens." He circled carefully around Pym's lance, searching Branwen's face. "Ye be what we've heard, lady? Aye or nay?"

Branwen was silent.

"The Lady of the Ravens." The words were whispered from group to group along the street. Ahead of them the roadway opened as the men stepped back respectfully.

They continued without incident, turning into a narrow side street. Bright lights spilled from the open door of a tavern. Turning Beornwig's bridle over to a boy who stood waiting, Pym took Branwen through the hall and into a small back room.

"Any trouble, Pym?" Thorkell asked, reaching out with

one hand to take the girl from him, while his great dog nosed her torn tunic.

"None worth mentioning, Thorkell."

"That'll be all then."

Pym turned and was gone.

He drew her to him, holding her for a long time, until she relaxed, forgetting her strangeness, her antagonism, forgetting the role Edmund had cast her in, until she was merely Branwen again, glad to be held at last by the man whose heart spoke to hers.

"Have you eaten?" he asked.

"No. Rations are in short supply, I'm afraid." She laughed honestly.

"How short?"

"Oh, we've enough," she hedged.

"Branwen," he began but then he stopped. "Come here. Eat. Let me pour you some wine."

"Not too much, Thorkell. I'm a long way from home."

He laughed. "Why? What are you doing here with that wagon? What are you hiding?"

"It's Edmund's field equipment," she said. "He had to leave it behind. He asked me to bring it through to him."

"He what!"

"Now Thorkell, you must realize that Edmund's resources are very limited at the moment. He uses what he has desperately."

"I want you to go home, Branwen. In the morning. Back to Thornbury."

"But, my love, I can't," she said simply. "He asked me to bring the wagon to him and I said I would. The men with me wouldn't get two miles left to themselves."

"I'll get those wagons to Edmund for you, if you'll go back in the morning."

"You don't even know where they are going."

"I know."

"Where?" she asked, incredulous.

"To Thetford and the Lady Ealdgyth."

"You're guessing."

"Am I?"

She was silent, eating hungrily, leaning into the shelter of his arms.

"My fleet's back," he said, breaking the silence.

She stopped chewing, waiting for him to go on.

"Eadric brought the ships up the Severn to Tottenness and returned the crews as a token of good faith when he threw in with Knut."

"So now you owe him one," she said frowning.

"Perhaps," he said, thoughtfully. "He's pressing Knut to hunt Edmund down now and kill him. Knut is wavering. He knows Eadric's advice is sound, that the prince should be killed now while his strength is gone, but Knut has no stomach for Eadric and doesn't want anything to do with his advice if he can avoid it." He waited a moment and then said, "If you agree to go home, I will speak to Knut and urge him not to go after Edmund. He'll listen to me."

"And if I don't?" she asked softly.

"If you won't go, I will lead a troop and personally see to it that Edmund is found and destroyed. Then you will have no reason to wander the roads any longer."

She knew she should be angry with him for trying to bargain with her but she was not. She would be glad to get home. Edmund would gain nothing by her refusal.

"He will be humiliated," she said.

"It's better than being dead," he said, adding, "but I think he'll just laugh. He's always played lightly for very high stakes."

Looking up at Thorkell's stern face, waiting for her answer, she offered him a plump, juicy blackberry. "You are irresistible, my love," she smiled, popping the berry between his parted lips. He pushed her back into the pillows and kissed her roughly so that the taste of blackberries was in her mouth as well.

In the morning, she woke, her poor clothes strewn about the room, her dignity preserved only by his rough field cloak, thrown over her. Thorkell was gone but his dog slept across the doorway. She dressed hurriedly and was combing out her hair when he came back carrying a sack of food.

"Good morning," he said absently, his mind already moving away from her. "I've not much time; we're moving out. Pym will take you back over the bridge to see you on your way. I've dispatched six men to see the wagon safely through to Thetford."

"And how many men will you send to see me safely back to Thornbury?" she teased.

"Don't be facetious, Branwen." He smiled. "Here's a letter for Toki. He won't bother you. And here," he said, handing her five heavy coins, "take some money for food—and perhaps a new pair of boots," he added frowning.

"When will I see you again?"

"Probably not until winter."

"Take care, my love."

He ran his hand roughly over her hair, turned and was gone.

Chapter Thirteen

SHE TRAVELLED SOUTH slowly, for there was no reason to hurry.

The weather held sunny. Beornwig cropped in the warm meadows while Branwen gathered wild herbs to trade for their dinner at the heavy-roofed cottages along the road. Blaec stayed close, circling lazily in the clear blue sky.

It was mid-June when they forded the Kennet and started across the Salisbury plain. The gently rolling countryside was dotted with sheep. Many of the fields were unworked, their hedges broken, their furrows unplowed and weed-choked, for there was a layer of chalk under the downs and grain grew poorly. She had never been in this part of the land before, these central downs, bordered on the north by the Kennet River and drained toward the south by the gently flowing water of the Avon. Wandering over the land she stumbled upon the grass covered mounds and barrows of a forgotten people. There, among the ancient tumuli, she felt a new closeness to that race which had once gathered here to worship and bury their dead. It was nothing that she knew clearly or could have put into words, just a sense of recognition, a kind of memory, of a time long ago when the barrows were open, decorated with flowers, filled with offerings of honey and freshly baked bread.

Branwen climbed one low, broad hill, larger than the others by far, and looked out over the land. The sound of people singing and laughing washed over her although she was alone under the sun with Beornwig. Blaec rode the same warm summer breeze which ruffled the tall grasses around her. She felt a sense of peace enveloping her. She sighed, unafraid, unsurprised. There was something here she did not understand, but it was not frightening. She sat on the hilltop for a long time, listening to the voices which were singing words just beyond her understanding. Finally, when the sun started to cast longer shadows, Branwen started down from the hill, climbing over the rows of ridges which ran around the slope. She could not remember seeing ridges like that on any other hill. She wondered what they meant or if they meant anything at all. The voices from the past faded as she walked south along the banks of the Avon.

That night the sun set but they went on through the twilight looking for some sign of shelter in the empty land. Blaec flew down at dusk and settled on her shoulder. The sky grew dark and filled with stars. Only a little light still lingered in the west when they topped a rise and there, standing before them, were grey stones rising up out of the shadows, looming like great, grey ghosts. The plain was completely still. Branwen dismounted and led the stallion quietly along the roadway. There were no small insect sounds, no scurryings; even the breeze had stopped. The horse's hoofbeats rang loudly through the stillness as they approached the great circle.

The unicorn stepped out of the shadows. He gleamed white in the starlight. *Leave the stallion and the king of birds outside the circle, daughter of the Mother, for the ground within is sacred.*

"Will they be all right?" she asked quietly.

What harm can there be where the Moon shines this night? The whole world awaits Her coming to bless the land and the fruits thereof which now grow full with life.

"I don't understand," Branwen cried, tears of frustration glistening in her eyes. "Why do you always talk in riddles?"

You will know and understand, child—in time.

The ring of stones was silent, empty, towering over her as she stepped toward it. The unicorn waited just beyond the northern trilithon. She stepped through the chill of the stone's shadow. The unicorn stood quietly, watching her from the bottomless depths of his lavender eyes. Even as she buried her face in the long-remembered softness of his pale velvet fur, a sudden weariness came over her and she sank down onto a carpet of summer flowers and slept, while the sacred messenger kept watch.

A distant chanting woke her. The looming grey stones were gone and in their place was a tall bank which circled the place where she had slept. Higher than a standing man, bright white, glowing in the darkness, it rose around her, four hundred feet from rim to rim. She stood up, turning toward the sound of the approaching chant. There, through an opening in the embankment, a roadway stretched between gleaming white mounds. Along the course so bounded walked the singers, lit by a myriad of flaming torches.

Branwen stood quite still, alone. The unicorn had gone. She watched the procession approach the entrance. Just outside, the torch bearers stopped and fell back toward either side, forming an avenue of light. Through this light the women came. Dressed in white robes and crowned with pale flowers, they came into the darkness within the circle.

Branwen waited calmly, knowing in the very depths of her being that this was as it should be, that these were the voices she had heard earlier. She, too, wore a long robe of whitened animal skins, intricately worked with tiny, white beads. When the women had come halfway into the circle, still a hundred feet from her, they turned and began to form a ring within the great chalk bank. Beyond the wall, as well, Branwen could see an outer ring being formed from the light of hundreds of flaming torches. When each circle was complete there were two women who stood apart, watching her, waiting.

"Come. Stand with us, daughter of the Moon," one of the women said.

Branwen moved closer.

"Greetings, and welcome to our ring of light, Mother's child," the second woman said as Branwen came near.

When she had taken her place beside them, the first woman called out in a loud voice, "Let it begin."

And suddenly there was a great blaze of light as men carrying torches mounted the chalk ring. The flames from their pine brands scattered the darkness and the women within began to sing. Joining hands they danced an ancient circle dance, singing as they moved of the glory of the Eternal Life Giver, the Mother of All, from whose womb the universe was born.

> In the beginning the Eternal dwelt alone.
> In the fastness of the north She dwelt.
> Where there is neither life nor death
> But only the unending turn of the Wheel,
> There She had Her abode.
>
> So are we born to delight the Creator of All.
> So are we born to delight the Holy Mother.

When the song ended, the dancers stopped and turned toward the east, where there was a dark gap in the ring of torches.

"Let the darkness of the earth come upon our spirits," the priestess called out.

At her words, the torches were put out and only the pale starlight shone upon the Salisbury plain. They waited, facing the east. The sky lightened. There was a gentle susurrant from the men who stood atop the mound and Branwen knew they had prostrated themselves before the first light of the rising Moon. And then She was there for all to see. Rising above the artificial horizon of the chalk embankment She illumined Her worshippers.

The priestesses who stood next to Branwen in the center of the ring raised their arms and began to chant time-honored prayers begging the Goddess to bless the fruits of the midsummer fields. While the Moon rose they prayed until the bottom rim of the rising deity cleared the edge of the embankment.

Then a tiny tremor ran through the ground, as if time and the world had blinked. A deep silence enveloped Branwen and she saw the Great Mother Herself step down from the shining orb and stand alone on the top of the mound. The worshippers, the priestesses, were gone. The meadow was empty, the great stones once again shimmered and grew solid, the massive ring of Stonehenge. The glow of the chalk ring faded and disappeared beneath a covering of poor grasses, slumping lower so that it was hardly remarkable at all.

Come, I will take you to Her. The unicorn stepped out of the shadows beside her. Together they walked toward the waiting Goddess.

"Greetings, winter child," the Goddess said, smiling warmly.

Branwen knelt and bowed her head.

The Goddess stood, waiting.

"What was here, Mother?" Branwen asked at last. "Tell me who those people were. Please," she begged, "I want to know, to understand."

"Four thousand mortal years ago, two hundred generations in the past, your people raised the gleaming rim of chalk in a sacred circle and marked out the cycles of the rising Moon. They were the first growers of grain who had learned from My holy women the simple skills they needed. The land was rich and fruitful. Game ran through the forests, fish swam in the rivers. No one went hungry and skilled were the healers so that disease was no burden to them. Their wants were simple and easily supplied. They lived in peace for their numbers did not yet fill the land. This was the millennium, the golden age, before the coming of the herdsmen from the east. This was the millennium when the mystery of motherhood was the only link between the children of the earth and the eternally spinning Wheel.

"The sons of women were hunters, coming among women for shelter and the pleasures of hearth and home. But they came, not as kings, but as lesser beings, to be cared for and nurtured, for the gift of new life was withheld from them and their fruitfulness was held to be the fruit of the hunt and their gift of life was death itself.

"They raised this circle almost too late, my daughter, for as they dug the ditch and raised the mound, the rumor of change was upon them even in this remote island on the edge of the world. The worship which had been paid to the Mother from the depths of primeval caves and ancient mounds, developing slowly over twenty-five thousand years, peaked here at this holy place."

"Then the great stones were raised to your honor?"

"Oh no, child," the Goddess laughed. "They came later. These great stones mark the rising of the Sun, the new God of power and might. They were raised here, in this place, because all recognized the sanctity of this ground."

"Didn't anyone try to stop them? Didn't anyone speak out?"

"The fruit of man is death. The priestesses who stood against the profanity lie buried here, beneath the ground.

"The golden age ended when the blood of war desecrated the fields of grain. When Gwydion stole the pigs of Pryderi; when Gilvaethwy took a woman against her will, then was the fabric of the heavens rent and a new age begun."

"I've never heard these names," Branwen said.

"I know. In time you will. They are part of a long cycle once sung all over this land. Now there are only a few left in the western hills who know the words. I will send one to you and he will sit by your fire in the cold and dark of winter and sing sad songs of the ending of an age, of the time when My beautiful Arianrhod was forced to bear a child against her will, when that child so born was tricked from her. It is a long story, Branwen, the story of the ending of an age, the loss of the supremacy of love and the victory of brutal power. And still the sons of the earth wallow in it," the Goddess said, Her voice tinged with anger.

"Can't You do anything?"

"I cannot stand against the river of time. All growth is painful, child; but the alternative is death."

They stood in silence for a long moment and then the Goddess said, "It is almost daybreak. Listen, the birds are waking. It is time for you to go home."

As Branwen watched, the Goddess faded, and was gone.

Two days later they came to the top of the last hill overlooking the Coombe valley and Thornbury. Branwen's feet were bare, her tunic faded, stained, fraying at the hem. A small wind carried sounds from the harvesters in the fields below. She shrank back from their voices.

Glad to be home, Branwen? Blaec mocked from a branch in the leafy shade.

She was silent for a while, searching the furlongs below. "And you," she said finally, "you must be glad to be back. You're a king here."

Blaec croaked. It was impossible for the bird to laugh. This was as close as he could come.

"Will you have to fight?" she asked.

Of course. That's the nature of kingship.

She sighed and started off the hilltop. Beornwig followed. The bird watched them go. No one noticed her, scuffling through the dust between the hedgerows.

Aelle was asleep in the afternoon shade by the kitchen door when she came into the courtyard at Thornbury. The dogs opened one eye and then, reassured, went back to sleep. There was no sign of anyone else. She unsaddled the horse, filled his grain bucket and brought him water. Aelle slept undisturbed as she filled the cauldron in the laundry with water from the well and kindled a fire under it. As the water warmed, she walked slowly around the buildings which had always been her home. Idly, strangely disembodied, she noted that all was as it should be. The gardens were weeded, bare spots showed where the harvests were being collected carefully. There was new thatch on the part of the barn which had leaked last winter. She opened the door of her little hut and went into the stuffy darkness. She opened the shutters and a breeze swept curiously around the room.

"It's only me," she said softly to the worried field mouse poking her head out from behind the faded cupboard which filled one wall. Reassured, the tiny mother set about her more important tasks.

She turned and went out again. Crossing the dusty court-yard, she came into the great hall. The heavy door closed behind her and the sound echoed through the empty room. The floor was bare, the trestle tables folded up against the wall. The window was shuttered, the hearth clean and empty. There was a thin film of dust on the side board and the head table as if the room, having been set to rights, had been forgotten.

"Poor hall," Branwen said softly, "where are the voices which brought you to life?" She felt a moment of doubt, a flicker of regret that she was not really mistress here with her children growing strong around her. She thought of Thorkell, for the first time in days it seemed, and a rush of loneliness washed over her. For a long moment she thought how simple and good it would be to live as his wife, to bear his children and watch them grow. Why, she wondered, did she want more?

Opening the shutters to let in the light, she knelt beside the chest which stood under the window and removed a blue tunic, coarsely woven, meant as a work dress. The slack saddle bags which had gone to war with her lay on the earth floor next to her. She opened one, drawing out the tarnished, silver belt from another age. She laid it carefully beside the thin, gold circlet still wrapped as she had left it. She turned a bag over and five gold coins fell onto the floor. She picked them up carefully, holding them heavily in the palm of her hand before stacking them in one corner of the chest. She reached into the other bag and pulled out Thorkell's letter to Toki. It had gotten wrinkled and she laid it on top of the chest, smoothing it with her hands. I'll send Wiggs off with it later, she thought.

When she returned to the laundry, the water in the caul-dron was hot and she ladled it into the tub. Peeling off her ragged tunic and the disreputable shreds of her undergar-ments, she stepped into the tub. She sat there for a long time, feeling the weariness flow out of her. The soft, fresh soap from the tallow of Thornbury sheep billowed around her. The boar bristle brush caressed her skin roughly, scratching pleasurably at the itchy places bitten by bugs, rubbing off the scabbed bramble scratches around her ankles. Oh, but it was good to feel clean. When she had finished rinsing her hair with rainwater from the barrel in the garden, she dressed carefully. Out in the sun, she sat on Ansgar's rock, and began to comb the tangles out of her dark hair.

Beyond the stockade she could hear the running laughter which meant that the harvest hag was being passed as one reaper after another finished his fields. She had just finished when Dyffed came into the garden.

"Welcome home, Branwen!" he said, startled.

She smiled at him. "Thank you, Dyffed."

"I am sorry there wasn't anybody to greet you."

"It's just as well," she said with a laugh. "You've taken good care of Thornbury while I was gone."

Dyffed said nothing, watching her, waiting. She stood up and walked between the clumps of pot herbs before she answered his unspoken question.

"There was no battle. Edmund was betrayed."

"Killed?"

"No, but there is nothing left for him. My brother is still with him, and Leofric, too, I think. They're moving through East Anglia but there's no hope now of raising an army."

"Who betrayed him?"

She looked up at him, ashamed because he knew she had not always hated Eadric, and her face colored.

"Streona," he said, spitting out the word as if it left a bad taste in his mouth.

"Knut is sweeping unopposed through Warwickshire and the Danelaw," she said.

"Even where Edmund was such a hero last fall?"

"Even there," she said sadly. Then she added, "At least he's still alive, Dyffed."

"But not for long. The Danes will hunt him down."

"No," she said, "they won't do that."

She could see the anger mounting on the man's face as he chafed, wanting to know the whole story, courtesy and position standing in his way. Suddenly she laughed, a sound rusty at first, and then warm and familiar. "All right, Dyffed," she said, "I'll tell you everything. Only let's get a jug of ale and some cold meat. I haven't had anything to eat today and I'm hungry."

There were long tables set out along the gravel bank of the Coombe as Branwen rode through the village on her way to the monastery the next morning. It must have been Tukka who had taken home the harvest hag—the doll, woven of straw, passed from reaper to reaper as each finished his field, coming in the end to spend the festival with the man who was last in the countryside to finish reaping his field—for he held the jug. Judging from the laughter around him, he must have had to pour out many rounds although it was not yet noon. There were Danes among the harvesters, laughing with them. Branwen remembered Dyffed saying, "Toki is not hard on us. It's good you have friends in high places."

"Branwen," a voice called, "welcome home. Come and join us."

"Not now, Wade." She laughed. "Perhaps later."

She rode on, waving to the neighbors she had grown up among, unable to shake her feeling of distance. She was no longer one of them. They were familiar strangers to her.

Carefully tended roses filled the air with their sweetness as she walked up to the convent gate. She found Aelfthryth sitting in the formal gardens shaded by a magnificent copper beech.

"Branwen, child," the old woman said.

"My lady," she answered, curtseying with a gentle grace more fitting a richer dress and slippered feet.

"How is my grandson? Have you come to take me home?"

"No, not yet," she answered slowly. "The prince is well. My brother is with him in East Anglia." Quietly then, and reluctantly, she told the queen mother the news she had earlier told Dyffed.

"So, it will be a while longer before we can open the treasury at Holcombe. I hope it was strong magic you used to seal it, to last so long."

"The seal will not be broken but, oh my lady, I'm afraid we'll never be able to open it for Edmund," Branwen cried.

"Nonsense, child. Edmund will be king. You are too impatient. He is destined for the throne. Take the word of an old lady who has seen much of kings."

"I pray you are right, my lady."

Aelfthryth laughed. "I find it hard to imagine you praying, Branwen," she said.

"Why do you say that?"

"It has been a long time since you have been in church. Father Anselm is worried about your soul."

"Are you?"

"You are young. I am not worried yet."

Branwen was silent in the westering sun of the garden. Finally, she said, "I have seen The Mother, and I have talked to Her."

"The Mother," the old woman said slowly. "So She still walks among Her daughters—and you." She smiled. "It does not surprise me."

"You believe me?" Branwen said.

"Were you so sure I would not?"

"You worship the Christian mysteries. There is no Goddess in this cathedral."

Aelfthryth laughed. "No, my dear. Father Anselm would not take kindly to Her altar in his sanctuary, I dare say."

"And so you worship the God of power and might, the God who teaches men that to be powerful is to be god-like, sharing in the divinity of Him from Whom all power comes."

"No, child," the gentlewoman said, quietly. "I worship the Deity Who is beyond our understanding. Surely man's greatest conceit is believing he can know the Eternal Infinite. No, my dear, I do not believe the Deity can be grasped by mere human understanding. I think that we must be like the rye the sower sows in April to reap in July. Does the growing plant know or understand the one who gave it life? So it must be with the Deity I adore."

Branwen watched a bumblebee which flew heavily from

one rose to another before asking, "Yet you say you believe me when I tell you I have seen the Ancient One, the Great Mother. Who is She, to you? How can you worship another?"

"It is a pity you have no children yet, Branwen," Aelfthryth said, thoughtfully. "Do you remember how your mother taught you to be a woman? When you were very young she had a small broom made, like her big one, so that you could imitate her in the simple tasks. As you grew up, she taught you the more difficult work of being a woman, each new lesson coming as she thought you were ready. Even so, my dear, the Infinite Life Giver sent The Mother to the children of the earth when they were very young. She was our first glimpse of Divinity."

"And growing up is never easy, is it, Lady Aelfthryth?"

His voice startled them and they looked up to see Father Anselm, his breviary in his hand, standing in the garden pathway. He smiled at them warmly and said, "If God did, in truth, reveal Himself to His people as The Great Mother of All, is it not strange the Bible is so silent? There is no mention of Her in the story of creation nor was She present in the Garden of Eden when God first made man."

"I wonder, Father," Aelfthryth asked, unabashed, "if man's sin in that garden was to reject the Goddess and the love She asked of Her children? Perhaps that is why Christ, redeeming us from that sin, taught once again that the greatest commandment is love."

"Ah, perhaps that is possible, my lady, but we can never know, can we?" His face was grave and he continued, "Here at St. Martin's we must worship God as Christ taught us and the mysteries you speak of are forbidden us."

"Are there no answers for the child here, Father? Is there nothing we can do to help her in her search?"

"We will remember you in our prayers, Branwen, that the way you travel will not be beyond your strength, for the solitary traveller follows the harder road."

"Thank you, Father," Branwen said quietly.

Aelfthryth smiled and held out her soft hands to Branwen. Taking them in her own brown, roughened ones, Branwen noticed how fine the old woman's skin was, thin and translucent over thick blue cords, long fingers ending in clean, rounded nails. Aelfthryth noticed, too, and, holding Branwen's hands in her own, she turned them over and said, "How different our hands are, my dear. Yours are still so strong and useful-looking."

Branwen laughed ruefully, not understanding the compliment.

"Come back soon, child," the old woman said. "It's always good to see you."

"I will, my lady. Good afternoon, Father Anselm," she said, with a smile as she turned to go.

"Dominus vobiscum," he said, raising his hand to bless her.

"Et cum spiritu tuo," she called back over her shoulder.

Chapter Fourteen

THE HOGS WERE slaughtered and salted away. A fine, light snow was falling through the early evening twilight when a lone rider came through the gates at Thornbury.

"Pym," Branwen said, holding out both hands to him as he came into the great hall. "This is a surprise. Come in and warm yourself. Wiggs," she called, "bring some metheglin and tell Aelle to heat up the meat pasty we had at dinner."

After he had eaten and warmed himself with the fire and the metheglin, he put his goblet down on the table and looked up at her. "Thorkell sends his greetings, my lady," he said. "He bids you join him in Salisbury. Knut and Aelgifu are holding a mid-winter feast there."

Branwen looked up in surprise. " 'Bids me,' Pym? Is that what he said?"

Pym shuffled his feet uncomfortably. "Well, no, my lady, I mean . . . er . . . he wants you to come. He just sent me to ask if you would, that's all."

Branwen laughed. "Well," she said, "I thought for a moment. . . ." She shook her head. "It doesn't matter. A mid-winter feast at Knut's court. I wonder why he wants me to come? He knows I'd be out of place there! I wouldn't know anybody. What would I wear?" She walked over to the window and watched the snow blow against the glass, drifting into the corners. "Tell him I cannot come, Pym. I'm sorry."

"He'll be awful disappointed, Branwen. He really wants you there. Hemming hoped you would come, too. Ulf and Eilaf are there. You know them. They were here last spring, don't you remember?"

Oh yes, I remember Ulf, she thought with a smile, and his laughing brother.

"And the men of the Raven's Wing," Pym went on, "we all want you to come. He really misses you, my lady," he finished up awkwardly. "He said to tell you he doesn't think he will be able to get out here at all this winter. After Salisbury, they're moving north to Berkhamsted."

"Does he have to go with them? Why can't he come here for a few months? There'll be no campaigning until spring."

"Him and Knut—they're very close, my lady."

"Are they?" she asked archly. Reaching out to touch the soft wax at the bottom of a candle which burned beside the window, she said thoughtfully, "Well, I had better go then. Who knows? Perhaps I can change his mind."

"He wants to send an escort, Branwen, one fitting your rank," the Norseman said hesitantly.

"No!" she said, whirling toward him. "Tell him I won't ever ride through my country with Viking escort. Tell him I'll come as my father's daughter. He'll have to settle for that," she added more gently.

When she rode through the frozen streets of Salisbury two weeks later she was alone, wrapped closely against the icy chill in the magnificent grey squirrel cloak Thorkell had given her one bitter cold evening long ago. Her head was bare but for the crown of holly she wore.

All eyes turned to her as she stood in the entrance of the great hall where Knut and court were gathered. A sudden hush fell over the room. Even the clatter of plates and mugs grew still. Under the table the dogs stopped growling and looked up curiously at the change. Branwen seemed coldly unaware of the effect she had caused as an attendant took

her cloak, revealing the richness of her black dress with its
gleaming silver girdle, her undertunic showing silver grey
at the cuff. She stood quite still there in the back, allowing
her eyes to travel slowly along one side of the room before
coming to rest on the figure of the king lounging in his high
seat.

He straightened up under her gaze, pulling his arm free
from the beautiful woman at his side whose rich gown
seemed suddenly garish. "Welcome to our court, Lady
Branwen," he said.

She crossed the room slowly, hearing familiar voices calling her from the long tables against the walls. She looked to
neither side. In her heart she was a Saxon and all who saw
her cross the room that evening felt her pride—the
undefeated dignity of a people not yet wholly conquered.

She stopped five feet from the head table and curtsied
deeply. Her head unbowed, her eyes still raised to Knut's,
she said, "Yule greetings, noble lord. I bring you a gift
from the west country."

The king looked at her curiously, for she stood empty-
handed in front of him. She smiled and raised her right
hand high over her head. Knut tensed. There was a rasp of
drawn swords. A dog growled. Branwen laughed and
called out in a strange tongue. An enormous black raven
flew down through the thin smoke from the high windows,
open under the roof. He settled on her arm, his eyes red:
glittering symbols of the Viking warrior.

The crowd was suddenly on its feet, cheering. Branwen
spoke softly to the bird and Blaec hopped off her arm onto
the table where he began to peck disrespectfully at the food
on the king's plate.

At her side Thorkell laughed. "Well done, Branwen,"
he said, his voice barely audible above the cheering. "You
are, indeed, your father's daughter."

When the hall was quiet again, Knut, leaning back in his
chair and laughing softly, obviously pleased with the bird,
said, "We thank you, Lady Branwen. We had heard you
have a way with these birds. But now we are in your debt
and would give a gift in return. Tell me, what would you
like?" The strong wine he had been drinking all afternoon

had made him over-generous.

Branwen smiled. She felt Thorkell stiffen. She wondered if he knew what she would ask.

"A boon, my lord," she said, her voice clear and unafraid. "There is much work at Thornbury since my father died that needs a man to see to it. Give me your chieftain, Thorkell—until the buds swell in the spring."

Knut's face clouded but Hemming's great laughter boomed through the room. "You should have spent more time with your books, Knut. There have been many heroes who've rued the day they said, 'Ask what you wish.' "

"Well, Thorkell," Knut said, "what have you to say?"

"It's fairly asked, Knut. She leaves us little choice," he answered with a frown.

"Very well, then. But only until spring. I want you back with the thaw and ready to move out when we take London."

Thorkell nodded and led Branwen to a seat next to his brother at the end of the head table.

"Hemming, merry Christmas," she said, sitting down beside him.

Hemming was still laughing. "Branwen, Branwen. This is one feast that will be talked of for a long time, I'll wager. But you deserve a better helper than my brother. I'm afraid he's not good for much."

"He'll do, Hemming," she said with a smile. Turning to Thorkell, she asked softly, "You don't mind, do you, my love?"

"Does it matter?" he answered.

"Don't be angry," she said.

"I'm not. It's just that there will be a lot of decisions before spring. I hope you won't be sorry that I'm not with Knut when they are being made."

"Oh Thorkell, I hadn't thought about that."

"No, I'm sure you hadn't."

Then he relented. "It's all right, Bran. It will be good to see Thornbury again—and you," he added. "It's been a long time. Did you get those boots?"

She laughed. "What did Edmund say when your men delivered his equipment?"

"They did not see Edmund. He had left Thetford before they got there."

"Tell me who these people are," she asked brightly, changing the subject. "I know I've met some of them before."

"The woman next to Hemming," he said quietly, "is Cwenhilde. She's a friend of Aelgifu, over there," he nodded, "next to Knut."

Branwen looked down the table at the beautiful girl sitting next to Knut. Aelgifu combined the best qualities of the two peoples who co-mingled in the Danelaw where she had been born. Her hair was golden, her eyes dark, her mouth strong and willful. She was very young.

"On the other side of Knut, the woman with the grey hair, that's his half-sister, Gytha. She has come down from Norway to join Eric for the winter with their son, Hakon. There's trouble brewing along the fiords and Eric wants them both safely out of it."

Eadric, the Grasper, sat beyond, turned away talking with Harald, now the king of Denmark. As if he felt her glance, Eadric turned toward her. His eyes were intense and there was no trace of a smile. With what she hoped was cool disdain she looked past the traitor, smiling at Pym and Ragnar who sat along the side wall with the other men of the Raven's Wing.

Nearer were Eilaf and Ulf, who had been at Thornbury in the spring. Ulf's wife, Estrid, Knut's youngest sister, was hopelessly trying to soothe a fretful baby who was too distracted by the music of the pipers and the uproar of voices to nurse peacefully. Even as they watched, the young mother rose and took the child out of the room. Branwen smiled.

"So you see," Thorkell was saying, "he has all his family with him to celebrate his victories."

"Is his victory complete?" she asked, her eyes lowered to the silver plate in front of her. "What of Edmund and my brother? I've had no news in months. Are they still alive?"

"They're alive, Bran. They're spending the winter in London. Edmund couldn't raise any support last summer, you must know that. He eventually wound up with that old warrior, Ulfkytel. And then, sometime around the middle of November, Ethelred came out to join them near Colchester. The aetheling died sometime in October, did you hear? Ethelred may have gone to Colchester to acknowledge Edmund as his successor. Nothing's come of it though. As far as we know they went back to London together. Godwin was with them."

Branwen felt tears start in her eyes and she blinked them away.

"When we take the city in the spring, I will do whatever I can to see that your brother is safe."

"I know, Thorkell. Thank you."

Later they danced and, as they changed partners through the pattern, Branwen came to Knut.

"Aelgifu is right," he said abruptly. "Thorkell has been too stingy with his treasure. Why hasn't he given you any jewels to wear? God knows he has chests full of the stuff."

"My lord," she said, smiling innocently at him from the figure of the dance, "Thorkell's treasure would serve him ill if it were mine to use."

"What do you mean?" he probed.

No trace of drink blurred his voice now. In his clear eyes burned the light which gave him power over men. Here again was the conqueror who frightened her. But despair dulled her fear. What did it matter? She had little hope now of ever defeating the Dane. But it wasn't over. Not yet.

"My loyalty is to Edmund, my lord," she said heedlessly, her voice steady. "It is only by your grace I have leave to spend this evening with you."

"Pah, Edmund will be dead by summer," he said angrily. "Don't push me too far, lady."

"I should leave Salisbury in the morning, then," she smiled.

"You should come to your senses. I need Thorkell here, happily bedded with a loyal wife. If not you, he can learn to love another."

"Thornbury is not so far, my lord. He will grow restless when the willows turn yellow. Don't grudge us respite."

"Not at all, my dear. On the contrary. I spoke with Toki a little while ago. We may go to Holcombe in a few weeks.

Perhaps we will remain there until spring."

"I hope you will not find the quiet country life too boring, my lord," she said gaily, hiding her dismay. Holcombe. Not Edmund's Holcombe. What had she done? It had seemed so simple. What would she do if he came to Sherborne?

She spoke to Thorkell about it a little later. He laughed. "Don't worry," he said. "They won't come. Aelgifu wouldn't stand for it."

In the morning, like horses let out of the barn at the end of winter, they were away, racing over the frozen roadway toward the west and home. Thorkell's personal guard, the men of the Raven's Wing, followed more slowly with the wagons.

The winter passed slowly. Thorkell was right. Knut never came to Holcombe. After a while Branwen was almost sorry he had not. Thorkell was restless at Thornbury. There were messengers back and forth between Sherborne and Berkhamsted almost every day. She was surprised, because she had never really believed that he was so close to Knut. Often she would wake in the middle of the night to see Thorkell pacing restlessly or hunched over a map of London spread in front of him in the candlelight. She could no longer ignore the fact that he was planning to take the city in the spring, that he knew all its secrets, its defenses and weak points, and that with his help Knut would succeed where his father had failed. There was a strain between them that grew worse as the winter went by. There were more and more things they could not talk about. So they were both relieved when, for the first time in many years, a wolf hunt was planned for February. In the excitement of preparation, London could be forgotten for a few days.

"Are you coming, Bran?" Thorkell asked, knowing how difficult hunting was for her whose mind echoed the cries of the animals and birds.

She looked at him, startled that he should ask. "It's my place, Thorkell. These are my people. I am their thegn. I owe them protection for their homes and flocks."

And he stood there, hands on his hips, feet apart, looking down at her. She was so small. It was hard to imagine her protecting anyone. It should have been funny but it wasn't. She was right. Toki was thegn in name only; he had seen that these past few weeks. Too many times Dyffed and the others came to her with problems they should have taken to Toki. Even this business of the wolf hunt. Toki had gladly given her the lead. It would be cold and would probably rain. It always rained in February in this godforsaken climate. I'll have to speak with Toki, he thought. It's time Branwen stopped being thegn and started being more of a wife. He laughed to himself. It had better be carefully done though, or Branwen would be furious. And she'd have every right to be, too, he thought ruefully. Still, if she's going to be my wife, she's going to have to leave Thornbury. One more season. We'll take London. Ethelred will be forced to flee and Edmund . . . well, we'll have to wait and see what Edmund does. By fall, the whole thing should be settled once and for all.

Branwen went out alone that night before the hunt, walking up into the hills. The road was bathed in moonlight. Grey shadows gathered around her and she spoke with them.

"There will be a great hunt at dawn. Men will come with dogs to kill you. You must flee now before it is too late."

Where will we go, hairless one? When men war among themselves, the hills grow crowded with our kind.

"I only came to warn you and the pack, Grayfax. Leave my people. Go away or you will die."

Perhaps, but I think we are not so easily killed, the old leader said.

What would you have us do with the cubs who are too small to travel? a ragged bitch, her dugs hanging low, asked quietly.

I, for one, won't stay on their account. There is always another season. Cubs are your concern. You had them, you protect them. Even in the moonlight Branwen saw how strong the young wolf was.

Spoken like a man, Grayfax growled, the ultimate insult.

*Let us stay until the cubs are old enough to travel and then
we will leave. You have my word.*

"It will not do, Grayfax. There is no honor between the
people of the wolf and mankind. You must leave now."

We will not.

"So be it."

She turned back the way she had come.

At dawn a circle was drawn around the hills, a line of
hunters too thin to prevent a lone wolf from breaking
through. It wasn't the single male they hunted today but
the female, denned with cubs. The dogs were loosed and
the circle began to close. The first den was found before
noon. The big grey male stayed to fight and was killed, too.
There were nine killed that morning and two dogs.

They ate lunch standing in a frozen field and were off
once again.

Branwen was riding at Thorkell's side when the dogs
picked up the scent right in front of them. The male was
gone when they discovered the den. The female was gaunt,
no match for the dogs. She was dead before the horses rode
up. Branwen dismounted without waiting for the others to
arrive and was in among the cubs, her knife dripping as she
cut their throats quickly so the dogs wouldn't get them first.

It rained fitfully all morning, but not hard enough to
bring the men indoors. Branwen stood at the window in the
main hall, looking down across the fields to where the willows were an unmistakable yellow along the riverbank.
There was a sudden clatter of horse's hoofs in the cobbled
courtyard. It sounded like a single rider. She turned away
from the window and walked toward the door. Eadric was
just handing the reins to Wiggs as she came out into the
rain. She stood silently watching him, glad Thorkell was
not here; it would have been hard to shield her feelings
from him.

Eadric turned and came toward her across the muddied
cobbles, stripping off his grey gloves. She waited in the
doorway, watching the way his long, black cloak swirled
around his high boots. He pushed back his hood. Rain
streaked his face.

"Are you alone?" he asked.

"Thorkell is out with his men. They've taken the hawks. I expect them back any minute; it's almost dinnertime."

"Did you get what you wanted from him?" he asked.

She smiled sweetly at him. "And how is your lady wife?"

When they had gone into the empty hall, he pulled her into his arms, shutting the door behind them with his foot.

"Don't, Eadric," she said.

"You didn't get what you wanted from him," he sneered.

"Eadric, I love him," she said.

He kissed her and incredibly she felt her mouth go soft. His scent haunted her with memories long forgotten.

"You're a fool, Branwen," he whispered. "Does he ever make you feel like that?"

"Please let me go, Eadric," she said. A hunger raced through her body. She struggled, disbelieving, against it.

"A pity you didn't pack a picnic lunch for them," he said, releasing her, as the courtyard filled with the sounds of dogs and returning riders.

"Some wine, my lord," she said formally, moving across the room, "to warm you after your long ride."

Branwen had her back to the door when Thorkell came in. Her face was quiet and composed as she turned to greet him. He stood there looking from one to the other.

"How long have you been here?" he asked.

"Not long enough." Eadric laughed.

She could feel Thorkell's hatred for this man, like a thick, viscous liquid rising around her.

"Well, Eadric," he said coldly, reaching for the goblet Branwen held out to him, "what brings you so far from court?"

"Knut wants you back. He sent me to tell you."

"I get messages from him every day. They are seldom brought by such important messengers," Thorkell said.

Eadric smiled. "It's his way of reminding me that he's the king and I'm his to command."

Thorkell laughed. "Well, he's learning."

The tension in the room was broken as Thorkell's hungry men pushed through the door, elbowing for a place at the fire. Moments later Elin brought in the pies.

Before they sat down to eat, Thorkell turned to Pym and said, "See that everything is made ready. We'll move out in the morning."

"What will you do this summer, Bran?" Thorkell asked her after they had made love that night.

"Take a lover," she said. "Perhaps Toki. He's a little overweight and not too clever but at least he doesn't ride off when the warm weather comes."

"I'd kill him," he said, only half matching her laughing tone.

"I know," she said, all the laughter gone from her voice. "Why, Thorkell? If you killed my lover, would it make me love you more?"

"Oh, for God's sake, Branwen, I don't want to talk about this now. I've got to go in the morning."

"Yes, I know. You go to kill my king and probably my brother as well."

"Would you rather they killed me?"

But she was crying and couldn't answer him. He held her close and after a long while she said, "I love you. Be safe. I won't give you a reason to kill any man, not this summer."

He kissed her and they made love again as the sun rose, so that the troop was mounted in the courtyard, waiting for him, as he came out of her room.

As she watched them ride off she never questioned the deep enduring love she felt for the tall Dane; a love which seemed hardly touched by the sharp fierce flame which burned for the traitor who rode with him. The Dane turned at the bend in the road to wave back at her but the other never looked around.

Chapter Fifteen

BAREFOOT, BRANWEN STROLLED along the river bank collecting lady's smock which was blooming in the sunny places. She raised her eyes, shielding them with her hand, at the sound of a rider galloping down the road to Thornbury. His coat was bright blue in the morning sun—Edmund's blue. She jumped up, grabbing the handle of her willow basket, and ran up the bank to meet him.

"Step aside, wench," he called to her rudely. "I have a royal message for the Lady Branwen."

"Stand and deliver, knave! I am the Lady Branwen."

"I know," the rider said, laughing. He removed his helmet.

"Leofric!" she exclaimed.

He swung easily out of the saddle and gave her a hug. When she had caught her breath she asked, "What's happened? What are you doing here?"

"Now, now, Branwen," he chided, "what would your father say? First you must see to my refreshment and no questions until I am washed and my thirst is slaked."

"Very well, good, gentle sir. Wouldst come to Thornbury with me and I will see to your needs anon?" she mocked.

Not until a full hour later, when he was washed and fed, did Leofric tell her why he had come. "Ethelred is dead. He died last month."

"Poor Ethelred. I hope he has found peace at last."

"Poor Ethelred be damned! He almost cost us a kingdom. With him dead the shires are rising for Edmund. We are going to march against the Viking at last."

Branwen was quiet, hardly daring to believe him.

Dyffed, standing behind her, said, "Go on."

"You should have been in London with us when the news went out that Ethelred was dead. The whole city was screaming to make Edmund king."

"King," she whispered, stunned.

"Aye. Archbishop Lyfing rode up from Canterbury and crowned him on the steps of St. Paul's where everyone could see. What a day!" he said, his eyes bright. "Edmund stood in the sun, the crown new-set on his head, and vowed to drive the Vikings from the sacred soil of Britain. The crowd was wild. They cheered him day and night."

"Where is he now?" Dyffed asked.

"Moving through Sussex. Everywhere men rally to his standard."

"What of the Danes?" he asked.

"The fools are still laying siege to London. They don't seem to realize that all the while Edmund's army is getting bigger and bigger. Why, Branwen, it's three times the size it was last summer!"

"Oh Leofric, it's too good to be true. And what of my brother? What news from Godwin?"

"He rides at Edmund's right hand these days. They're never apart."

"And you? What are you doing here?"

"Edmund plans to be in Holcombe in three days. I came on ahead to see that it is ready."

"That explains the great bustle there this morning," Dyffed said. "Toki is leaving. I wonder how he knew?"

The monastery bells of St. Martin's began peeling at dawn. The dust of the road from Cowstead and Nettleden had no chance to settle as families made their way to

Holcombe, once more Edmund's. When the small boys keeping watch on the eastern hilltop gave the cry, the very air pulsed with excitement.

Branwen was still arranging bowls of flowers in the great hall when the cheering began. She wiped up a last drip of whitewash which had eluded an earlier inspection. Untying her apron, she went out through the crowd to a place under the old oak where Aelfthryth sat waiting. Leofric stood to one side, laughing happily with the excited villagers. Branwen took the old gentlewoman's gnarled hands in her own.

"You alone never doubted, my lady," she said.

"He has a greatness to him, Branwen, that will not be denied."

Branwen smiled. Her hair curled softly around her face. Around her head she wore the thin circlet of gold Edmund had given her. There was a growing maturity about her eyes and mouth now. The fragile, wild beauty of a few years back was fading. She seemed completely relaxed, sure of herself.

Suddenly the outriders were in the courtyard, their horses holding back the crowd to clear a space. The noise rose higher. The dogs barked frantically from the kennels where they had been shut.

And then Edmund was among them. He wore the great crown of Alfred and it was not out of place. His flashing blue eyes, his rich, full, black beard, the massive power of his broad shoulders and the strength of his bare hands gripping the reins, seemed to perfect the image of a sovereign.

He dismounted and strode, unhesitating, to where his grandmother sat. Aelfthryth rose, leaning heavily on Branwen, as he approached. With determination she forced her stiffened knees to bend and she knelt before him. In hushed silence the entire crowd in the courtyard followed her example.

Edmund leaned down and helped the old woman up. He embraced her and seated her gently back in her chair under the oak. A great roar went up and under its cover Edmund turned to Branwen and said, "I missed you. Don't disappear. We have a lot to talk about."

Godwin was there then, hugging her. He looked older suddenly. Full-bearded now, like Edmund; and there were wrinkles around his eyes from the long days in the saddle, squinting in the sun. But there was an exuberance in his manner which was still boy-like.

"Oh Bran," he said, "what a great time this is! You should have been with us in London. The people were wild for him; and now, everywhere we go, men stream into camp. It's hard to believe the agony and despair we went through just last year."

She had no time to reply. Edmund was speaking to the villagers.

"We are not here to stay this afternoon. There is much to be done to drive the invader from the sacred soil of our land. Those among you who will join us are welcome. We need good Dorset men to join the brave men of Kent and Sussex. We will leave at dawn tomorrow, moving north."

"At dawn, Godwin? Must you leave so soon?"

"There's no time to waste," he whispered. "Knut has started to move against us. We dare not delay. We've got to rally what strength we can before we have to face him on the battlefield."

"I'll come with you."

"We won't be sorry, to be frank. Edmund hoped you'd add your strength to ours. Can you be ready?"

"Of course I can, Godwin. Do you think I've become the sort of woman who must pack carts to accompany her?"

At dinner Aelfthryth's gentleness quieted them. They sat at table listening to the old woman tell of the secret storeroom where Edmund's treasure had been kept safe from the Danes, locked with a magic charm.

Edmund turned to Branwen with a shrewd smile and said, "There is no end to your talent, is there?"

"Edmund," she said quietly, "please don't think of me as just a talented trickster."

"But you are so useful, my dear," he said, his eyes laughing, "and pretty, too." He leaned over and kissed her chastely.

"I still love the tall Dane, Edmund. Nothing's changed."

"Do you know how many eager neighbors have passed that information on already? 'Do you know, Your Majesty,' " he mocked, " 'they lived together at Thornbury all winter.' "

"You don't mind?"

"I've also heard of a certain midwinter feast when you had the nerve to tell Knut to his face that I was the rightful king!"

"How did you ever hear about that?"

"Knut drinks too much—and apparently you made him very angry."

They moved out at dawn, leaving the fields around Holcombe trampled, the new crop destroyed. There were few men who stayed to reseed it. Elin went home, wiped the tears from her face, tied up her skirt and searched out the seeds to start over. Ten-year-old boys were suddenly older. Fourteen-year-olds were men who went to war, embarrassed by their mothers' tears.

And so it was all through Dorset and into Somerset as they moved north toward the Cotswold hills. Near Sherston they set up camp and waited for the stragglers. Leofric left, riding on to raise additional men from his father's lands as well as Edmund's holdings in the Danelaw.

Branwen was treating a young farmer whose foot had been badly bruised when it was run over by a cart wheel. Bathing it in an infusion of willow bark, she probed gently but found nothing broken. She was binding it up with linen strips when Edmund's outrider galloped into camp.

"They're here," he said to Edmund, who stood nearby. "Across the valley, just beyond those hills. Danes."

"How many?" Edmund asked sharply.

"Seven companies, three mounted."

"You're sure?"

"Yes, my lord, we rode beyond, searching for others, but there weren't any."

"Very good. Who leads them in the field? Could you tell?"

"They carry the banners of Thorkell the Tall and Eadric Streona."

"Ah," Edmund said thoughtfully. "That's an interesting combination. Would you say they are friends, Branwen?"

All eyes turned toward her. She kept wrapping the man's foot. "They are not friends," she said evenly.

"I wonder why Knut sent them out together."

She was silent.

Godwin said, "Wiltshire is Eadric's land. He held it from your father, no doubt confirmed by Knut, so he is a natural. Knut has no reason to trust him, however, and what better man than Thorkell to keep the traitor honest?"

"Well, no matter," Edmund said, his mind already turning to the battle ahead. "Pass the word among the men. We will fight at dawn."

Branwen felt his words like a blow and went off alone, sick with the sudden realization that what she had always feared was now at hand. Eadric's words rang hauntingly in her ears. "When Thorkell and Godwin face each other across a sea of blood; when they raise their swords and close to strike, what will you do?" he had asked so long ago.

She still had no answer.

When darkness covered the hills, she moved restlessly through the camp. All around her men were rolled in their blankets. Some watched the flames of their cookfires; but others, their loud snores bearing witness, slept soundly. Through the darkness she heard the sounds of Elfheah's harp and gradually she moved in that direction.

She stood in the shadows listening to the softly picked melody. The prince did not sing as he watched the beautiful youth who sat cross-legged in the firelight mending a broken buckle on his armor. She realized with a start that it was Cobbe, finely dressed in simple green, his hair long, shining. The leggings he had always worn were gone and he wore high leather boots. She stood, unseen for a long while, watching the harper watch the boy.

"Put it away, Cobbe," Elfheah said at last.

The boy looked up at the prince and Branwen felt her heart tremble as she watched. She turned away quickly, the shadows grown cold.

She moved unseen through the camp to the edge that looked out over the stream which would run with blood tomorrow. She knew that what she had been looking for was not on this side of the valley. She slipped easily between the guards and ran lightly down the hill, across the stream, and on up until she could clearly see the sentries standing guard around the Viking camp. She frowned then, concentrating, and her shape swirled, reforming once again as a grey cat which padded quickly, unnoticed, through the camp.

Thorkell sat against a tree, watching the night fire. He saw the cat prowl past the neighboring fire and frowned, for the dogs showed no interest in the intruder. He stood and picked up his sharpened battle axe. Crossing the sentry line with a password, Thorkell climbed to the hilltop overlooking the fires of both camps glowing in the dark.

"What you are doing here, I don't know," he said to the cat, which had followed him. "Go home. Tomorrow we are going to kill each other. Do you want to watch?"

"I don't want to watch," she said angrily, shrugging off the illusion, "but how can I not? If you die, I die too. Without you, I am lost."

"You shouldn't have come," he said, taking her roughly in his arms.

There was a rustling along the path they had climbed.

"Who goes there?" he called, pushing her behind him.

"You all right, Thor?"

"Yes, Pym. I came up to have a word with the Lady Branwen."

"Branwen, Thor?" Pym asked, stepping into the moonlit clearing.

"You seem surprised to see her," Thorkell said.

"Oh no, Thor. Nice night, Lady Branwen."

They muffled their laughter in each other's shoulders for they did not want to disturb the quiet though they laughed long as the tension broke in each of them.

Finally Pym said, "You stay as long as you like. I'll go down a ways and keep watch."

They sat quietly together on the hilltop, leaning against a glacial erratic deposited there how many eons ago? Branwen smiled softly when she realized that the mighty warrior she held in her arms was sleeping peacefully. She woke him at first light, calling his name softly, trying to wake him gently, but he was instantly alert. He glanced at the sky, paling in the east, still an hour before dawn. "I want you to stay here today," he said. "Don't go down until the battle is over."

Branwen sighed. "I'll stay here," she agreed sadly, "for if I go back across that little stream. . . ." She stopped, looking up at him. "If I cross that stream today, Edmund will ask me to fight at his side, wielding what magic is mine to command."

"And would you do it?" he asked softly.

"I'll stay here and he won't ask."

"And if my need is great, and I ask you, will you fight beside me?"

"I won't *ever* fight," she whispered fiercely. "If your need is great I'll turn you into a small, brown field mouse and keep you safe."

He laughed, kissed her long and hard, and was gone, skittering down the hill.

The blare of horns, the distant thunder of horses' hoofs, and the clash of arms woke her. The sun was up. She had slept at last. She stood, letting the morning sun warm her, but her heart was cold as she watched the battle begin below. She located Thorkell by his raven banner. He rode a mighty chestnut war horse with a blonde tail and mane. Across the meadow Edmund's great black stallion reared, eager for battle. She searched in vain for some sign of Godwin.

Branwen traced the movements of the armies by the litter of darkness they left behind them. There seemed to be no way of telling who was winning, for the trails led back and forth across the meadow. The fallen lay everywhere.

The sun climbed higher in the sky and she knew she could not stay, watching the slaughter idly. "I'm sorry, my love," she whispered, "but I have to go."

In the deserted Viking camp she found a water bucket and a dipper. She started off to fill them for she knew that thirst would torment the wounded who lay in the sun.

She had not gone far when she came upon a body, twisted among the nettles. Flies buzzed eagerly over a great, sticky rent in his head. Branwen retched. She turned away from the evil sight but there was another lying in front of her, his belly opened, spilling out through fingers which must have tried in vain to contain it. Panic rose in her. A moan escaped from the body at her feet. He wasn't dead.

"Oh, my God," she said, looking around frantically. There was no one near to help. She knelt by his head. His eyes opened and he saw her. Incredibly, a smile flickered over his face. Her mind reeled under the waves of pain surrounding her.

"The angel of death," the boy whispered.

She blinked back her tears. She laid her hand over his eyes, closing them tenderly. She blanketed his pain with her mind, severing the threads which held him tied to this world in agony. He was dead before the smile faded from his lips. She got up numbly and went on. It was a wide plain and long. The heaviest fighting seemed to be taking place beyond the trees, on the other side of the brook. Eventually she reached the stream and filled her bucket with water which no longer ran clear.

Staying out of the way of the fighting men, the wheeling horses, the bloodied weapons, she filled the bucket many times as the morning wore on. Once, as she crouched at the edge of the stream, she saw Edmund in the front line of battle. His knees gripped the red-eyed war horse he rode; his shield was chipped, great gouges hacked from the edge; his sword was black with the blood of his enemies. Even as she watched he yelled a paean at the man he fought, driving the sword deep beneath the other's shield, wrenching it out as the dead man fell from the saddle. She took the bucket and turned away.

Some time after that she met Godwin watering his horse behind the lines. "Where the hell have you been?" he snapped. "Edmund is furious. We both thought we could count on you." Without waiting for her answer he was gone, swinging easily into the high saddle, unmindful of the weight of his coat of chain mail.

The hours dragged by. She stopped counting the souls

she loosed from shattered bodies; stopped thinking of the words she spoke to comfort others who merely drank from her dipper. Dyffed rode by, alive as the sun sank in the west. Pym was dead. He gazed unseeing at the sky. She had washed the fleck of blood from his mouth, his mouth that would not laugh again. She had tried to close his eyes. She was too late.

She had lost sight of Edmund, almost too tired to care, as the sun went down. Suddenly, out of nowhere, Eadric, astride a foam-flecked exhausted mount, surrounded by cheering Wiltshire men, held up a bloody head, black-bearded.

"Give up, fools! Edmund is dead!" he roared.

The clash of arms faltered. Branwen stood stunned, feeling the blood drain out of her as surely as if she had been pierced by a sword. Men looked at each other in dismay, not knowing what to do.

"To hell, traitor. He lives," roared Edmund. Standing tall in the stirrups, he urged his charger across the battlefield. Holding his sword in his left hand behind his shield, he tore the helmet from his head. A ragged cheer went up from the tired men of his army. Branwen saw Thorkell, then, ahead and to one side of Edmund. As in a dream, she saw the mighty Dane throw back his arm. A lance, stained with the day's work, poised and then, gathering speed, flew straight at the open side of the charging king.

"No," she screamed, deflecting the shaft with the force of her will.

Edmund saw it coming at the last instant. He made a small, shrugging gesture, but the lance merely hit him on the right side and glanced off. Its fury was unspent, and it buried itself effortlessly through the leather armor and thick body of a foot soldier who stood to one side. A great gasp went up around him. Edmund laughed. Branwen looked at Thorkell, who met her eyes from twenty yards away. He saluted her stiffly, wheeled about and rode away slowly.

The battle was over—for the day.

The sun had set. Men from both sides went among the

wounded, sorting out those who could be mended from the dead and dying. Branwen went unnoticed behind them and left quiet where before the peace of the evening had been disturbed by the hopeless moans of the dying.

So it was that eventually she found Cobbe, pinned to the bloody ground by a long lance which quivered in the air when he moved. It had penetrated through his body just under the collar bone.

"Can you get it out, Lady Branwen?" he asked, blood trickling from the corner of his mouth.

"I'll get help, Cobbe," she said desperately.

"That won't be necessary." It was Elfheah, his face ashen. Cobbe looked up at the prince. The boy's eyes were filled with love and trust. He could not know that life would flow out of him when the lance was withdrawn like dark wine from an opened cask. Elfheah knew. He knelt by the boy's head.

"You must be very brave," he said, smiling gently.

"I will not shame you, my lord," Cobbe said, coughing.

"No, you will never shame me."

He stood up and grasped the lance.

"No," she said, "wait."

She bent down and touched the boy. He smiled and closed his eyes. She waited for a moment, smoothing back his hair, and then stood up.

"He's dead," she said. "Pull it out."

She didn't stay to watch.

Edmund's army lay over at Sherston for a day, licking its wounds as the Vikings fell back toward their main force around London. Dyffed and many of the men who had come north with Edmund left now, carrying their wounded with them. The army, however, was not diminished. From every side men rallied to the man now called Edmund Ironside.

The sun was sultry as they marched northeast through meadows of ragweed and St. Johnswort. Branwen rode beside Edmund and her brother. If Edmund had been angry with her as he went into battle, he had forgiven her by evening. Perhaps Godwin had explained about the lance. It didn't matter. Others might say that the Battle of Sherston was a victory for neither side, yet Edmund's army knew they had faced two powerful and experienced commanders that day and had held the field. It was glory enough.

They marched toward London now in a wide sweep that would bring them down on the city from the north. Topping a small rise ahead of the army they saw a single rider approaching, his pennant hanging limply in the still air.

"Who do you suppose that is?" Godwin asked.

"This is Wiltshire. He can be carrying a message from only one man. He hasn't come far. See, his horse isn't even sweaty and a pennant like that is hard to carry with one hand for any distance. You," Edmund said, turning back to his standard bearer, "Saeweald, straighten up. Look sharp. Ride down and see what that man wants."

They watched as the two men met a little way off. The message was brief and Saeweald trotted back smartly.

"Lord Eadric sends you greetings, your majesty. He invites you to join him for dinner at Bryony just to the north, there where the River Ouse flows."

"The hell you say," Godwin exploded.

Edmund laughed.

Branwen watched the two men.

"I could use a good meal. What do you say, Godwin? Let's go. He always kept a good cellar."

"You're mad! It's some kind of trap. You can't go."

"Branwen will come. She'll weave one of her magic spells and protect us, won't you, my dear?"

Branwen said, "We've got to go, Godwin, or Eadric will have it said the new king is a coward."

"God's blood!"

"Ride back, Saeweald, and tell him we will be pleased to accept his invitation. Godwin, tell the captains to see that the men make camp along the river. We'll stay the night and perhaps tomorrow as well. It's too hot to travel anyway. The river will make a welcome break."

There were pennants flying from the stockade and the gates were open as Edmund rode up, his army fanning out along the river behind him. Eadric knelt in the shadows of the old trees outside the walls, immaculate, cool, unperturbed.

"Well, Eadric," Edmund said, looking down from the saddle. "This is a pleasant surprise. We had not looked for such hospitality."

"Wiltshire recognizes its king. Could I do less?" he asked, his face smiling with child-like simplicity.

Edmund dismounted. "Get up, Eadric. I am hot and thirsty. Politics will wait, although I've half a mind to run you through and be done with it."

Eadric shrugged and stood up. "Surely not in front of your sister, my dear wife," he said, still smiling.

"Ah yes, of course, Eadgyth is here," Edmund said slowly. "How nice. It's been such a long time between visits. We missed her, you know, at the funeral last spring."

They walked through the cool hall. The thatch, thick overhead, kept out the heat of the sun. The floors were newly laid with the blue flag which grew at the edge of the river.

It was in the cool of these inner rooms that Eadgyth sat with her women at the looms. They rose like startled birds, richly feathered, as Edmund entered the room.

"Edmund," Eadgyth said happily, crossing quickly to embrace him. "But I must kneel to you for Eadric tells me you are king now. Poor father. I pray daily for his soul."

She was older than her brother and the years did not sit easily on her face, but there was a calm, a remoteness about the woman that Branwen felt would be seldom breached. She was dark like her brother. Her black hair was thick and bound into a net of gold. It was too hot for jewels, but she wore easily a large uneven pearl hanging on a gold chain about her neck. The soft, warm color of the pearl matched the pale warmth of her skin.

What has brought her here? Branwen wondered. She and Eadric see so little of each other. Why now? What has he promised her? And then, looking around at the house and garden, she realized that this must be Eadgyth's home. Eadric must have come here to her.

They sat on lovely carven oak seats in the gardens which sloped gently down to the river. The old rowans threw dark shadows across the greensward and a breeze ruffled the grass. Branwen felt renewed, clean, dressed in her fine sandal jumper. It was good to feel like a lady again. She sat quietly, saying nothing, sipping chilled wine, while the great men sparred with each other. Elfheah stood nearby, his face drawn. He took no part in the conversation around him and she dared not speak to him, nor had she since Cobbe's death.

Not until it was quite late and she was very tired did Edmund, assuming the full dignity of the monarchy, say, "Are we to assume you wish to throw your forces in with ours, Eadric?"

"You have been crowned king, your majesty. I would, of course, serve the king loyally as Earl of Wiltshire."

"Earl? And are we merely to forget the unpleasantness of a year ago? Are we merely to forget that but a fortnight ago your loyalty was to a different king?"

Eadric smiled, still charming, and said, "A year ago you were not the king. Your army was ragtag and you thought the men of my command would recognize you as their leader. I disagreed. There seemed only one course of action at the time to protect my people from devastation at the hands of Knut's forces. One does what one must."

"And what of next month, if the tide should change?"

"The tide is flooding for you, Edmund. Between your army and my own we can drive the Dane into the sea, brother."

"I think we'd be better off without your help, brother."

Eadric's eyes narrowed. His voice was soft and casual. There was only gentleness in his manner, but he said, "And would you take the time to destroy my forces or would you move against the Dane with my armies at your back?"

Suddenly Godwin laughed—a rich, evil laugh that Branwen had never heard from any man before. "With your permission, my liege, I'll put an end to this farce."

"No, Edmund," Eadgyth said quietly from the darkness where she sat.

"It may come to that, my friend," Edmund said, laying his hand on Godwin's arm. "But perhaps not here and not yet."

Turning to Eadric, Edmund said, "So be it." But he did not smile, nor did he offer his hand.

* * *

They turned southeast now into the Chiltern hills. Edmund's strength continued to grow with each passing day. Though he had tried unsuccessfully to raise an army from this same region only a year earlier, now men flocked to his standard.

They had halted along the Thames just outside of Brentwood where a large force of Danes held the bridge and the road leading to London. As they prepared to force the crossing, Leofric returned at the head of a large contingent of men from Staffordshire and the Danelaw. He brought good news as well from the queen. Ealdgyth had borne Edmund a second son. Leofric had stood at the font in the ancient Saxon church of St. Paul's in Lincoln as the baby was christened Edward.

And so in high spirits they fell upon the bridge. There were heavy losses on both sides before they forced the Danes to fall back. Late in the day, when the road was clear, Branwen rode across, her eyes on the road ahead, careful not to look down to the river below where the stone channels of the bridge supports were clogged with bodies.

The delay of heavy fighting at Brentwood had given Knut the cover he needed to abandon his siege of London, moving southeast into Kent.

Edmund, at the head of his army, reached the city by evening. A great crowd had gathered along the roadway leading up to the main gate. The air was filled with their shouts and cries of welcome to the king who had delivered the city from the invader. Edmund was distracted, though, paying scant attention to the crowd, for the sky in the southeast glowed with light like a second sunset and the air had the bitter taste of too much smoke.

"The Danes are burning the land as they go," he said to Godwin and Leofric as they rode. "How are our supplies? There will be precious little here for us, or for the cottars," he added bitterly.

Burning the fields was a desperate measure, seldom used. War was to be fought by brave men on the field of battle. Burning peasant fields and cottages was stained with dishonor.

"We can't afford to wait, Edmund. Two days and the

men will start to feel it in their bellies."

"And what are we to feed the horses?"

"In two days the Danes will have reached their ships and escaped. I won't let that happen. I don't want them back to fight again—they must be crushed *now*. Pass the word. We will not enter the city but will press on. A hard march tomorrow and we can drive the bastards against the Medway. Leofric, take your men around the lines to burn the bridges at Otford. See to it the work is not done until the armies are committed to that crossing. If God wills, when the sun rises on the second day, it will watch the destruction of the Viking horde once and for all."

The sun never rose that dawn. The sky was blanketed in heavy rain clouds. Commands went out through the gloom as Edmund's army swept down on the Vikings arrayed before them. By noon it had begun to clear and steam rose from the men as the late summer sun heated their wet leather armor.

Now Branwen went into the field with the leeches and bonesetters. Hour after hour they followed the trail of the battle, moving the wounded to the shelter of the trees, out of the way of the heedless hoofs of the wheeling, charging war horses. She worked without thought, her tunic bloodied. Her hands, wiped on her skirt, were blackened around and under the nails, the cracks and crevices darkened with death.

She knelt beside a mutilated body, quiet now, its agony over. Suddenly Thorkell was there. She'd not seen the tall Dane since the Battle of Sherston—since the moment their eyes had met when she'd turned Thorkell's lance away from her king, turning his victory into defeat. He stood silent, looking down at her, barely recognizable under his helmet, his battle axe no longer shining.

"You've won," he said finally, his voice weary. "We're going to try for the boats. It's our only chance. Bran, I . . . ." He fell silent again.

"Take me with you," she said.

He looked down at her. She looked like a boy drafted too young to fight in a war he had thought would be glorious. Her face was grey, smeared with dark stains. Her clothes were torn, filthy. Her hair was pulled back, tied with a frayed bit of bright ribbon.

"Please," she whispered hoarsely, reaching up to him.

He pulled her quickly into the saddle in front of him. He kicked the stallion and they tore across the field, thundering over the bridge even as flames ate at the support posts.

The clouds returned as the sun set; the night grew very dark as they rode through the countryside. They rode slowly, lingering among the stragglers of the retreating army, urging the men along. Someplace during the night he found a dead man's horse and Branwen rode, unthinking, the reins held by the rider ahead of her whose mind was closed to her. She wondered if Edmund's army would overrun them the next day. She wondered if they were looking for her among the dead and wounded.

About midnight, they came down to a sandy beach that led across the tidal reach to the Isle of Sheppey. The tide had ebbed. They were able to ride far out on the firm sand before the water rose around them for a few moments, then dropped off quickly as they climbed out on the far side.

Once on the island, Thorkell turned aside from the ground trampled by the feet of Knut's retreating army. Alone they walked their horses along the edge of the sea until a gentle curve hid them from the others. There was a hollow in the dunes; on the other side a tiny freshet ran through sweetgrass down to the sea. He tethered the horses and carried her into the hollow. They fell asleep without speaking and slept for several hours.

She woke with the dawn. Thorkell sat a few feet away, watching her, his face grey. She felt his despair as if it were her own and suddenly she was glad she was there. Nothing else mattered. Everything else would change again and again. The only thing that went on was their love. She looked down at her blackened hands, her stained tunic and shrugged. When she looked up at him again, he was smiling at her. She got up and went to him.

"You're right, of course," he said, holding her close, "but, still, we could use some food."

"Later, my love," she said, "later."

Afterwards, there in the hollow of the sand, he said, "This day will be our last, Branwen." He spoke softly, looking back across the tidal race now in full flood. "Edmund has us trapped here. The fleet cannot get here before tonight at the earliest. When the tide goes out at mid-day, he will fall on us and. . . ."

He looked down at her and she knew he felt no fear but only regret for what might have been. Then he smiled. "Come on," he said. "Knut's camped not far from here. At least we can get something to eat."

"Let me wash up before facing the world," she said with a smile.

"You won't disappear?"

"I'll come back to you, my love."

But it was not to wash that she left him standing in the sun that morning. Beyond the dune, with the early morning light casting shadows from the clumps of coarse grass, with the cries of sea birds filling the air, she began to weave an illusion more powerful than any she had ever tried before. Concentrating all the strength of her mind, focusing it with her will and her desperation, she began to reach out to a power she had never tapped before. Not knowing how, opening herself, letting it flow through her, she began to focus the power of the earth itself, a power which had slept undisturbed since the coming of the new tribes. Like a dragon, it rose up around her and she controlled it, used it, forced it to do her will. And she knew nothing of price, nor did she care.

"Forgive me, Edmund," she whispered as it began around her. "I will not let you kill them."

And the old power, newly roused, hung like a mist over the island and the sea lane north beyond the mouth of the Thames. In that mist men saw what she willed, but not the tall Dane and not the men of Knut's shattered army huddled on the far shore. The grey mist hid them in the early morning sunlight because that was what she willed.

So it was that Edmund saw the Viking fleet depart on the dawning tide, bearing with it the survivors of the battle of Otford. So it would be later in the day that when he crossed to the island at low tide, he would see no one, nor would any man see him.

It took only a little while, only a few moments to wake the sleeping dragon, and when it was done, she stooped at the little brook and rubbed mechanically at the grime on her hands with clean sand. When she started back toward the Dane there was a part of her that was sealed off, a part of her that he would never know.

Ragged and unkempt, she rode beside the defeated Viking across the island. She was too tired to notice that the world had gone out of focus. There was a blurring around the edges as if reality were not quite real anymore.

"What the hell is *she* doing here, Thorkell?" Knut demanded when they rode into the midst of the Viking confusion. All around her men stood staring. Blaec croaked loudly and flew down, settling on her shoulder.

"It's been a long time, your kingship," she said quietly to the great raven.

"I found her on the battlefield yesterday. She stays with me."

"Keep her out of the way then," Knut growled, frowning.

"Why are you here, Branwen? You've won. You should be on the other shore where they are whetting their weapons for the kill." Hemming's head was bandaged and his leg as well. His eyes were deadened with pain and despair.

"I have no side, Hemming," she said. "And who has won when there are so many good men dead?" She reached out and touched him gently, feeling his pain.

"Stay here," Thorkell said. "I'll get us some food."

"Who bandaged you like this, Hemming?" she asked, noting the slack in the wrappings.

"What does it matter? Edmund will hack us limb from limb before sunset." He shivered as the fever of his wounds racked him. "What keeps him? Hasn't that damn tide gone out yet?"

"If he comes, I'll turn you and your great, hulking brother into toads and Edmund will never notice you."

Hemming laughed without humor. "How will we explain

that to the fleet when they arrive and find us alone, surrounded by dead men? Better to die, lady, than that."

"Maybe he won't come."

"He'd be a fool not to. If the fleet gets here first, we can withdraw along the north coast, lick our wounds, and fight again. He must know that. He'll come."

Branwen turned away, her heart like ice within her.

The day passed, the illusion held, for she could not condemn these men to slaughter. Night fell and before it did they saw on the horizon the first and fastest of the Viking fleet. During the night, by the light of driftwood fires, Knut and his men boarded the ships and sailed across into Essex. Branwen stood with Blaec heavy on her forearm, watching the shore where Edmund camped fade behind a rise of black water.

Chapter Sixteen

THE GOLDENROD AND bluebells were blooming in the hedgerows. Everywhere the air was full of the buzzing of bees in the still heat of late summer. Branwen walked alone, her feet bare in the brown dust. Like last summer, she walked in a torn, stained tunic. Her hair was bound up in a bit of new ribbon, shyly offered by a boy whose wound she had cleaned and bound. She had come to the edge of a river, under the trees, looking for the late looming asphodel to curb the flux which gripped the Viking army on short rations. She had grown used to the peculiar haze which hung over the land even when the sun was high. No one else seemed to see it. Perhaps there was something the matter with her eyes. She rubbed at them absently with the back of one soiled hand. But there was also a feel to it, like a rumbling so low it couldn't be heard, just felt, like distant thunder. Why was she the only one who knew? What was the matter? What had happened to her?

She pushed aside a low branch and stepped out onto a sandy pocket of beach not ten feet across, the dark roots and forest litter undercut around the edges, in deep shadows. She stood blinking in the sun, rubbing her feet absently on the warm sand. There was one tree whose roots reached farther along the littoral than the others and whose canopy of leaves was taller and broader than the others as well. Its bark was thick and dark, deeply incised like the richest of oak carvings. From among the topmost branches of this ancient oak came the jangle of hawk bells. She looked up and saw a great barred harrier.

She called to it in the magic words she alone knew. "Who has dared to bell you, king of the wind?"

The bird answered her, nobly defiant. *What does it matter? It is done.*

"Come down and I'll untie you so you can fly again across the sky."

Never.

"You'll die up there with the jesses trailing from your talons. They will get tangled in the trees and then you'll die slowly in the sun."

Better a captive of the trees and the sun, than of man.

"Come down," she said then and her voice carried the power of her will. The great bird of prey flew down to the gnarled root which hung over the beach near the place where Branwen stood. She loosed the jesses quickly, cutting through the leather straps with her small, sharp knife. The bird eyed her for a moment and then rose heavily into the air, his wings beating powerfully, carrying him up to the thermals where an effortless grace would be his.

Branwen watched him go, holding the leather straps with their finely worked, silver bells.

"That was a valuable bird you loosed, lady."

She turned, startled, toward the voice. There on the high bank across the river stood a man. His face was wrinkled, deeply incised like the bark of the oak although not as dark; his hair was grey and thin, straggling out from under his straw hat, wide-brimmed to shade his pale blue eyes from the sun.

"That bird was lost to you before I cut his jesses, sir," she said simply.

"He would have come down when he got hungry."

"Never. Not that bird. You took him too old from the sky."

"And how do you know that?"

"It's true, isn't it?" she asked. "Do you want your bells back?"

"There is a boat just beyond you, there," he said indicating a second beach only separated from the first by a stubborn willow tilting over the river.

She pushed the coracle into the stream and poled clumsily across. The old man met her on the other side.

"You owe me something for the bird," he said.

"What price did you have in mind?" Branwen laughed, holding out her torn skirt. "As you can see, there is little I can pay."

"It's not money I want," he answered. "My sister waits dinner for me. You will come eat with us. It will be good for her to have company. Take her mind off her worries," he said eyeing her narrowly.

"Who are you, sir?" she asked.

"My father named me, Ulfkytel."

"I've heard of a great warrior named Ulfkytel," she said. "Among the Vikings he is called Snellinger which means the Valiant. Around their fires they say he was the greatest of swordsmen, the bravest enemy they ever faced."

"Many are the stories told by men in camp which grow in the telling, like shadows cast by firelight."

"Yes, but the story of Ulfkytel the Valiant was told me by a Viking warrior just the night before last. And the man who told me still bears a scar, whitened with age, that he received in deadly handplay with the great man outside of Thetford."

"Enough," the old warrior said gruffly. "My sister will be angry if we delay dinner longer." He led the way through the narrow edge of trees to an open oat field, newly cut. A groom waited patiently, holding the bridles of two horses.

"Can you manage astride?" the old man asked.

She laughed. "Aye, my lord, I can manage."

And they raced, showing off to each other like children, across the hills toward a brooding hall set on a low cliff above the sea, smoke rising slowly into the still air. The groom sighed, watching them, and started home on foot, hoping there would be some dinner left when he got there.

Ulfkytel led the way into the coolness of the main hall where the great shutters on the cliff wall were open to the sea breeze. An old woman rose from her seat by the loom as they entered. She was fine featured, her wrinkled skin white as cream; her white hair was coiled thickly around her head and her eyes, like Branwen's, were large and black. Branwen felt a sudden chill as she saw herself an old woman, youth lost to her.

"Ah, Ulf," the woman said slowly. "Where did you find this pretty child?"

"She loosed the harrier," he said, as though that were all the introduction Branwen needed.

"I am called Branwen," she said quickly. "I come from Thornbury."

"That would make you Wulfnoth's daughter, eh?" Ulfkytel interjected. "Now there's a man whose deeds are the stuff of legend! Defied the king, he did, right enough, rather than order his men into a battle they could not hope to win."

"Hush, Ulf, and let the child speak! It's few enough strangers we see in these parts," Ulfkytel's sister chided. Ulfkytel grinned at her, unabashed.

Branwen joined the pair for dinner, answering their questions about her family good-naturedly. The pleasant reminiscences, the wine, and the sea air combined to make her feel quite drowsy, and she did not object when the old woman led her through a curtained archway into a sun-filled room where an enormous bed stood gleaming with clean linen. Dazedly, Branwen exchanged her soiled, torn clothes for the thin, blue shift a maidservant held out to her. With a deep sigh she fell untroubled across the bed.

Hours later she awoke. The room was darker now, although the sky outside the window was still blue. Her ragged jumper was gone, but across one corner of the bed was a green woolen tunic, softened by many careful washings so that it had that richness new things never have. She slipped it over her head and noted with pleasure that there was some fine hand work around the yoke—small birds and flowers stitched carefully into the wool. Then she stood still for a moment, staring down at the design. The flowers on this old tunic were the same flowers she had seen on a loom in an enchanted meadow in the hills above Lydney.

"You know them then, my dear," the old woman said, standing in the archway. "I thought as much."

"Who are you, my lady?" Branwen whispered.

"I am an old servant of Her Who Is Forgotten, as you are, my child. My name is Penardim."

"Penardim," Branwen said slowly. "I have heard that name. . . I think there are many things you must explain to me, my lady."

"Perhaps, but not now. Later we will have time. My brother wishes to speak with you first."

She found him walking along the sea cliff, his face grave. Ulfkytel listened closely while she told him all she could of the recent war, and Edmund's victories.

"Will you go with me?" he asked when she had finished.

"Where?" she asked, her heart cold with foreknowledge.

"Why he didn't destroy the invader on the Isle of Sheppey, I do not know. But this I do know: He cannot let many days go by before their armies clash in combat once again. Can I then, in honor, remain away? Nay, lady, this very night I will call up the men who answer to me.

"We will ride at dawn to join our king."

While the great hall was filled with the excitement of men preparing for war, the old woman sat and sent the shuttle back and back again, steadily, without looking up from her work. Her hands were blue veined and gnarled with age. Branwen took up the cloud of wool which lay at her feet and fed it evenly between her fingers, spinning the fine yarn as she had learned at her mother's side. They worked quietly until the peace around them was settled. The others left them alone; there was no need to disturb them.

Branwen, unwilling to think about what tomorrow would bring—more death, more broken bodies—all somehow her fault, tried to concentrate on her work. It would have been over if she had not been with Thorkell on

Sheppey. What had happened there, she wondered. Everything seemed so wrong now. What had she done?

"There was an old man," she said suddenly, afraid to speak of the other, "who taught me many things the summer I was fifteen. Once he spoke of a woman he had loved who had seen a unicorn. His name was Ansgar."

"Ansgar," the weaver breathed and the shuttle was still. "Ansgar. I had not thought to hear his name again. It was so many years ago and yet the memory of the months we shared has never faded. Does he still live?"

"No, my lady," she said softly. "He died that fall. He was not sad to go. He had no fear and slipped gently from this world."

"I am glad the way was easy. How strange that he should find you in the end. Did he know you for what you are?"

"He told me I was very like you."

"And so you are, my child."

Then they were silent and between them was only the clatter of the shuttle and the rattle of the spindle.

"Of late I have dreamed that the unicorn walks once more upon the earth," Penardim said.

"I have seen him twice. Twice he has taken me to the Mother of All."

"Yes, that is what I've dreamed. I wasn't sure the voice I heard spoke truly. One learns in old age to distrust the mind's wanderings. He told me. . . ." she hesitated, gazing at the pattern on the silent loom.

Branwen waited.

After a while Penardim went on, "You have waked the sleeping powers, you know."

Branwen said nothing and a cold fear wrapped around her.

Putting aside the shuttle, Penardim got up and went over to the window which was open toward the dark sea beyond. "There is a pattern to our lives, Branwen, which you have disturbed. Don't you feel it?"

"Yes," Branwen whispered, "since Sheppey. What have I done? I only wanted to save them. I didn't want them to die. Not all of them."

"You wanted to save them," Penardim said sharply,

turning back to her. "But who are you to call up such magic to do your will? Do you think the power is there only for your taking?"

"I didn't know."

"No, I suppose not," the old woman said with a sigh. "Still, what's done is done."

"What will happen?" Branwen asked, the words dragged out unwillingly.

"You must pay the price! You must put it right once more."

"But I don't know how," Branwen cried. "Don't you see? I don't even know what it is I've done! How can I put it right?"

"I don't see why you've been given all this power if no one has ever bothered to explain the rules," the old woman said, half to herself, busying herself at the loom once more. She banged the shuttle over and back twice before saying, "Hasn't anyone ever told you that everything has its price? Even magic. Oh, little magic has such a little price sometimes you hardly notice—unless you let the bill run up, that is. But the greater powers. . . ." She shook her head. "And waking the *dragon*—tsk, tsk," she clucked.

Angry color rose in Branwen's cheeks but her voice was tight and carefully controlled. "What dragon?" she asked.

"Well, it's not a real dragon," Penardim laughed. "It's the way we refer to the magic which lies all around us—the earth magic. No one uses it anymore. It's too strong. The price is always too high."

Branwen, angry, not trusting her voice, waited for her to go on.

The old woman glanced at her out of the corner of her eye. "They've never told you anything, have they? Well, well. It's a wonder you didn't cause more trouble before this. It's like a balance, my dear. If you upset it with magic everything takes on a tilt. Nothing looks quite right."

"The haze," Branwen said.

"Of course. Nothing has been quite clear all week and instead of each day going along smoothly there's a rumbling, as if the cart wheel's come loose. If it isn't fixed soon, Branwen, it will get worse."

"But I can't fix it. I don't know how," Branwen cried angrily.

"You don't have to shout, child. I can tell you what must be done. It's quite simple really. Even you should be able to do it quite nicely, I think."

Branwen glared down at her hands and said nothing.

"You used the magic, now you must let it use you," the old woman said. "You must let the magic flow through you to rebalance the scales. You must let yourself be nothing, you must deny your will, your feelings, everything. You must come to understand your own unimportance, child. You can't fix the world. You are too small and insignificant. Empty your heart of yourself and let the powers use you as they will."

Branwen stood up with a bitter laugh. "I don't know what you are talking about. I can't understand what you are telling me to do. You're as bad as the unicorn, talking in riddles. I don't understand either of you! And I am very tired. What I do know tonight is that there will be more war, more killing. That is real. I can understand that. This other is fantasy and I do not believe it—not any of it."

"If you choose not to believe what you know in your heart is the truth," Penardim said wearily, "then you will cause great evil."

"No. It is not so!"

"It was no small illusion you worked to hide your lover from death at Edmund's hand. You called up an ancient magic to serve your will on the Isle of Sheppey. Because of you, men who were meant to die did not die. Because of you they lived to fight again, and the war that comes will be more terrible than any that have gone before."

"It's not my fault!" Branwen cried.

"Are you sure?" Penardim asked.

"I am going to try and get some sleep now. We're leaving early in the morning," Branwen answered, turning away.

Penardim said nothing. The loom moved evenly, up and down, for a long time before she, too, tried to sleep.

In the morning light, the warm smell of the horses and the good-natured calling of the men who rode with

Ulfkytel reassured Branwen. See, she thought, it can't be as the old woman said. This is what is real—the ground beneath the horse's hoofs, the warm sun in the sky. Last night's words were only the ramblings of an old woman. What had happened on Sheppey was a simple illusion, nothing more. She squinted, trying to bring the trees along the road into focus.

They reached Edmund's army late in the afternoon. There, in the low lying coastal hills outside the town of Ashington, the armies had camped. There was little fire in the men's eyes as they awaited the dawn, for these were veterans who had tested the enemy and knew the stench of death. It had soured their taste for battle and their hunger for victory.

"Well met, Ulfkytel," said Edmund, rising from his seat as they came into the firelight. "You are a welcome soldier whose valiant heart all men know. We will be proud to have you fight at our side tomorrow."

Ulfkytel knelt on one knee to the young man who was his sovereign, and those who had ridden with him did the same. Edmund smiled and helped the old man to his feet.

"And who is this who kneels in your shadow? Did you think we wouldn't notice you, lady? Where have you been? There are those who care enough to worry about you, or did you forget?"

"If you worried, my liege, it must have amused my brother," she said, smiling at him and the man who stood behind him. "Didn't you tell him not to worry, Godwin?"

"No one knew where you were, Bran. Of course, we worried about you."

"I was with Thorkell."

"And what are you doing back here now?"

And when she didn't answer he laughed and their thoughts once again turned toward the dawn.

They moved out at first light. The Danes had camped in an ancient hill fort, a position too strong to be taken easily or quickly. A large force had been left on the river bank with the fleet. If Edmund's army had been a lesser one these two arms of Danish might could have crushed him between them, but in the light of the new day the flood plain was blackened with Edmund's men. Thorkell, who commanded the fleet, threw aside that caution which is wisdom, and, as the heat of the rising sun stirred the breeze, and the raven banner on the mast of his ship broke free, he signaled for the attack.

Knut, watching from the stockade, laughed as a man must who is caught up in madness. He ordered the gates opened and his men prepared to sweep out against an army they could have little hope of defeating. Singing, the Vikings sallied forth.

Tall in the saddle, between the blue standard of his own Huntington and the red of Godwin's newly awarded Dragon of Wessex, Edmund Ironside, king of the land, urged his army forward to what must be total victory.

A great shout went up from the opposing armies, mingling with the blare of horns and the screams of the war horses, spurred on to battle. The plain became a seething sea of color and sound as each group moved forward, each group flying a pennant, each group forgetting its fear of the night before, each group anxious to win glory, anxious to begin the fight, anxious to kill.

Suddenly the whole left of Edmund's army sheared away. Branwen watched in horror from her vantage point on a small rise where she waited with Ulfkytel and his men who were being held in reserve. She watched as almost half of the forces on the field turned west away from the coming battle. What was happening?

"Eadric," she whispered, her heart ice within her. "He has betrayed Edmund again."

The old warrior knew instantly what was happening. He raised his arm, waving his command forward to cut off the traitor's flight. But only the old man was mounted; only the old man spurred his war horse across the marsh to stem the flow of Wiltshire men who rode west, away from the battle.

She watched Ulfkytel struggling to turn the army back. She could not hear his voice but saw how the men around him hesitated in the face of his bravery. Ulfkytel, the Valiant. And he was turning the troops. Perhaps not all, but several columns had halted.

Then, while she watched, an arrow pierced his armor,

toppling him slowly out of the saddle. The old war horse he rode, seasoned in battle, marked where he lay, unmoving as the men from Hereford and Wiltshire swept past.

All day the armies hacked at each other. More evenly matched now, neither side could gain an advantage. Through the heat of the day they fought, their throats dried, sweat running into their eyes and down their arms making their hold on sword or spear slippery so that their arms cramped from gripping tightly.

The sun set over a plain that ran with blood and still the armies hacked at each other. The men could tell friend from foe only by the light of the moon, grinning in the sky above them.

Surely it will end soon, Branwen thought as she knelt holding a cup of water to a boy's lips while they waited for others to carry him off the field. It must end soon.

She looked up and saw her brother towering over her on his great war horse. Just past him, with the moon behind him was Thorkell, watching him.

She rose to face them.

"You can't go on like this," she shouted, "you'll *all* die."

"Go away, Branwen," Thorkell said.

"No," she cried.

"Leave her," Godwin said. "Let her watch." His great war horse reared as Godwin pulled him around to face his enemy.

"No," she screamed, "no."

She stretched her arms out toward them both, struck numb by horror and despair. Unthinking now, she stood drained, empty, without hope. And as she stood there, the power of the earth itself flowed through her. The forgotten power of the ancient ones flowed through its vessel and out over the battlefield. A silence grew, a sudden stillness hung in the air. As Branwen stood motionless, an overwhelming weariness descended upon those who fought that day. Exhausted men let their weapons drop. As if bloodied bandages fell from their eyes, they saw the carnage that lay around them and it was loathsome to them. In a light which seemed to radiate from the upraised arms of a small woman, they saw the evil they had called good and they were sickened, and there was none among them who could lift his sword any longer. When she dropped her arms, there was silence, but for the moans of the dying.

Tears ran unheeded down Branwen's cheeks. Why had she waited so long? So many brave men were dead because she had been afraid to believe, afraid to accept her role. She stared around her, unable to speak, and when Thorkell came and held her, she clung to him the way a frightened child will to any nearby adult. Godwin followed them. The three of them sat for a long time without speaking, and Thorkell held Branwen close, stroking her hair until finally she slept.

"Do you know what happened tonight?" Thorkell asked Godwin quietly. "What will she do?"

"I'm not sure. There is a power which answers her call but what that power is, or how she controls it, I don't know."

"It's taken something from her. She seems so fragile."

"Someone will have to take her away. She can't stay here."

"I'll take her."

"You can't, Thorkell, not any more than I can. The battle may be over but nothing is settled. Neither of us can walk away from this, not yet."

"I'll take her with me. Hemming will take care of her."

"He's dead," Godwin said quietly.

"Dead?"

"I'm sorry."

"I'll take care of her," Thorkell said, his voice thick. "She'll be all right."

"If you say so," Godwin said wearily. "Look, I've got to get back." Walking slowly across the field, he left them alone.

In October 1016, both sides, exhausted by their fighting, met on an island in the Severn River near Olney in Gloucestershire. They divided the country between them—Knut getting Anglia, Essex and the unconquered city of London while Edmund held the rich lands of Wessex, Somerset, Dorset and Kent.

Within a month Edmund was dead, perhaps of an old battle wound, perhaps poisoned. The chronicles are strangely silent. He was twenty-two.

By Christmas Knut was betrothed to Emma, the still-young widow of Ethelred, the Unraed, and became undisputed monarch. He was twenty.

Godwin and Leofric switched allegiances, whether easily or not is unrecorded, and continued their rise to power in the land.

Thorkell the Tall became Earl of East Anglia.

NOTES

1. P. 52 The song "King o'Luve" is quoted from Folkways Records Album No. FW 928, 1957.

2. P. 83 The Beowulf passage is quoted from the translation by Burton Raffel, *Beowulf*, New American Library of World Literature, No. 63.

3. P. 159 The song "Whittingham Fair" is quoted from the above mentioned Folkways Record.

4. P. 163 The bit of Welsh poetry is quoted from Joseph P. Clancy, *The Earliest Welsh Poetry*, Macmillan, St. Martin's Press, 1970.

ACKNOWLEDGMENT

Every author hopes, I think, to create scenes and characters which are not easily forgotten. The death of Cobbe on the battlefield grew out of such an unforgettable scene written by Mary Renault in *The Last of the Wine* which I read years ago and which has become a part of me.

If you enjoyed AN UNKINDNESS OF RAVENS, you won't want to miss the exciting sequel, DEATH OF THE RAVEN by Dee Morrison Meaney, coming in November 1983 from Ace Fantasy Books. Here's a small sampling of this magical, romantic tale. . . .

There was the unmistakable scrape of spades cutting into the rough gravel flood plain. Men who had slept only a few hours bent grimly over the work—digging the grave for those who had fallen in the battle.

There was one who stood and watched. He was a tall man. His hair was brown, cut short because in a fight a man's life can depend on such small things as cropped hair which will not blow suddenly across the eyes. Stiff leather armor encased the upper part of his body. It was not pretty to look at, undecorated, marked with random scratches and gouges, some darkened by years of careful oilings, others lighter, newer, and some bright, still virgin, never having known a soldier's rough caress. One of his arms was bound neatly with a strip of white linen. He held it still against his chest. The man's name was Thorkell, called the Tall. He was a great chieftain in the army of Knut, the Dane.

Knut, who would be king of this island his father had conquered once before; Knut, who had led his army against the army of Edmund Ironside in a battle which had raged from dawn until long after dark; a battle which might have raged until no man remained standing, for there had been an unnatural fury upon them; Knut, who stood now on the low hill overlooking the plain and watched, his helmet under his arm, his clear northern blue eyes, which missed little, coming back time after time to watch the small figure who worked beneath the trees among the wounded.

"I'll see her in hell for this, Harald," he said bitterly to the grey-haired warrior who stood beside him.

"For what, brother?" the man asked derisively. "If it is true that she somehow magically ended the battle last night—which I doubt—be grateful. Another hour, we would all be dead." He spit.

"By Thor," Knut snapped. "Another hour and we would have wiped them out."

"Don't be a fool," Harald said.

Knut ignored him. "Eric saw her do it. He stood with me and we saw her, standing there, and we could not lift our arms."

" 'And with the moonlight streaming over her, she forbade the battle to go on.' I know. I know. Everywhere the men are whispering of it. Exhausted men dream strange things, especially when they are standing hip deep on a bloody battlefield long after any sane commander would have made truce for the night."

"Truce," Knut hissed, "truce! We had them beaten, another hour and the island would have been mine."

"You're mad! We were all dropping in our tracks. We couldn't have fought another fifteen minutes and you know it. My arm aches today like it never did before," he added, rubbing his massive shoulder for emphasis.

"Believe what you will, brother," Knut said, "but I know what I saw and I won't rest until that witch is destroyed."